A SHEETCAKE NAMED DESIRE

Jacklyn Brady

CHIVERS

British Library Cataloguing in Publication Data available

This Large Print edition published by AudioGO Ltd, Bath, 2012.
Published by arrangement with the Berkley Publishing Group, a division of Penguin Group (USA) Inc.

U.K. Hardcover   ISBN 978 1 4458 2370 6
U.K. Softcover   ISBN 978 1 4458 2371 3

Copyright © 2011 by Penguin Group (USA) Inc.
A Piece of Cake Mystery

Printed and bound in Great Britain by
MPG Books Group Limited

For Lorelei

ONE

The Mississippi riverboat cake tilted on the table in front of me, its fondant paddle wheel askew, gashes of lemony yellow cake gaping in its once-smooth white surface. In all the years I've been working as a cake artist, this was the worst disaster I'd ever seen. Repairing the badly damaged three-foot cake would have been a daunting task under ideal conditions. In my current situation, the job was almost overwhelming.

Trickles of nervous perspiration snaked down my back as I studied the wreck from every angle. I could feel the staff of Zydeco Cakes watching me intently as I sorted through possible ways to proceed.

First priority: stay calm. Not easy under the circumstances. The stakes were as high as they got in the world of professional cake decorating. The cake was due in less than three hours at the grand opening of a new riverboat cruise line, for folks with money

7

and influence. Failure to deliver on time would have a far-reaching impact on Zydeco's reputation. For a cake artist, reputation is every bit as important as talent.

The staff at Zydeco had already suffered a blow today. I couldn't let them down again.

The air conditioner was cranked up to keep the work area cool, but the intense heat and humidity of New Orleans in July still managed to creep into the building somehow. The undercurrents of tension that ebbed and flowed through the room didn't help me keep my cool either.

My name is Rita Lucero, and I'm a trained cake artist, a graduate of the French Pastry School in Chicago. Currently wasting my fancy training by working as sous chef in my uncle Nestor's Mexican restaurant in Albuquerque. So what was I doing sweating over a cake in New Orleans?

It was the same pending divorce that had left me chopping onions by the bushel that had brought me to the Crescent City for a few days. But now, instead of getting my ex's signature on our divorce settlement, I was standing in his bakery, shaking the dust off my cake decorating skills.

Taking a deep breath to calm my nerves, I closed my eyes and counted to ten — a trick my aunt Yolanda had taught me when I was thirteen and angry with the world. It didn't always work, but I hadn't given up trying. I needed to focus, but concentration was hard to find in a room full of tense, anxious people.

When I opened my eyes again, Zydeco's manager, Edie Bryce, was staring up at me, a deep scowl accentuating her round face and the almond-shaped eyes she'd inherited from a Chinese grandmother. To the uninformed, Edie resembles the stereotypical porcelain doll, but I learned a long time ago not to underestimate her.

"So?" she demanded. "Can you do it or not, Rita?"

"I'm thinking."

"Think faster! That cake is due for delivery in less than three hours."

Not helpful. "Nobody's more aware of the clock than I am," I assured her. "Just back off a little, okay? Pushing through this too quickly is guaranteed to make things worse."

Edie's frown deepened, and impatience flashed in her dark eyes. She muttered something under her breath and turned away, but I knew she'd be back soon. Patience has never been one of her virtues.

I glanced around at the others, some of whom I'd known since pastry school. The rest I'd met just a couple hours earlier, and

9

I was still struggling to remember their names. "We're going to need buttercream," I said to no one in particular. "Lots of it."

It had all started just two hours earlier, at precisely ten o'clock a.m. It was a Saturday morning in July and already steaming. I'm from New Mexico, so hot I can deal with — but I'm used to dry desert heat, and the humidity here weighed me down even as it made my curls frizz up.

I dragged myself and my duffel bag out of the taxi I'd taken from my hotel near the French Quarter. I'd booked the room back when I thought I'd get in some sightseeing while I was in town. Big laugh. Maybe I should have let Philippe know I was coming, but I'd been afraid he'd put me off. I'd spent the entire day yesterday trying to catch him, and I was back this morning to try again.

Zydeco Cakes — Philippe's business — occupied a gleaming-white, beautifully renovated antebellum mansion near the Garden District. Philippe couldn't have picked a more perfect setting for his new business. The surrounding neighborhood was upscale and trendy, the nearby restaurants and boutiques looked eclectic and inviting, and the renovated mansion could

10

have been used on the set of *Gone with the Wind* or *Jezebel;* it looked ready to receive carriages filled with gentlemen planters and hoopskirted belles. Philippe, with his old-money roots, must feel right at home here; I felt dazzled but intimidated and totally self-conscious about being a poor, orphaned Hispanic girl who was out of her element in this town.

Already wilting from the humidity, I let myself inside the building. Photographs of elaborate and elegant cakes adorned the crisp white walls of the foyer, and the familiar scents of chocolate, sugar, lemon, and almond filled the air. An ornate staircase rose to the second floor, its rich dark wood gleaming in the sunlight. So far I'd only seen the reception area, which was pretty incredible. I was dying to get a look at the rest of the building.

Edie Bryce — Zydeco's business manager — shot to her feet from behind the reception desk when she saw me and stated the obvious. "You're back."

With a nod, I lowered the duffel bag to the polished hardwood floor at my feet. "I told you I would be. Could you please let him know I'm here?"

Edie's eyes narrowed slightly, and she glanced toward the door I'd already deduced must open into my ex-husband's office. "Philippe? Sorry. You just missed him."

Hearing Philippe's name pronounced correctly always gives me a little jolt. It's Fil-*eep,* not *Fill*-ip. He's tolerant of folks who don't get it right (approximately 99 percent of the population), but heaven help the fool who says it wrong in front of his mama. Miss Frankie can take the hair off a dog with one look when someone crosses her. I know. I've been the dog a few times.

I've known Edie for almost a decade, and she's not exactly a poker face. She stared at me without blinking, but she had guilt smeared all over her expression. I understood why. She was lying to me.

For the past few months I'd suspected that Edie was running interference between Philippe and me. But he'd called earlier while I was in the shower, so apparently she'd told him that I was in town. He'd left a voice mail on my cell phone asking me to meet him at Zydeco, so I *knew* he was here. The layer of defiance that showed through her expression like chocolate cake through a thin crumb coat of buttercream was harder to understand. Maybe she could tell that I wasn't being entirely honest with her either.

I'd spent the past two years getting over Philippe and nursing the wounds he'd inflicted when he left. It had taken me a long time to reach this point, and now, just when I was ready to take control of my life, get the divorce finalized, and move on, Philippe had left a message that made me wonder if he wanted to get back together.

I'd played it half a dozen times already, trying to figure out whether I was interpreting it correctly, and I knew it by heart.

Rita? Philippe. Listen, Edie told me that you came by yesterday. Sorry I missed you. Actually, I'm glad you're in town, babe. We need to talk. I made a mistake when we split up. Probably the biggest mistake of my life. You gotta admit, we were good together. Come by Zydeco this morning. Around ten? I want to talk to you about starting over.

Okay, so he hadn't actually asked for reconciliation, but he *had* admitted that he'd made a mistake, and those words were like music to my ears. On some soul-deep level I still loved him and probably always would. But the rest of me — the part closer to the surface — hadn't forgiven him for hurting me. I had no idea which side would win when we met face-to-face. I supposed that would depend on whether he seemed genuinely sorry.

"I can't believe I missed him again," I said, serving up a cheerful smile to cover my confusion. Apparently, Philippe hadn't told Edie that he'd asked me to meet him. I wondered what that meant. "Honestly," I said, "I have the worst luck. Guess it's a good thing I came prepared to wait, huh?"

I carried my bag to the nook by the window and settled into an early Victorian chair covered with peach brocade. It was by far the most comfortable chair in the reception area. I knew, because I'd tried them all yesterday. Its location by the window was also the best for a lengthy sit-in thanks to its unobstructed view of the reception area, the staircase, and all the doors leading into it.

Scowling, Edie came out from behind her cluttered U-shaped desk. "Wait a second, Rita. You can't just *sit* here all day again." Edie may be short, but she can still look formidable when she tries. I'm sure that's why Philippe hired her as his manager. After spending time in pastry school with her, I can safely say it wasn't because of her superior skills in the kitchen.

I dug a bottle of water from the bag at my feet and opened it. "I'm not going to stay here all day. I'll leave as soon as I've talked

14

to Philippe."

She frowned as she bore down on me. "Look, I gave Philippe your message yesterday. I'm sure he'll call as soon as he has a break in his schedule."

"He called this morning, as a matter of fact. That's why I'm here."

She stopped in her tracks. "He *called* you?"

I retrieved the paperback novel I'd picked up in the hotel gift shop and settled in. "He did. So don't mind me. I'm prepared to wait as long as I need to."

"But I *do* mind," Edie practically snarled at me. "You can't just sit here with your water bottle and your . . . *stuff.* We have an image to maintain."

I met her eyes briefly over the rim of my water bottle, but her expression made me uncomfortable. I looked away and cracked open the book. A breath of cool air wafted down from the overhead ceiling fan, and the air conditioner kept up its steady hum as it worked to keep that big old house comfortable — not an easy task on a day when the temperature had topped 80 before eight in the morning. "Why don't you just let Philippe know that I'm waiting? I'll leave as soon as he signs the documents in my bag."

We'd had this same conversation yesterday, so I didn't hold out much hope that Edie would do what I asked, but I had to try. I wasn't going to leave New Orleans without Philippe's signature on the divorce agreement. Of course, there was a possibility that I'd forget about the signature. I mean, you know, if Philippe really had come to his senses and really wanted me to forgive him and stay in New Orleans. And *maybe* I'd agree. But the chances were slim.

Edie darted an uncertain glance at the door that led into the back of the house. "Philippe is busy. I have strict orders not to disturb him."

"I don't mind waiting," I assured her. In an effort to lighten her mood a little, I grinned and added, "He can't hide from me forever."

Instead of smiling at my little joke, Edie ticked her tongue in irritation. "He's not *hiding* from you. He's busy." She thrust out a hand and wiggled her fingers in my face. "Just give me the papers. I'll get him to sign."

She was seriously starting to piss me off. She had no idea what was going on between Philippe and me. *I* didn't even know what was going on between us.

Brushing aside the urge to slap Edie's

16

hand out of my way, I managed a regretful smile. "I wish I could, but I've lost track of the number of phone calls and e-mails he's ignored in the past two years. He ignored the papers I mailed him six months ago. And the documents I faxed three months ago. And he never returned the agreement my attorney sent him last month."

Remembering all of that made the warm glow I'd been feeling since I heard Philippe's voice this morning on the recording cool considerably. "I'm through with go-betweens, Edie. Just give me five minutes with him and I'll get out of your hair — forever."

Just then, the door to the inner sanctum opened, and the scent of freshly baked cake grew stronger. I turned toward it eagerly, swooning a little at the smell of warm chocolate but annoyed with my heart for racing with anticipation.

Along with the overload of pleasant aromas came the sound of loud, angry voices and a young blonde woman with wide, blue eyes and a frantic look on her face. "Edie! You have to —" She stopped abruptly when she realized Edie wasn't sitting at her desk and glanced around helplessly. She spotted us and shot across the room toward us. "Edie. You have to do something. They're

17

going to kill each other!"

A loud crash reverberated through the bakery, and Edie set off toward the open door. The young woman wheeled around to follow her, and I brought up the rear. What can I say? I've always been the curious type, and I'd been dying to get a look at Philippe's operation.

I stepped through the door and found myself inside a huge open workspace interrupted only by four large support beams. The aromas of citrus and chocolate were even stronger back here, and memories of pastry school filled my head. My stomach growled, and I regretted skipping breakfast, but I didn't have time to worry about being hungry.

Across the room, a small crowd clustered around a wide metal door that led onto a loading dock. Edie made a beeline toward it, and the young woman who'd raised the alarm trailed after her, talking a mile a minute.

"It was the cake. The paddle wheel, you know? Ox and Philippe were going to deliver it, and then . . . I don't know what happened. It was just ruined!" Another shout went up from the crowd at the door, and the next few sentences got lost in the noise. "And then Philippe went after Ox," I

18

heard her say, "and Ox . . . well, you know how he gets. Should I call the police?"

Hearing my old friend's name made my step falter. Ox was working here, too? Since when? And why hadn't anyone bothered to tell me?

I tamped down my hurt feelings and tried to pay attention to the more important issues. Like the fact that Ox and Philippe were apparently trying to kill each other. Surely I'd heard that wrong.

"Don't be ridiculous," Edie snapped at the blonde over her shoulder. "Everything will be just fine."

Her certainty made me feel better. The two men had been like brothers in pastry school, and they'd grown even closer after graduation. No way they were going at each other with fists flying.

Edie and the blonde moved away, but I stayed where I was and took a good, long look at my surroundings.

Each of the four walls was painted a different color — bright hues of gold, fuchsia, teal, and lime. In a smaller room the almost neon colors might have been overbearing, but in this large space they worked. Huge white-paned windows overlooking a lavish garden let in bright summer sunlight and added another layer of cheer to the workspace. A workspace I'd sketched more than once while Philippe and I were married.

I counted at least a dozen gleaming metal tables, half of which were in use, judging from the fondant, icing, and pastiage scattered around them. Countless sets of aluminum shelves were filled with every piece of baking equipment someone in my profession could hope to own.

Seeing my dream laid out in front of me made the breath catch in my throat. The shouting died away, but I could still hear excited voices coming from outside as I turned slowly in a circle to take it all in. This was my idea, my design, *my* bakery. How dare Philippe take it and make it his?

I'm not sure how much time passed before footsteps sounded behind me, followed by a startled, "Well, hello!"

I whipped around at the unexpected voice behind me and found myself staring at one of the most attractive men I've ever seen. Tall. Tanned. Athletic. Great body and a killer smile. I gawped like a prepubescent schoolgirl and got out a one-word response. "Hello." Brilliant.

He shrugged into a chef's jacket and buttoned it slowly. "Who are you and what are you doing here?" His voice was warm and lazy, an unhurried drawl that conjured up mint juleps and porch swings. I think my toes curled at the sound of it.

I dragged my gaze away from his shoulders and forced it back to his face. "I'm here to see Philippe."

Adonis glanced around at the now-empty room. "Philippe Renier?"

"You have more than one Philippe working here?"

One of those shoulders rose and fell in a shrug, and his gaze drifted briefly toward the loading dock. "He's kind of tied up at the moment."

What? Who? Oh. Yeah. Philippe.

"I'd be glad to help you," he said, flashing that smile again. "Burt McGuire at your service."

His tone was flirtatious and playful, and I don't mind admitting that his interest did wonders for my ego. I might have stayed right there, lapping up his apparent admiration, but a new round of excitement rose up from the loading dock, and I couldn't ignore it. I nodded toward the open door. "Trouble?"

"A little," he admitted. "Nothing important." He put one hand on the small of my back and tried to steer me back toward the front office.

When I realized what he was doing, I

slammed on the brakes. "If you could just point me in the right direction, I'd appreciate it. I only need a minute of Philippe's time."

Burt shook his head slowly. "Sorry, darlin'. Wish I could help, but I don't think he's here. I'd be happy to pass on a message when he gets back."

Aw. Darn. Strike one. I hate being lied to. "Thanks, but this is a personal matter. I'm sure he's around somewhere. Rumor has it, he's knocking the stuffing out of his best friend Ox on the loading dock."

"Don't believe everything you hear." Burt leaned against an empty table and grinned as if we were BFFs. "So it's personal huh? What did he do? Stiff you with the tab last night? Not call when he said he would?"

I wondered if unhappy women showed up looking for Philippe on a regular basis and added that question to the growing list I intended to ask Philippe when I found him. "Maybe you could just tell me where he was the last time you saw him."

With a shrug, Burt picked up a spatula covered in pale-blue buttercream and wagged it at a door across the cavernous room. "Last time I saw him? He was in the kitchen talking to Abe. But that was an hour or two ago. Abe's usually gone home long

22

before this."

My head snapped up so fast, I felt a twinge in my neck. "Are you talking about Abe Cobb?"

"Yeah. Why? You know him?"

"We've met." Apparently, Edie and Ox weren't the only old friends who'd joined Philippe in his new business. I wondered if any of them would have come running if I'd been doing the hiring, but I was afraid to ask. Philippe had always been the gregarious one. I'd been more reserved, and I'd never been sure whether our friends had really liked me or if they'd hung around because that's where Philippe was. Guess I had my answer.

None of that mattered now, I reminded myself. I was moving on to a new life — whatever that turned out to be. There wasn't room in my new world for the old insecurities.

Burt grabbed a clean latex glove from a nearby box. "I doubt Philippe's in the kitchen anyway. He's supposed to deliver a cake in a little while, so he probably *is* out on the loading dock."

Exactly where I intended to go next since Philippe was allegedly involved in the trouble, which seemed to be escalating. I started to walk away but stopped and turned back to ask one more question. "Aren't you even a little curious about what's going on out there?"

Burt shook his head and snapped the latex glove onto one hand. "Don't have to be. I know what's going on."

"Oh?"

"Just a couple of guys blowing off steam. It's been building up for a while now, but they'll be okay."

With Philippe and Ox involved, that's probably exactly what it was. But part of me wanted to see for myself — the part that resented Philippe for choosing work over me, for stealing my dream bakery, and for signing on half our friends behind my back. That Rita needed to know there was trouble in her ex's new paradise. And who was I to deny her?

I made my way through the cavernous room toward the back door and stepped out onto the loading dock, where the oppressive heat slammed into me. The heaviness of oxygen at sea level landed on my altitude-loving chest like a fifty-pound bag of flour. I resisted the urge to run back inside and instead tried to catch up on the excitement.

I found half a dozen people milling about on the loading dock and Edie trying to calm the chaos from the back of a white van bearing the "Zydeco Cakes" logo. I might have chosen a different image than the cartoon alligator playing an accordion beside a five-tier wedding cake, but I appreciated the fact that Philippe had come up with at least one semi-original idea.

The blonde who'd alerted us to the trouble had given in to tears, and a plump, middle-aged woman with red frizzy hair was doing her best to offer consolation. A sour-faced young woman with pale skin and lips painted as black as her hair watched the chaos from one corner of the dock, careful to stay out of the sun, and Burt wandered outside behind me.

The van's back door and driver's door were both wide open, and I could see a big cake in the shape of a paddle-wheel boat leaning heavily to one side. Several large holes had been hacked into the showpiece, causing chunks of cake to fall away which left yellow patches gaping in the smooth white fondant.

I recognized the recipe immediately, but I wondered why Philippe had used it for such a huge job. The cake had a lovely, light lemon flavor, and the lavender cream between the layers was heaven on earth, but the cake itself was moist and heavy in texture, and that made it difficult to work with. Philippe was one of the most skilled cake artists around, but even for him this seemed an unlikely choice for a cake this size.

As I watched, a glob of buttercream icing slid from beneath the fondant, forming a lumpy pool on the plywood used to create a solid foundation during transportation. Apparently, the cake didn't like the heat and humidity any more than I did.

In spite of my irritation with Philippe, my stomach twisted in unexpected sympathy as I looked at the carnage. That riverboat must have taken at least a week to put together, and the damage was so severe it would take someone with incredible cake skills to repair it. I knew of only two cake artists I'd trust with a job like that. From what I was picking up from the cacophony around me, one of us was nowhere around.

"Get the cake inside," Edie ordered. "If you leave it out here any longer, it will be totally ruined."

Good call. I wanted to suggest that they put it straight into the refrigerator to prevent further melting, but it wasn't my place to say anything. I swallowed my advice and moved deeper into the shade of the dock, not only to avoid the oppressive heat, but because it seemed like a bad idea to get in Edie's way.

Leaning against the coolish wall, I mopped sweat from the back of my neck. When the door behind me squeaked open again, I whipped around, still expecting to see Philippe. Once again, I got a blast from the past as Dwight Sonntag, shaggy and bearded and wearing a faded T-shirt and holey jeans, flew past me and hopped from the dock to the parking lot.

Et tu, Dwight? I was beginning to think Philippe had hired *all* our friends to work at Zydeco. And yeah, I was annoyed by that, but the fact that none of them had mentioned it to me bothered me a whole lot more. It wasn't as if we talked on the phone once a week, but we were all Facebook friends and stayed in touch through the occasional e-mail. They could have said something, and the fact that none of them had mentioned it, even in passing, made me wonder if I'd uncovered a conspiracy.

The conversation rose and fell around me as the staff tried to decide what to do and argued mildly over who was in charge. I heard a couple of people blaming Philippe and Ox for the ruined cake, but I wasn't sure they were right. Even if those two had been locked in combat, both would have protected the cake. That's just how they were.

As the minutes ticked past, people stopped speculating about the cake and started asking other questions. Had anyone seen Ox? Where was Philippe?

That's what I wanted to know. The Philippe I knew should have been right in the middle of this mess, taking charge and barking orders. The Philippe I knew should have been there to meet me after asking me to come by that morning.

Beneath the confusion, I felt an undercurrent that made me uneasy. Something was wrong here. I could feel it in the air. And the longer I stood on that loading dock, the more convinced I became that a ruined cake was the least of Zydeco's worries.

Two

I stayed in the background as long as my conscience would allow, but as Dwight and Burt carefully carried the cake into the bakery, followed by the others, I took the short flight of stairs to the parking lot and moved closer to Edie's command-post near the driver's door so I could share my concerns with her. Keeping my voice low, I said, "I heard a couple of people mention Ox. He's working here, too?"

Edie nodded and a flicker of guilt darted through her eyes. "From the beginning. He's been Philippe's right hand for the past couple of years."

That shouldn't have surprised me, but it did. The proof of my naïveté stung. But again, I pushed my hurt feelings away — this wasn't the time to deal with them. I nodded toward the now-empty van. "Some of your crew seems to think Ox did this."

"Yeah, I know." Edie sighed heavily. "But

they're wrong. You know Ox. He wouldn't do this."

I would've agreed, but I hadn't been around for a couple of years. People can change. "Any idea where he is?"

"Ox?" Edie shook her head. "There's no sign of him, no sign of Philippe." She frowned and chewed her bottom lip. "It's not like them to just disappear like this, especially when there's trouble with a cake." She glanced over her shoulder at the van, and her scowl deepened.

I met her gaze with a frown. "So both of them are missing."

"It looks that way." Edie shifted slightly, making it possible for me to see a set of keys dangling from the ignition and a pair of sunglasses abandoned on the dash. Expensive sunglasses. The brand Philippe had worn while we were married. He never went outside without them.

"I think we should try to find them," I said.

"Agreed, but I don't want everyone wandering around. We have no idea what happened here yet." Edie shaded her eyes with one hand and scanned the area slowly. From the dock, I'd been able to catch glimpses of the rose garden behind the trees, a gazebo off to one side, and a driveway curving around the house toward Prytania Street. Now that I was on ground level, the trees and undergrowth were so thick I felt a little claustrophobic. Anybody could be lurking out there. Anything could happen, and nobody would notice.

"Did you see anyone else?" she asked. "Anyone who doesn't belong here?"

I shrugged. "How would I know who belongs and who doesn't? But I only saw the people who were on the loading dock, and they've all gone back inside."

I walked to the end of the parking area to get a better look. I could see cars whooshing past on the street at the end of the long driveway, reminding me that I wasn't as isolated as I felt. I called out for each of the missing men as I walked toward the gate, but only the sounds of traffic and the breeze stirring in the trees broke the silence.

About halfway down the drive, I passed a cluster of flowering bushes that had been blocking my view. I saw an opening in the trees a few feet farther on, and just past that, a lump on the ground near the open gate. It took only a second for me to identify the lump as a person. A man, lying face-down on the ground.

My heart jumped straight into my throat. "Edie! Over here!"

Edie looked where I was pointing, let out a cry of alarm, and took off, running past me. I set off right behind her. Sweat poured down my back from the exertion, and I could feel my carefully straightened hair frizzing a little more with every step I took. My lungs burned from the unnatural exertion, and all that extra oxygen squeezed my chest like a fist. Or maybe it was fear at the thought that Philippe had been hurt. Whatever.

My legs are longer than Edie's, so even though I'm seriously out of shape, I caught up with her halfway down the long drive and passed her a few feet later. As I drew closer to the man on the ground, I realized that he couldn't possibly be Philippe. His skin was the color of mocha cake, and dark stubble covered his head, not Philippe's shaggy blond hair.

Ox. I heard him groan, and relief sucked the breath out of my lungs. Dizzy and light-headed, I hunkered down beside him and dashed sweat from my eyes before giving one shoulder a gentle nudge. "Hey. Are you okay?"

He responded with another groan just as Edie caught up with me. She yelped like a wounded puppy and dropped to the ground beside me. "Ox! Are you all right? What happened?"

He tried to sit up, but his elbows buckled and he sagged against Edie. On the ground where he'd been lying, a ball cap bearing the New Orleans Saints logo lay crushed and stained with something dark. I tried telling myself it was dirt, but the blood matted on his temple and trickling down one cheek made it hard to delude myself.

Edie put an arm around him and asked again, "What happened? Where is Philippe?"

Ox seemed confused by the questions. He shook his head gingerly, but even that small amount of movement seemed to be more than he could bear. Holding his head with both hands, he croaked, "I don't know."

"That's okay," Edie said gently. "Don't try to talk."

I stared at her in disbelief. "With all due respect, Edie, we need him to tell us what he knows. Philippe might be hurt, too." I offered him a reassuring smile. "When you're ready, Ox. Take a minute to think."

He nodded and took a deep breath. "I came down to open the gate. I think somebody hit me from behind." His voice was thin and reedy at first but gained strength after a few words.

"You didn't see who it was?"

He gave his head another careful shake.

"What about Philippe?" I asked. "Did you see where he went?"

"No." Ox rubbed the back of his neck and very carefully tilted his head in my direction. He blinked a couple of times and slowly focused on my face. "Rita? What are you doing here?"

"Hoping to see Philippe," I said shortly. No need to elaborate now. I stood and swiped at the sweat beading on my forehead. "If you were attacked, I think we ought to call the police and probably the paramedics, as well."

Ox shook his head and struggled to his feet with Edie's help. "Don't worry 'bout me. I'm okay." He took a step but his knees gave way, and he sagged toward the ground again. Since I'm taller and stronger than Edie, I slipped in to offer him a shoulder. "I think we should get you inside. Any idea where we should start looking for Philippe?"

Ox took a couple of limping steps toward the bakery. "He took off that way, and I came this way. If he's not in the van, maybe he's in the garden."

"You think he went for a walk?" With a cake to deliver and employees under attack? That didn't sound likely.

Ox scowled at me. "No. He said . . . I

think he . . ." He broke off with a growl of frustration. "I don't know."

We had to start looking somewhere, and I supposed it made sense to eliminate the fenced-in grounds before branching out into the rest of the world, so I nodded. "The garden it is."

Ox touched his temple gingerly, wincing a little. "We should split up. We can search faster that way."

"There is no 'we,' " Edie said firmly. "You're in no condition to do anything but sit inside, where it's cool."

"Not a chance," he argued. His voice was growing a little stronger, but I was still worried about him.

"Edie and I can look for Philippe. You need to lie down and rest."

I trailed the two of them back to the bakery, where we elicited firm promises from Sparkle — the young goth woman — and Burt that they wouldn't let Ox out of their sight. Isabeau, the perky blonde, gently wiped the blood from Ox's face while Dwight and the plump redhead — Estelle — wrestled with the paddle-wheel cake. With everything in the bakery under control, Edie and I decided to divide and conquer the garden.

I wanted to call the paramedics, but since

there was still no sign of Philippe, I gave up trying to talk sense into Ox and resumed the search.

Edie set off toward the gazebo, and I strolled down the rose-garden path past blooms so big they seemed almost unreal. The extensive garden added to the illusion of days long gone, as did the muted sounds of Dixieland jazz playing on a nearby radio. Only the noise of nearby traffic kept me grounded in the here and now.

I breathed in the scents of gardenia, jasmine, and roses, and another ribbon of envy curled through me. I would have given my right arm for a shop like Zydeco. Philippe knew that. Was this why he wanted to talk to me? Was he feeling guilty?

Another thought occurred to me, and my step slowed. Was it possible that he'd done this on purpose? Was he trying to win me back? Is that why he'd refused to sign the papers for so long? Had he created my dream so he could show me how sorry he was? If so, it was a wonderful gift. Elaborate. Over the top, just like Philippe himself.

My heart softened, and I wondered again what I'd say if Philippe did ask me to take him back. Would it really be possible to put the past behind us?

By the time I'd followed several twists and

turns in the path, I'd moved from "what if" he asked to "when." Uncle Nestor would have a fit, but Aunt Yolanda would understand. I knew she would.

I spotted a gate in the distance and paused to get my bearings. It looked like the gate let out onto an alley rather than a street, and from where I stood, I could see a heavy padlock on the latch. Obviously, Philippe hadn't left the grounds this way. Neither had Ox's attacker.

I was just about to turn back to explore another branch of the path, when I spied the toe of a running shoe poking out from beneath a low hedge. I froze in my tracks, and the breath caught in my throat. Somehow I knew I'd found Philippe, and I prayed he was in no worse shape than Ox.

Hurrying toward the end of the path, I called out, "Philippe? Are you all right?"

He didn't answer.

Dread churned through my veins, but I told myself not to overreact. "Philippe? It's Rita. Are you okay?"

I prayed silently that he'd respond, but the only voice I heard belonged to an announcer on the radio talking about an upcoming jazz festival. The scent of roses was strong and heady. The heat oppressive. Nervous perspiration trickled down my

37

back as I reached the end of the path and peeked over the hedge.

The man I'd married lay on the grass, his handsome face twisted in pain. A chef's knife protruded from his chest, and blood slowly pooled beneath his body. I retched and backed a step away, but I couldn't tear my gaze away from his eyes. Once, they'd looked lovingly at me. Now they stared sightlessly at the pale-blue sky. I knew instinctively that it was too late for him.

I gagged again and covered my mouth with both hands. The smell of blood filled my nostrils, and I backed up again, almost stumbling over my own feet as I tried to get away from that horrible odor.

Tears burned my eyes, and my heart felt as if it had been shattered into a million pieces. Philippe had been my friend, my lover, my husband, and, for a while, my worst enemy. I'd come to New Orleans, determined to finally detach my life from his, yet for a few hours this morning I'd contemplated reattaching. Had he been planning to ask for a second chance? I'd never know. Philippe was dead and I was finally free to move on . . . but I've never wanted anything less.

THREE

"Now, then, Mrs. Renier, why don't you tell me what happened this morning?"

I glanced up from the table in the conference room above Zydeco's kitchen and looked toward the door, fully expecting Miss Frankie, Philippe's mother, to be standing there.

"Mrs. Renier?"

I looked back at the owner of the voice, realizing slowly that the scowling police detective was talking to me. He was a large man. Fit, not fat. His light brown hair was buzzed short, making him look like someone who meant business. He leaned forward, a pair of muscular forearms resting on the polished tabletop, watching me intently as he waited for my answer.

"It's Ms. Lucero," I said, trying to shake off the mental fog that had settled in as soon as I had finished repairing the paddle-wheel cake. I'd had to cut out the whole midsection of the cake, stack and carve a replacement section. While the staff worked on creating new detail work out of fondant and gum paste, I'd given the new stack a quick crumb coat, then iced it with buttercream and covered it all with fondant. A few well-placed gum-paste windows and pillars had hidden the patch job, but the work had taken a toll.

"Rita," I clarified as I blinked away exhaustion. "I kept my name when we got married for professional reasons. And don't try to make anything out of that. Women do it every day."

"Duly noted," the detective acknowledged with a thin smile. "So Rita, what happened this morning?"

The question irritated me, mostly because he already knew the answer. I played along anyway. "My ex-husband was murdered, and one of his employees was injured in the attack."

The detective — Sullivan, if I remembered right — looked at me through a pair of eyes so brilliantly blue they were a little disconcerting. "I'm tryin' to piece together the details," he drawled. "Start from the moment you arrived." He sat back in his chair, and I realized that he'd been blocking one of the windows. With his shoulders out of the way, afternoon sunlight poured into the room, hitting me squarely in the face.

I squinted, holding a hand over my eyes to cut the glare. "Do we have to do this now? I'm so tired I can barely think."

Those blue eyes turned to ice in a heart-beat. "If you don't mind, ma'am, I'd like to catch the person who did this."

Heat crept into my cheeks, and a flash of resentment found its way through the sadness. "Me, too. But I don't know anything."

"Why don't you let me be the judge of that?"

"Fine." I shifted in my chair to escape the sun. Exhaustion made every muscle in my body ache, and a yawn snuck up on me without warning. I tried to stifle it, but Detective Sullivan kept his eyes locked on me, so I was sure he'd noticed. I rubbed my face with both hands, trying to wake up. *Keep it simple,* I told myself. *Answer his questions so you can get out of here.*

"I told that other officer everything I know already," I said, hoping Sullivan would trot off to get my statement from the other cop.

He didn't move.

"I don't remember his name," I said help-fully, "but he was one of the guys who responded to my 911 call."

"I'm real glad to hear the firsts did their

41

job. Now how about answerin' my question?"

I'd had a rough day. I could have used a friendly smile and a little compassion. Apparently, I wasn't going to get either from this guy. "Fine. I'll try."

Reluctantly, I walked the detective through my arrival at Zydeco that morning and my discovery of Philippe's body.

"And then after calling 911, you decided to spend the time . . . decorating a cake?" He sounded incredulous.

"If we hadn't fixed that cake and gotten it out the door, there was a real chance that this whole business would collapse," I replied defensively. "I couldn't do that to Philippe." I didn't mention that I hadn't even wanted to get involved, but Edie, of all people, had insisted I take the lead on salvaging the damaged cake.

It had been a while since I'd taken the lead on a decorating job, and I don't mind admitting that it felt good. Creative muscles I hadn't used since moving back to Albuquerque two years earlier had stretched as I worked, and I'd remembered why I'd gone to pastry school in the first place.

"But now I'm exhausted," I told the grim-faced cop. "I'd really like to go back to my hotel."

"I'll let you do exactly that . . . in a few minutes." Detective Sullivan flipped a couple of pages in his pocket-sized notebook and looked up at me with eyebrows raised. "You came here all the way from New Mexico?"

I nodded and tried not to squirm under the weight of his gaze. "To talk to Philippe."

"You couldn't have called?"

The pain in my head began to throb. "I needed to get his signature on some legal documents. I couldn't do that over the phone."

Sullivan's left eyebrow rose a little higher. "What kind of legal documents?"

I assumed the detective already knew the answer to that question too, which meant he was trying to trip me up. Did he consider me a suspect? Suppressing a shudder, I moved my chair a little farther from the sunlight so I could think. "I needed him to sign our divorce agreement, okay? Would you mind lowering the blind? The glare is giving me a headache."

Sullivan glanced toward the window as if my request surprised him, but he stood and did as I asked. "Better?"

"Yes, thanks."

"Good. Now, the divorce agreement. You sayin' you had to bring it to New Orleans personally?"

"I'd already tried dealing with it from a distance. Philippe kept ignoring me. I wanted to get his attention."

Sullivan's eyes iced over again. "So you wanted the divorce, but he didn't?"

"Philippe wanted the divorce as much as I did. He just had a habit of putting things off. If it had to do with his business, he was all over it. Anything else got shoved to the side and forgotten." I didn't mention the message he had left me that morning or admit that I wasn't sure how Philippe felt about me. No sense confusing the issue.

Sullivan wrote something in a notebook. "The decision to end your marriage made you angry?"

"No, it made me sad."

"So you left here and went back to Albuquerque."

I shook my head. "We were living in Chicago at the time. New Orleans was home to him and he wanted to do something to help with the recovery after Katrina. He came here. I went home to New Mexico."

"This was how long ago?"

"Two years."

"And why did you decide to get the divorce agreement signed today?"

"Because it's time. I grieved for a while, but I'm ready to move on with my life. I couldn't do that with our marriage in limbo."

Sullivan made another brief note. "How long you been in town?"

"I arrived Thursday afternoon. I came here yesterday, but Philippe wasn't available. I left a message with Edie and went back to the hotel last night. I came back today to try again."

"You didn't try calling his cell or pay him a visit at home?"

"I didn't have his current address or cell number," I said. "Since he came back to New Orleans, I've only been able to reach him at the shop."

"You couldn't have reached him through a relative?"

"I didn't want to involve his mother."

The detective cut another one of those intense glances at me. "That's unusual, isn't it? Not knowing how to stay in touch?"

"I wouldn't know," I said, trying not to look nervous. "This is my first divorce. We didn't have children, so there was really no need to stay in touch."

Sullivan jerked his head toward the duffel bag the uniformed officers had gathered from the front office. "So you came back this morning. What were you fixin' to do? Move in?"

Was he trying to be funny? The complete lack of expression on his face made it hard to tell. "I came prepared to stay until Philippe signed the divorce agreement."

"You were serious about getting rid of him."

Nervous perspiration beaded on my nose and upper lip. "Look, Detective, I know what you're thinking, but you're wrong."

"You have to admit, it's quite a coincidence. You come to town, and two days later, your estranged husband is dead."

My stomach lurched, and the hair on my neck grew damp. "But it *is* a coincidence. I didn't have anything against Philippe. I just wanted him to sign the agreement so we could make the divorce official."

"And did he sign?"

I shook my head. "The first time I saw him was when I found him in the garden . . . so no."

He pulled back and looked me over. "So now you're technically his widow?"

"No! I mean, maybe. Technically. But not really. We were separated."

"So you said."

"We were in the middle of a divorce," I reminded him.

46

"And your husband died before it became final. Now that he's gone, what do you suppose will happen to his property?"

I *really* didn't like the direction he was going. "I don't know. I suppose his mother will get everything as his next of kin." My stomach gave a nervous flip. Was it possible that *I* would inherit? One glance at Sullivan told me that's exactly what he was thinking. "Whoa! Wait just a minute! If the business is successful, I think that's great. I'm happy for Philippe." I flushed and wagged a hand in front of me as if I could erase what I'd just said. "He was an incredibly gifted cake artist, and he deserved success. He worked hard to be the best." My voice caught and tears blurred my vision. "I never would have hurt him. Not to get Zydeco. Not for any reason."

Detective Sullivan shrugged. "Seems to me you had the most to gain."

"But I didn't know that was even a possibility until you just told me. Maybe the killer wasn't someone Philippe knew. Maybe the killer saw an opportunity and just took it."

"An opportunity to mess up a cake?" Sullivan shook his head. "That's doubtful."

"Maybe the killer was after money."

Sullivan shook his head. "Both men had

47

their wallets on them. They weren't touched."

I took a calming breath. In. Out. It didn't help. "Maybe the guy wanted the van. Or maybe he thought he could steal something valuable from Zydeco."

Sullivan leaned forward slightly, caught my gaze, and held it. "The perp didn't take the van or make any attempt to gain access to the bakery."

"That you know of," I pointed out.

Sullivan rolled his eyes in exasperation. "We're looking at homicide, Mrs. Renier. Probably premeditated."

"Rita," I said automatically. Premeditated? That made it worse. A crime of passion was one thing, but premeditated meant that someone had watched and waited. Someone coldhearted and calculating.

"It wasn't me," I said again. "And what if you're wrong about Philippe's property? What if he made a will and somebody else gets everything? Maybe somebody else had something to gain from his death. Have you even considered that?"

Sullivan dipped his head, just once, without taking his eyes from my face. "I have. You're not the only person of interest in the case."

I was a "person of interest"? Frightened

tears filled my eyes and a wave of grief and self-pity washed over me. Philippe was dead. I hadn't even had a chance to absorb that before the police started accusing me of murder. Maybe Philippe and I hadn't been able to make our marriage work, but I'd still wished him the best. I'd spent two years convincing myself that I no longer felt anything for him, but that wasn't true. My chest felt as if someone had reached inside and torn out my heart, leaving a huge, painful hollowness in its place. I'd thought losing him to divorce was painful, but this was a thousand times worse. Who could possibly have hated him enough to want him dead?

Sullivan produced a couple of bottles of water from somewhere and put one on the table in front of me. "Are you all right, ma'am?"

Now he wanted to play nice? "No, I'm not," I snapped. "My ex-husband has been brutally murdered and you think I did it. I'm most definitely *not* all right."

Sullivan sat there, watching me, until I'd composed myself.

"Assuming for the sake of argument that you didn't kill your husband —"

"Ex," I interrupted. "And I didn't kill him. No assuming necessary."

"Husband according to the law," Sullivan insisted. "Now, ma'am, if you didn't kill him, do you have any ideas about who did?"

"None." I twisted the cap off the water bottle and took a long, cold drink. It wasn't a miracle cure, but I did feel a little better. "Like I said, I haven't even spoken to him in a year. I have no idea what his life is like now or who his friends are."

"Or his enemies?"

"Or his enemies."

"What about Mr. Oxford?"

It took a second or two for me to realize he meant Ox, whose full name was Wyndham Oxford III. "No way. He and Philippe were like brothers. There's no way he could have done . . . that. Besides, he was attacked, too."

Detective Sullivan opened his own bottle of water but stopped short of drinking. "You said that you came to New Orleans to get Philippe's signature on the divorce papers. Maybe you changed your mind once you saw his operation. Maybe you decided you didn't want the divorce after all."

"That's *not* what happened."

"How about when you found out that he was seeing someone else?"

I swallowed wrong and spent a minute coughing before I choked out, "He was *what?*"

Sullivan's eyes bored into mine. "Are you saying you didn't know?"

"I had no idea."

"That's not why you suddenly felt the need to come all this way to see him in person?"

The heat in the room climbed a few degrees higher. "No," I insisted. "I had no idea he was even dating again. But why shouldn't he see someone else? We've been separated for two years." I tried to convince myself I meant that as I said it.

Sullivan ran a long look over my face, and I wondered what he saw there. Embarrassment at learning that Philippe had moved on with his life? Confusion over why he'd left the message asking me to meet him here? Or just my bone-deep exhaustion? I snapped a little. "Listen, I know you have a job to do, and I don't mind answering questions, but while you're talking to me, Philippe's killer is out there doing who knows what. He could be destroying evidence, for all you know. Covering his tracks."

Sullivan's mouth quirked up on one side. "You think I'm wasting my time talking to you."

"Yes, I do. I don't know anything about Philippe's life now. Like I've been telling

51

you, we've been separated for two years, and it's been a year since I even spoke with him on the phone."

"So he didn't know you were coming to New Orleans?"

I shook my head. "I didn't tell him."

"Why not?"

I hesitated for a second and then voiced a suspicion I'd been trying to ignore for the past few weeks. "Because I wasn't completely convinced that he was getting my messages or the documents I've been sending him. I thought I'd have a better chance of actually reaching him if I showed up in person. I was wrong."

Detective Sullivan glanced up from his notebook. "You think someone has been intercepting your messages?"

"A little less cloak-and-dagger than that, but yeah. Sort of."

"You're talking about Ms. Bryce?"

I shrugged. "Maybe. She's a friend, but she's always been overly protective of Philippe, even when she had no reason to be."

Sullivan pondered that for a moment, then asked, "What about the rest of his staff? How did he get along with them?"

I shook my head slowly. "I don't know all of them. Philippe and I went to pastry school with Edie, Ox, Dwight, and Abe. We were all good friends . . . Obviously, they've kept in touch with Philippe, since they're all working here. As for the other staff, I have no idea what his relationships with them were like, but Philippe was a great guy. Friendly. Fun loving and easy to get along with. I just can't imagine someone hating him this much."

"So why did you split up?"

"We wanted different things."

"Who pulled the plug on the marriage?"

"He did. But that was a long time ago."

Sullivan scribbled something in his notebook. "What about family? Any of them have a grudge against your husband?"

"Ex," I reminded him. "Philippe has several cousins, but as far as I know, he got along great with all of them. Other than that, it's just him and his mother. Philippe was an only child, and his father died when he was eleven or twelve." We'd had that in common. I'd lost both my parents when I was a child. Philippe had understood that part of me, and I'd gravitated to his empathy. Thinking about that made the lump in my throat grow large and painful again. "His mother," I choked out around it. "Miss Frankie. How did she take it?"

Sullivan shook his head. "She doesn't know yet. I'm heading over there next."

I think my mouth fell open. "You haven't *told* her?"

"I've been a little busy."

"But that's horrible! You're here wasting time talking to me, asking me questions, and treating me like some kind of criminal. Meanwhile, Miss Frankie could be finding out that her son was murdered from somebody else!"

"That's not going to happen," Sullivan assured me. "My men are keeping an eye on everyone who hasn't been interviewed yet. No one is allowed to make calls."

"But —"

"I've got it under control." He started to rise, and panic rose up in me at the same time. How could I just walk away and leave my ex-mother-in-law alone at a time like this?

A few minutes ago, I couldn't wait to get away from Detective Sullivan. Now, suddenly, I didn't want the interview to be over. Crazy? Maybe a little. But what can I say? When trouble hits, I panic. It's what I do.

FOUR

I gripped Sullivan's arm. "Take me with you."

His gaze dropped to my hand and lingered there. He didn't say anything, but the message came through loud and clear.

Sheepishly, I pulled my hand away and mumbled, "Sorry. But you have to listen to me. Miss Frankie can't be alone when she finds out that Philippe is dead."

"This isn't the first time I've had to talk with the family of a homicide victim," Sullivan assured me. "I know what I'm doing."

"But you don't know Miss Frankie. She's going to need someone with her."

He almost smiled. Almost. "And you think *you're* the person she needs?"

"Yes I do." He made a noise of derision and the urge to grab his arm rose up again. I linked my hands together in my lap instead. "The divorce wasn't my idea. She was never angry with me."

Sullivan looked interested in that. "She was angry with Philippe?"

"No!" I sighed in frustration. My relationship with Miss Frankie was difficult to explain. Here in the United States, we like to tell ourselves the class system doesn't exist, but, of course, the truth is it's alive and well. As a poor Hispanic girl from Albuquerque, New Mexico, with no immediate family of my own, I'd felt *way* out of my league around the Thibodeaux-Renier tribe, with their old money and even older customs. But from the start Miss Frankie had welcomed me, the woman who stole her babyboy's heart, and treated me almost like her own daughter. Philippe and I had been together seven years total, five of those as man and wife. During that time, Miss Frankie had helped fill the void left by my own mother. I'd missed her almost as much — maybe even more — than I had her son over the last two years.

I scowled at Detective Sullivan, trying to figure out how to make him understand. "It's complicated, okay? But I need to be there when she finds out. Please?"

He stared at me for a long time. "There's no other family?"

I shook my head and tried to come up with a more persuasive argument, or maybe

56

a plan B. Maybe I could call a cab and hope I made it to Miss Frankie's before Sullivan delivered the bad news. He couldn't stop me from doing that, could he?

"Are we through here?" I asked as I reached for my bag.

"For now."

"Good. Any reason I can't take my things with me?"

Sullivan shook his head. "Fine by me."

While I gathered myself up, Sullivan crossed to the door and opened it. But there he paused with his hand on the knob. "Well?"

"Well what?"

"Are you coming or not?"

My head snapped up and gratitude bubbled to my lips, but he'd already left the room. I lurched out of my chair and hurried after him. "You're taking me with you?"

"Isn't that what you wanted?"

"Well, yeah, but —" I broke off and hurried to catch up with him as he turned the corner. "Yes. Yes, it is. Thank you. I can't tell you how much I appreciate this."

He glanced back at me. "You can be there for your mother-in-law if you'll keep your mouth shut and let me do the talking. Can you do that?"

"Absolutely." I rounded the corner behind

him and caught a glimpse of my reflection in a window, gasping aloud at what I saw. My hair looked as if I'd spent the morning playing with a light socket, and the makeup I'd put on at the hotel had melted off my face like the fondant on the paddle-wheel cake. Dirt smudged my forehead and cheeks, making me look like a kid who'd found the cookie jar.

And I panicked. "Hold on," I said. "I need five minutes."

Sullivan ground to a halt and frowned at me. "You what?"

"I need five minutes," I said again, waving my hands around my face and hair. "I don't want to show up on Miss Frankie's doorstep looking like . . . this."

Sullivan shook his head. "Either come as you are, or forget it. I'm not waiting around while you do whatever it is you do."

"But *look* at me. I can't go anywhere looking like this."

"Fine. Stay here then." Sullivan started to turn away.

"I'm asking for five minutes," I argued. "The woman was my mother-in-law. Do you have any idea what that means?"

"That you were married to her son?"

"Exactly! I can't show up for the first time in years looking like a bag lady, especially under these circumstances."

He took a closer look at me, seemed to realize what a disaster he had on his hands, and relented with an annoyed shrug. "Fine. Five minutes. Any longer and I'm going without you."

I didn't know whether to be grateful or insulted, but I hurried to the bathroom before he changed his mind. Five minutes wasn't nearly long enough to repair the damage I found when I looked into the mirror, so I concentrated on the worst areas first, scrubbing at the dirt on my face and the streaks of mascara with a moist paper towel, then wiping off what little was left of my eye shadow.

With my face reasonably clean, I dug around in my bag for a hair clip. I found several empty gum wrappers, some loose change, and three receipts from Ortega's — the best place in Albuquerque for home-made tamales outside my Aunt Yolanda's kitchen — but nothing I could use on my hair.

As I tossed the receipts and wrappers, I checked my watch and realized my time was almost up. I gave up the search and plunged my fingers into the stream of water from the faucet instead. I plucked at the frizz, trying to tame it and make it look like stylish curls, but as usual, my hair resisted any effort that didn't include gel, pomade, and a heavy layer of hair spray.

With thirty seconds to go, I swiped a layer of Cinnamon Singe over my lips and stepped back to check the results. Not great. Not even good, but it would have to do.

I let myself out into the hall and found Sullivan leaning against the wall, one foot crossed over the other. He straightened when he saw me and gave me a once-over. "Ready?"

To take the worst news ever to my ex-mother-in-law? Not even close, but I nodded and fell into step beside him. We descended the stairs to the first floor and walked through the front office, where the staff sat in stony silence supervised by a couple of stern-faced policemen. "So what made you change your mind?" I asked, uncomfortable with all the unnatural quiet.

He flicked a glance at me. "Guess we'll find out if Mrs. Renier is as fond of you as you claim."

"That's why you're letting me tag along?"

He shrugged and pushed open the heavy front door, following me out into the heat. "I'm letting you tag along because I think you're right. I'm about to tell a woman that her son is dead. She shouldn't be alone."

He took the steps to street level two at a time and headed toward a red Impala parked at the curb. "But don't think this lets you off the hook. I still think you look good for this."

I had to run to keep up with him, and I was out of breath before I reached the street. "I'd argue with you," I huffed, "but I can't breathe."

Sullivan actually cracked a full smile and aimed his keyless remote at the car. "Hop in and buckle up."

I did as I was told, and a few minutes later, we pulled into traffic. Sullivan didn't talk much, which was fine with me. This was the first quiet moment I'd had since stumbling over Philippe in the garden, and I needed it to steel myself for what was coming next. I also needed to find a way to convince Sullivan I wasn't a murderer. I had what seemed to be a clear motive *and* I'd been at the scene of the crime.

Yep, clearing myself of suspicion ought to be a piece of cake.

FIVE

Twenty minutes later, we pulled up in front of Miss Frankie's house in Lakeview. I'm embarrassed to admit that I couldn't have found it on my own. I'd only visited New Orleans a handful of times while Philippe and I were married. Which, now that I thought about it, might not have been often enough.

My mother-in-law lived in an affluent neighborhood filled with graceful old houses, all untouched by Hurricane Katrina, all still surrounded by manicured lawns and ornate gardens. The community whispered wealth at every turn. Miss Frankie's house whispered as loudly as the rest, reminding me of all the reasons I'd felt uncomfortable the few times I'd been around Philippe's family money. Just as I began to wonder if I'd made the right decision by coming here, Sullivan broke the silence. "You okay?"

I nodded slowly. "Yeah. Sure." I took a couple of deep breaths as we climbed the stairs to the broad front porch, and did my best to beat back those old self-doubts. My place in the family wasn't an issue anymore. Making sure Miss Frankie was okay and that Sullivan wasn't going to badger her were the only things I should be worrying about.

Sullivan pressed the doorbell, and I heard several rich tones peal deep inside the house. A few seconds later, I heard the scuff of footsteps, and then I was looking at my mother-in-law for the first time since two Christmases ago, when I spilled red wine on her white carpet. My stomach lurched and nervous perspiration pooled beneath my arms.

Miss Frankie is several inches taller than I am, and rail thin. Her chestnut hair gleamed in the sunlight, sparkling with vibrant color that I knew came from her stylist, not nature. She looked confused, but only for a moment before I saw recognition dawn in her golden-brown eyes. "Rita? Is that you?"

Everything I'd planned to say got stuck in my throat, and I barely managed to nod.

"Well, my goodness, darlin', come here." She pulled me into a hug so tight I couldn't catch my breath. She smelled familiar —

spicy with a note of citrus, like Philippe's orange-spice cake. "I can't believe you're here! What are you doing in New Orleans, and why didn't you tell me you were coming?"

My eyes blurred and my throat burned. "I'm sorry," I croaked out. "I should have called."

Miss Frankie turned me loose and flapped a hand. "Don't you dare apologize. I'm just so glad to see you." She waved us in out of the heat, pausing to run a curious glance over Sullivan. I could see the questions in her eyes, but she was far too polite to ask and I wanted to wait until we were inside to explain.

"Y'all must be melting. Let me get you some sweet tea."

I tossed an uncertain glance at Sullivan. He nodded for me to accept, and we followed Miss Frankie into a spacious living room painted pale sea-foam green, accented with white crown molding and chair rails. I loved this room, with its rich brocade upholstery and soothing colors. Though as sunlight streamed in through a bank of French doors that led out onto a deck as big as my apartment in Albuquerque, once again I felt insignificant and out of place.

Miss Frankie motioned us toward the

same white-on-white sofa Philippe and I had sat on when we'd told her we were getting married. Then I'd been filled with giddy excitement. Now, sharp dread prodded uncomfortably. I sat. Sullivan stood behind me.

"Does Philippe know you're here?" Miss Frankie asked. I started to answer, but she raced on before I could get a word out. "Maybe we should call him." She tilted her head and seemed to reconsider, flicking a glance at Sullivan. "Then again, maybe you'd be uncomfortable. I don't want to push."

Sullivan cleared his throat. "Actually, Mrs. Renier, I'm here on official business. Detective Liam Sullivan, NOPD." He produced his identification and held it out for her to inspect. "Maybe you should have a seat yourself."

Her expression changed slowly from delight to confusion. "You're with the police?"

"Yes ma'am."

She sat in a wingback chair upholstered in the palest green and turned to me. "What's going on, Rita?"

Leaning forward, I took her hands in mine. "I'm afraid we have some bad news."

Miss Frankie's eyes registered shock, and

I knew that on some level she'd already guessed what we had to say. But denial is a strong emotion, and she clung to it desperately. "I don't understand. What are you doing here with the police?"

"I can answer that," Sullivan said. *Be gentle,* I begged him silently. "Your son and one of his employees were attacked this morning," he said. "The employee is stable, but your son was critically injured. I'm afraid he didn't make it."

I appreciated him softening the truth for her, but Miss Frankie didn't see it that way. Anger and pain flashed through her eyes, and she jerked her hands away from mine. "Is this some kind of joke?"

I shook my head, wishing I could say yes. "I'm so sorry. I'd give anything for this not to be true." Grief and sympathy for Miss Frankie's pain bruised my heart and made it even harder to breathe. I'd thought that I'd cried myself out at Zydeco, but now tears spilled over again and burned track marks down my cheeks.

Standing unsteadily, she backed away from both of us. "Philippe? Dead?"

"I'm afraid so," Sullivan said. He went to stand beside her, offering moral support without touching her. "Can I get you anything? Ms. Lucero here was visiting the

66

shop, so she agreed to come over, but is there anyone else I should call?"

Miss Frankie shook her head slowly. "No, there's no one." Her voice rasped in her throat, and every breath she took sounded as if she was choking. "My son is dead. There's no one else." She steeled herself and lifted her chin. "I'll be fine. Just tell me you know who did this."

"I wish I could." Sullivan put a hand on Miss Frankie's shoulder. "Why don't you sit down, Mrs. Renier? Maybe Ms. Lucero can bring you a glass of that tea."

Miss Frankie took her seat again and leaned her head against the headrest. "Yes. Thank you. Tea would be nice."

Eager to be useful, I shot to my feet. But before I could make it even halfway across the room, the front door flew open and a young woman with platinum hair and unnaturally large breasts burst into the foyer. She looked like any one of a hundred blonde-haired southern belles, all hair and eyes and . . . hips.

I disliked her on sight.

She slammed the door behind her and started up the stairs to the second floor. "Miss Frankie? Miss Frankie? Are you here?"

Miss Frankie closed her eyes and muttered, "Oh dear Lord." But when she opened her eyes again, her irritation seemed to have disappeared. "I'm in here, Quinn."

Footsteps clattered down the stairs again, and the blonde bombshell surged into the living room, her face tight with emotion. Or maybe it was Botox.

She wore an expensive-looking sheath dress belted at the waist and cut short enough to reveal a set of slinky long legs. On her feet were a pair of strappy white sandals that had probably cost more than I earned in three months.

When she spotted Miss Frankie, the blonde let out a wail of pain. "I *just* heard," she said, throwing herself on Miss Frankie's neck and sobbing as if she was the one who'd suffered the greatest loss. "What are we going to do without him?"

We?

Miss Frankie endured the blonde's hug for much longer than I could have, and then she gently pressed Miss Melodrama away. "What are you doing here, Quinn?"

Quinn. I searched my memory bank for the name but drew a blank.

Quinn's eyes widened in surprise. "I *had* to come. I *had* to see that you're doing okay." Without pausing for a response, she straightened up, swaying slightly and managing to look sexy and distraught at the same time. "The minute I heard, I told myself I just had to be here with you. Are you all right? Do you need me to call the doctor? I'm sure he could give you a sedative."

"I'm fine." Miss Frankie straightened her posture and folded her hands in her lap. "The detective here was just about to tell me what happened."

Quinn whipped around to face Sullivan and me. "You're the police?"

"Yes ma'am." Sullivan produced his badge and let her look it over for a moment. "You said you decided to come as soon as you heard," he said as he tucked it into his pocket again. "Would you mind telling me how you heard about Philippe's death?"

"Well, from Edie, of course."

Sullivan's eyes flashed with irritation. "Ms. Bryce called you?"

I felt a little flush of vindication. Hadn't I warned him?

Quinn made a pass at her eyes with a tissue and shook her head. "No. She didn't call." She took a breath deep enough to make her breasts strain against the fabric of her dress and exhaled as if she carried the weight of the world on her shoulders. "I stopped by the bakery to see if Philippe wanted to have lunch. The place was swarming with cops."

"I see. And you are?"

"Quinn Goddard. Philippe and I are . . . *were* . . . seeing each other." The last few words came out on a sob, and she sagged toward the floor, apparently on the verge of imminent collapse.

The melodrama made my gag reflex kick in, and I struggled to wrap my mind around the concept that this was Philippe's new girlfriend. Sullivan swept into action, offering support and guiding Quinn gently toward the sofa. No snarky cop voice for her. "I'm very sorry for your loss," he said soothingly.

Quinn lounged back on the sofa and turned her tear-stained face toward him. She looked more sultry than grief-stricken, if you asked me, and I caught her sizing Sullivan up as if she was trying to figure out which of her many feminine charms might work best on him.

"I can't believe that he's gone," she wailed again. "I saw him just last night. We . . . we had dinner together. And now he's dead?" She threw herself back on the sofa and draped an arm over her forehead in a classic "Woe is me" pose. "What kind of monster could do a thing like this?"

I expected Sullivan to laugh. Instead, he got all gushy faced and sweet. "I intend to find out," he assured her. "Do you feel up to answering just a few questions?"

"Me?" Quinn sat up sharply, looking as shocked as if he'd asked her to volunteer in a soup kitchen.

"If you don't mind." He looked at all three of us women in turn. "I know this is bad timing, but since you're all here together, it would be very helpful to my investigation if you could give me just a few minutes of your time."

Miss Frankie nodded. "Anything to help you catch the person who did this."

Her strength amazed me, but it didn't surprise me. She'd raised Philippe on her own after her husband died, and she'd done a pretty good job of it. Sure, he'd had his faults, but he'd been a good guy. One who worked hard and respected women. At least he had when I knew him.

Yet somewhere along the line, he'd apparently gone off the deep end. He'd started fighting with his friends and dating eye candy. And I couldn't help wondering how many other things had changed.

SIX

By the time Quinn had composed herself, the sun had shifted so that it painted afternoon shadows with the wisteria in the garden. Soon it would be dark, and I remembered all too well how much worse grief felt at night.

Miss Frankie stood quickly, her eyes blank. Functioning on autopilot. I knew that feeling, too. "Let me get the tea," she said. "I'm sure we could all use it."

Southern hospitality at its finest, serving refreshments to the folks who'd just shattered your life. I waved her back to her seat. "I'll get it. Is there anything else you want? Cookies? Cake?" I might not have visited often, but I remembered the drill.

"I believe there are some ginger cookies in the jar," Miss Frankie said, sinking back into her chair. "You could bring a few of those if you'd like."

Yeah. Those ought to help.

I turned to leave the room, but Quinn got herself up off the sofa and darted in front of me. "I'll go. I know where everything is."

Sullivan didn't offer any objection to her leaving, so I shrugged again and turned around. "Suit yourself."

She beamed as if she'd won the lottery and bounced from the room, leaving a trail of something flowery in her wake. Shampoo or some expensive designer perfume. Philippe had probably loved it. He'd always been after me to "do something" with myself, but I'd never thought he meant poison injections and plastic inserts.

"So she's Philippe's new girlfriend?" I asked Miss Frankie when Quinn was out of earshot. "Was it serious?"

Miss Frankie waved a hand in front of her. "Don't be silly. Quinn was a diversion, nothing more. But don't tell her that. She's an emotional little thing, God bless her."

A tinny-sounding laugh escaped me before I could stop it. "That's a bit of an understatement, isn't it?"

"She means well."

A dozen other Quinn-related questions flickered through my head, but Sullivan pulled his notebook and pen from his pocket, clearly eager to start asking questions. "How long were they together?"

73

Miss Frankie gave that a moment's thought before answering. "I don't know. A few months, I guess. Philippe didn't talk about her much in the beginning. I met her for the first time about a month ago."

Sullivan looked up from his notes. "Was that unusual?"

"Not particularly. Philippe and I are close, but he doesn't tell me every little detail about his life."

That wasn't true, but I didn't correct her.

"Yet you seem convinced that he wasn't serious about her," Sullivan said.

"I know for a fact he wasn't," Miss Frankie said firmly. "And I'm sure everyone in this room knows why."

I hazarded a guess. "Because he was embarrassed?"

Miss Frankie's lips actually curved slightly. "No, sugar. Because he was still in love with you."

Sullivan glanced my way, but I refused to look at him. I wasn't sure what he'd see on my face if I did. Did Miss Frankie know something I didn't, like why Philippe had left that message for me at the hotel?

"He was not still in love with me," I said, but I wasn't sure which of us I was trying to convince. "I've barely spoken to him since we separated."

Miss Frankie waved away my objection. "You know how stubborn he was. But I knew how he felt. A mother knows."

Warmth flickered in my chest, but even if she was right, it didn't matter now. "I came to town this week to get the divorce agreement signed. If I had seen him before . . . *before,* he would have signed it, and we'd have been divorced within the month."

Miss Frankie sighed heavily, but she put a hand on my arm and gave it a squeeze. "Leaving you was the biggest mistake Philippe ever made. You were good for him, Rita. The best thing that ever happened in his life."

I can't deny that made me feel good, but I wasn't so sure she was right. "That's kind of you to say, but I think he might have argued with you about that."

Sullivan leaned into the conversation again. "Why *did* he end the marriage, Mrs. Renier?"

Miss Frankie's mouth thinned and her eyes darkened. "I wouldn't know. That was between Philippe and Rita."

"He didn't talk to you about it?"

"No."

I didn't believe that either. Philippe had called his mother at least twice a day when we lived in Chicago, and he'd come home to New Orleans at least five times a year, often without me. I came with him for big family occasions like weddings and funerals, but he traveled alone for the other visits he couldn't seem to live without.

Apparently Detective Sullivan didn't believe her either. "That's unusual, isn't it? Since you say the two of you were close."

Miss Frankie's spine stiffened. I knew that look on her face. I'd seen it before, and it never meant anything good. "Are you accusing me of lying, young man?"

Sullivan shook his head. "Of course not, but it seems odd that he never said anything to you about his divorce. Maybe he mentioned something that you didn't consider important at the time?"

Miss Frankie lanced him with a steely look. "If you want to know why the marriage ended, ask Rita. She's sitting right here."

I gave Sullivan a little finger wave and tried to reassure Miss Frankie before she got too riled up. "He *has* asked me. I think he's trying to find out from you whether I'm lying or not."

Miss Frankie's head pivoted from me to Sullivan. Irritation flared into anger. "You can cross Rita off your list right now. She loved my son. She would never have hurt him."

Her loyalty both surprised and touched me. Sullivan opened his mouth to answer, but a loud crash cut him off. Quinn stood in the doorway, oblivious to the broken glass and tea on Miss Frankie's polished hardwood floor, staring at me with her mouth agape. "*You're* Rita?"

I nodded, but I have to admit that I was a little disturbed by Quinn's reaction. She seemed as appalled by me as I was by her.

"What are you doing here?" It must have been a rhetorical question because she turned on Sullivan before I could answer. "How dare you bring her here at a time like this? Miss Frankie has just lost her son. She doesn't need . . ." — she wagged a hand in my general direction and made a face — ". . . this!"

I felt almost as attractive as roadkill. "What Miss Frankie doesn't need," I said, "is a bunch of drama. Why don't we clean up that mess you just made and then we can answer the detective's questions?"

I thought my suggestion sounded reasonable, but Quinn boiled over like the filling in a lava cake. "Don't you dare start ordering me around! You don't belong here, and you're upsetting Miss Frankie by being here!"

"I don't think I'm the one upsetting Miss Frankie."

"You think *I* am?"

I'm not usually argumentative, but the day had taken a toll on me. I had no more patience, especially not for a skinny little *puta* with plastic parts. "You need me to spell it out for you? I'll use small words so you can understand. Yes, I think you're being very upsetting."

I'm pretty sure Miss Frankie said something just about then, but I couldn't hear her over Quinn's shouting. Sullivan perched on the arm of the sofa, his expression a mix of amusement, concentration, and morbid fascination.

Jabbing one acrylic-tipped finger toward the door, Quinn snarled, "I think you should leave."

When I made no move to obey her, she screeched, "I mean it! Get out of here now, before you upset Miss Frankie anymore!"

"You're the one who should leave," I snarled.

Quinn stepped over the broken glass and came at me. "You're old news, honey. Philippe loved *me*."

"Yeah? Then why did he leave a message

for me this morning asking me to get back together with him?" I blame exhaustion, grief, and shock. The words came tumbling out before I could stop them. And in the sudden silence that followed, I realized that I had some 'splaining to do.

SEVEN

Silence rang in Miss Frankie's elegant living room for about ten seconds before Quinn let out a feral yowl and lunged for me.

If the situation hadn't been so tragic, and if I hadn't been in such deep trouble with Detective Sullivan, I might have laughed. I held my ground outwardly, but those old insecurities nibbled at me from the inside. Quinn was tall, blonde, and gorgeous, with a figure straight out of a fashion magazine. From her Coach bag to her designer shoes, she belonged to a world I couldn't even hope to inhabit.

As I imagined steam pouring from her ears and nose, another layer of my hair frizzed, and my extra twenty pounds settled heavily on my hips. The jeans I'd picked up at Ross for a song and the blouse I'd ordered from a favorite online discount store had cost a grand total of thirty dollars. I felt dumpy and frumpy, like Philippe's used-up, worn-out castoff. But, I suppose, that's exactly what I was.

The headache I'd been fighting all afternoon pounded in rhythm with my heartbeat, and the sound of Quinn's screeching only made it worse. I was seriously thinking about using a few tricks on her that my cousins had taught me growing up, but Sullivan stepped over the coffee table to get between us.

"All right, that's enough. Both of you sit down and be quiet."

I didn't like being lumped with Quinn, but it seemed like a bad idea to argue. I circled back to my place on the sofa and sat. Quinn glared at me as she floated toward an empty chair near Miss Frankie's.

"Now, then." Sullivan looked at me as if he wanted to lock me up and throw away the key. "About that message . . ."

"I'm sorry. I know I should have told you."

"It's a lie," Quinn said with a smirk. She crossed her legs and jiggled her top foot nervously.

"Quinn, sugar, let's you and me stay out of this, shall we?" Miss Frankie's voice was syrupy sweet, but the expression in her eyes could have melted steel.

Blondie didn't like the suggestion, but she was smart enough not to argue with Miss

Frankie. She sank back in her seat and contented herself with shooting daggers at me with her eyes.

"The message?" Sullivan prompted. His mouth had thinned almost to the point of disappearing.

"Right. Well, like I told you, I left a message at Zydeco for Philippe yesterday. He called this morning while I was in the shower."

"What did he say?"

The message was still on my cell phone. I could have let him hear the whole thing for himself, but Miss Frankie would insist on hearing it as well, and that might be too much for her. Later, maybe. I summarized instead. "It was a very short message. He said we needed to talk and asked me to meet him at Zydeco."

Miss Frankie latched onto that. "Did he say what he wanted to talk about?"

"Not exactly, but he did say that he'd made a mistake when he broke us up."

"That's it?" Sullivan's voice was as tight and angry as Quinn's expression.

I shook my head. "He said that we were a great team and that things hadn't been the same since we split up."

Miss Frankie sat back with a satisfied snort. "See there, Detective? Isn't that what

I said before? A mother knows."

"Yes ma'am. You may be right." Sullivan turned back to Quinn, who looked downright murderous. "Now, Ms. Goddard, do you have any ideas about who might have wanted to hurt Philippe? Anyone who had a grudge against him? A jilted ex-girlfriend?"

Quinn pursed her lips and jerked her chin at me. "Just that one. Everybody else loved him."

Bite me, Blondie.

"Did he ever mention trouble at work?"

"No. Nothing. The business was doing well. He was making lots of money, and he recently picked up a couple of very important clients. Things couldn't have been better." Her gaze flickered toward Sullivan but didn't quite hit its mark. I had the feeling she was hiding something, but the detective didn't seem to notice.

"A few people at the bakery mentioned that Philippe had recently been having trouble with one of his employees — a man named Ox. Do you know anything about that?"

Quinn shook her head again. She recrossed her legs, revealing a length of shapely thigh and dangling one slim foot in its three-inch heel. "Not really, no."

"Which is it?" Sullivan asked. "Not really?

Or no?"

Oh, please! All that skin must be affecting his memory. "I told you already," I reminded him. "Ox would never have done this. You should be asking about the other employees. Or people who don't work for him. Or the neighbors."

Quinn shot me an icy glare, and the look Sullivan sent me was almost as cold. "How would you know what Ox would have done?" Quinn snapped. "You haven't even been around."

"No, but I know Ox, and I knew Philippe." And I knew them both a whole lot better than she could have. "They were as close as brothers."

"That may have been true once, but it hasn't been true lately." Quinn tilted her head to one side, and a silky curtain of sleek blonde hair fell over one bony shoulder. "Last time I was around them, they were barely speaking."

"Ox is Philippe's executive sous chef," Miss Frankie explained for Sullivan's benefit. "They met in Chicago, in pastry school. Ox came here when Philippe decided to open his own shop, and he's been at Zydeco ever since. I have to agree with Rita. Ox wouldn't have hurt Philippe."

"I understand your loyalty," Sullivan said,

84

"but the two of them were involved in an altercation this morning right before the murder. Several people on staff saw them fighting, and at least one person believed that one of them would kill the other before it was over."

"That was a figure of speech," I told him.

"Maybe. And maybe there's more going on at Zydeco than you know about."

What little color was left in Miss Frankie's face disappeared, and I worried that we'd put her through too much. "Time to wrap things up so Miss Frankie can rest," I said.

Miss Frankie waved off my suggestion. "Ox and Philippe? That can't be right. Someone was mistaken."

"Several someones, I'm afraid," Sullivan said.

Miss Frankie flapped a hand at him. "I don't care what they say. Ox did not do this."

"We'll know more after we've had a chance to interrogate everyone in more detail." Sullivan stood and tucked his notebook into his pocket, then handed each of us his business card. "I think that's all I need for now. Again, ma'am, I'm very sorry for your loss."

Sullivan stood chatting quietly with Miss Frankie, and when Quinn flounced out the door a few minutes later, I breathed a sigh of relief. I wasn't sorry to see her go, and I wondered about the look I'd seen on her face earlier, but exhaustion hit me like a slap in the face, and my brain felt as if it had been put through the blender. I couldn't wait to get back to the hotel. I wanted a hot shower and sleep. Time to decompress. To deal with the roller-coaster emotions that had been battering me all day.

"If you think of anything that Philippe may have said or done," Sullivan was saying to Miss Frankie. "Even something that may not have seemed important at the time, please call."

"Yes, of course." Miss Frankie got to her feet, but it seemed to require effort, and she wobbled slightly.

I moved to hug her, a promise on my lips that I'd stop by again before I left town.

She grabbed my hands and held on as if her life depended on staying connected. "You're not leaving, too?"

"I came with Detective Sullivan," I said. "And I have a flight out tomorrow afternoon —"

"No!" She tightened her grip on my hands. "Please. Stay. I don't want to be alone."

Visions of my hotel room danced in front

of my eyes, but they were no match for the pain in her eyes. She pulled me close and hugged me hard, and I felt the weight of responsibility settle on my shoulders. Reluctantly, I shoved aside my own needs and nodded. It wasn't about me. I owed her too much to walk away.

EIGHT

I couldn't sleep. I lay awake, listening to the unfamiliar sounds of night in Louisiana. The temperature had cooled off only slightly after the sun went down, and my desert-dry skin soaked up the moisture in the air as I listened to a chorus of frogs rivet, ping, and sigh outside. Every time I closed my eyes, images of Philippe lying dead in the garden filled my mind. I curled into the fetal position and wept until I had no more tears left. My reaction to Philippe's death confused me. We'd been apart for a long time. I'd moved on with my life, and so had he. Until I heard his message that morning, I'd never even considered reconciling. So why did losing him hurt so much?

Images of our first meeting danced relentlessly through my head. Our first kiss. Our wedding day. Philippe singing "Our Love Is Here to Stay" at the reception. It was our song, and I still couldn't hear it without thinking of him. I probably never would.

Around two in the morning, I gave up and crept downstairs. Baking has always been cathartic for me. Whenever I have a problem I can't easily work through, you'll find me puttering around in the kitchen.

I found some overly ripe bananas on the counter and dug around in the cupboards to see if Miss Frankie had everything else I needed to put them to use. Luckily for me, her kitchen was well stocked. I shouldn't have been surprised. Philippe had probably spent time here, and he'd have seen to it that she had ample supplies to keep him happy.

I pulled chocolate chips, flour, cinnamon, brown sugar, and vanilla from the cupboards and found eggs, butter, and sour cream in the fridge. I'd just finished coating a baking pan with butter and flour when a noise behind me brought me around so fast I almost dropped the pan.

"What's the matter, sugar? Can't sleep?" Miss Frankie stood in the open doorway wearing a nightgown beneath a threadbare robe — a gift from Philippe the year he left home. I wasn't at all surprised to see that she still had it, or that she'd chosen to wear it tonight. She'd scrubbed her face clean, and she looked frightened and vulnerable.

I shook my head. "I'm afraid not. Did I wake you?"

Miss Frankie dropped into a chair at the table. "Good Lord, no. I've just been staring up at the ceiling and wondering how much Philippe suffered. It just about kills me to think about him lying there hurt and alone."

I felt the same way. "I thought I'd make my aunt's chocolate-banana coffee cake so it will be ready in the morning. I hope you don't mind."

Miss Frankie shook her head and glanced around the room. "This is going to be a lonely old house now that Philippe is gone."

"He lived here with you?"

"No, he had his own place, but he was always around, fixing this and dropping off that. And I raised him here." She took another look around and released some of her pain on a sigh. "He's all over this house. I don't know how I'll stand being here knowing he won't ever come back. But I don't know where else I'd go. I've lived here myself since I was nothing but a twinkle in my daddy's eye."

I envied her roots. My childhood home belonged to someone else now, sold shortly after my parents died. Aunt Yolanda and Uncle Nestor's house just wasn't the same.

They'd taken me in after the accident, and they'd done their best, but I'd always been aware that I didn't quite belong.

Miss Frankie sighed again and propped up her chin in both hands. "I'm glad you came, sugar. It helps, seeing you. Makes me feel as if the whole world hasn't suddenly imploded."

I found a mixing bowl and a wooden spoon. "I'm glad you're holding up okay, but I'd feel better if someone could stay here with you for a few days."

"I'm a tough old bird," Miss Frankie said with a sad smile. "I'll survive this, though Lord knows I don't want to." She looked down at her hands and sighed again. "It's unnatural, a parent outliving her child. And for him to go like this . . ." She shook her head and fell silent. When she looked up again, steel and determination had replaced the pain and uncertainty. "I truly do hate the circumstances that bring you here, but I'm so glad you are. I always hoped you and Philippe would find your way back to each other. You were a good wife to my boy. I never stopped loving you, and neither did he."

I smiled tightly at her as I measured ingredients. I stirred the chocolate chips, brown sugar, and cinnamon together for the streusel topping, and the combined scents pulled me back to my childhood. I'd lost count of how many times I'd talked over some school problem with Aunt Yolanda while she made this recipe for breakfast.

Setting aside the streusel, I popped butter into the microwave for a few seconds to soften it, then creamed it in a bowl with the sugar, egg, and bananas. When I had the texture just right, I added the dry ingredients. Instead of using the mixer, I put my pain and confusion into stirring the ingredients into a smooth batter by hand.

Miss Frankie watched me for a few minutes before breaking the silence that fell between us. "I called Thaddeus Montgomery, our family attorney, and I have an appointment to meet with him tomorrow morning at Zydeco. I'd like you to come with me."

I stopped stirring. Batter dropped from my spoon to the bowl with a loud plop. "Me? But I'm going back to New Mexico. My flight leaves at two."

"You can't go," she said. "I don't want to do this alone, Rita. The attorney, the funeral, the arrangements . . ."

I left the bowl on the counter and sat across from her. "You want me to help you plan the funeral?"

She nodded and lifted her eyes to meet mine. "Would you?"

"You don't think people would talk? I mean, I'm the ex-wife."

"Not technically." Miss Frankie smiled sadly, trying to shine light into the dark corners of both our hearts. "And for the record, I don't give two hoots what anybody else thinks. I need you. I can't do this on my own. Will you stay for a while?"

"I guess I can stick around for a few days," I said. Uncle Nestor might grumble about me taking more time off from helping in his restaurant, but that was just his way. Aunt Yolanda would smooth things over for me. That was *her* way.

Miss Frankie patted my hand gently. "I've always thought of you as a daughter, not just a daughter-in-law. I guess you're all I've got left now."

My heart twisted. "I know it's early, but have you given any thought about what you'll do with the bakery in the long term?"

"I'll keep it open somehow. That's all I know. Philippe and I were partners in Zydeco. I put up the money. He provided the talent and the know-how. We set it up so that if one of us died, the other would inherit, but we always thought that *I'd* be the one to go."

I felt better knowing that Miss Frankie was behind the wheel at the bakery. "Well, you've got a good staff — at least the people I know. They're who I'd want to hire if I opened my own shop."

She tilted her head and studied me in silence for a moment. "*Do* I have a good staff? I thought so once, and I know Philippe felt he'd hired the best. But what if it was one of them who did this horrible thing?"

I thought about the staff — my old friends and the people I'd met that morning. Could one of them be capable of murder? "I'm sure the police will solve the case," I said, trying to convince both of us. "If anyone on staff had a hand in what happened today, they'll pay for what they did."

Miss Frankie looked up at me, her expression skeptical. "You have more faith in the system than I do. Read the paper. Watch the news. Murders go unsolved all the time. That young detective seems eager enough, but NOPD doesn't have the best track record. They say that NOPD stands for "Not Our Problem, Darlin'.""

"I'm sure Detective Sullivan will do everything he can to find justice for Philippe."

Miss Frankie nodded slowly. "He does

seem like a fine young man. Polite. Brought up right, it appears. But these things can take time, you know. And in the meantime, here I am with a business on my hands I know nothing about, and a staff I can't trust."

I gave the batter a stir, checking the consistency to make sure I hadn't accidentally overworked it. I didn't want the cake to turn out heavy or tough. "You can trust Ox."

"Can I?"

I checked the oven to make sure it had preheated, then poured the batter into the pan. "I thought you told Detective Sullivan that you did."

"I did. I *do*. At least, I want to. But he did get into a fight with Philippe this morning, and a few minutes later, Philippe was dead."

"I'll admit the timing looks bad, but all the police have is a bunch of circumstantial evidence. You could say the same thing about me."

"But you had no reason to want Philippe dead."

"I refuse to believe Ox did either," I said.

Miss Frankie shook her head slowly. "I don't know."

"Okay, then, what about Edie? She's been around for a while, and being manager gives her a bird's-eye view of the business."

Miss Frankie pushed air out between her teeth and swatted at the air between us. "Edie's a wonderful girl. Just wonderful. But you know Philippe didn't hire her for her decorating skills, and Zydeco needs a creative eye overseeing things."

That was true. Edie hadn't exactly failed pastry school, but she'd come close a few times. "Still, she might be a decent temporary solution," I suggested. "Or what about Dwight?"

"Dwight Sonntag?" Miss Frankie scowled at me. "Sugar, that man's not a manager. Even if he had the skills, he looks like something the cat dragged home."

An image of Dwight's shaggy hair and scruffy beard flashed through my head. Much as I liked him, I had to admit he wouldn't be good as the public face of Zydeco. "You might be right about that," I agreed reluctantly. "But there's no reason you can't trust him, is there?"

"I don't know," she said again.

"What about — ?"

She cut me off before I could finish. "Rita, there's just no other solution. You're the obvious person to take over. You know as much about cake decorating as Philippe did, and you're just as talented. Besides, you're technically still his wife." She slanted a glance at me and sighed again. "I might as well be honest. There's something else you should know."

"Oh?"

"There's been some kind of trouble at Zydeco for a while now. Philippe told me about it a week or two ago."

That got my attention. "What kind of trouble?"

"Strange accidents. Missing equipment. Disappearing inventory. Philippe was convinced that someone was trying to sabotage the business."

"What!? Don't you think you should have told Detective Sullivan about this while he was here?" I couldn't believe she'd kept this information a secret.

She looked at me as if I'd lost my mind. "Do you know what it would do to Zydeco's reputation if this got out?"

"It couldn't do more damage than murder."

She shook her head firmly. "The point is I don't know who I can trust. I need eyes and ears at the bakery. I want you to help me figure out who's doing this."

I gaped at her. "You can't be serious."

"I'm completely serious," Miss Frankie said. The set of her jaw and the steely look in her eye convinced me.

"But I don't know anything about sabotage," I argued.

"You know about running a kitchen. You know the business end of things. You know most of the staff. You're the obvious choice."

"I'm a cake artist, not a private investigator."

Miss Frankie waved off my arguments. "You're the perfect person to help me, sugar. I trust you. I need you."

I took a second to think about it. Half of me wanted to refuse. Stepping in for Philippe would be awkward at best. But the other half felt a little thrill at the idea of working in that beautiful kitchen and design center, even temporarily. "I have a life and a career back in Albuquerque, you know."

"Working for your uncle? Is that a better career than running Zydeco for me?"

No. Working as a sous chef in my uncle's restaurant couldn't compare with running my own cake shop, but the idea of running this particular shop made me more than a little uncomfortable. "Working *with* Uncle Nestor is a great opportunity," I said, out of loyalty.

Miss Frankie stood and pulled a couple of glasses from a nearby cupboard. "I'm not going to talk bad about your family, Rita, but you and I both know that what you're doing isn't worthy of you and your talents."

She certainly knew which buttons to push. "I can't just pack up everything and move here," I argued. "Uncle Nestor put me through pastry school. I owe him." I wondered what Uncle Nestor would say if I agreed to stay here in New Orleans. Or, rather, I wondered how long it would take Aunt Yolanda to calm him down. I contemplated the reactions of Philippe's staff. Would they be willing to take orders from me?

But in the end, it was the pain in Miss Frankie's eyes that convinced me. How could I say no?

"I'll stay for a few days," I agreed. "But just until you can find someone permanent to take over."

Miss Frankie threw her arms around my neck and kissed my cheek soundly. "Oh, thank you, sugar. You're a lifesaver. You won't be sorry, I promise."

Famous last words? I hoped not. I really wanted her to be right.

NINE

The next morning, I chased the aroma of fresh coffee, chocolate, and bananas into the kitchen, where I found Miss Frankie waiting for me.

She looked tired and pale, but she'd set out plates and mugs, sliced the coffee cake, and added a bowl of fresh fruit to the table. We ate quickly, reminiscing about Philippe. Miss Frankie shared stories about his childhood, and I told her about things that had happened when we lived in Chicago. Occasionally, we lapsed into long stretches of silence. I remembered Philippe as he'd been when we'd met, and I knew Miss Frankie was thinking about the five-year-old boy who'd broken his arm when he fell out of the towering oak tree near the property line.

After a quick detour to my hotel so I could shower, change, and check out (Miss Frankie insisted I'd be staying with her from then on), we walked through the front doors at Zydeco a few minutes before eleven. Unlike the previous two days, no enticing aromas filled the air. The hum of activity I'd noticed before was noticeably absent in spite of the fact that every chair in the reception area was occupied by a staff member. Apparently, Miss Frankie and I weren't the only people coming to the meeting with Philippe's attorney.

Once my initial surprise faded, it occurred to me that seeing the whole crew together might be a good thing. I still thought Ox was Philippe's most logical successor, and this might give me the chance to convince Miss Frankie of that.

Ox sat near the front window. A couple of deep bruises had formed on his face, and the cuts were covered with bandages. But in spite of his injuries, he looked strong and healthy. I told myself that was a good thing, but remembering Detective Sullivan's insinuations about Ox's possible guilt made me nervous.

I nodded at Burt as I passed and was treated to one of his flirtatious smiles in return. Isabeau's pale-blonde ponytail and perfect makeup couldn't hide the worry in her eyes. A flicker of surprise crossed Abe Cobb's narrow face when he saw me. He'd gone home before the attacks yesterday, so it had been a while since I'd seen him. He seemed even thinner and more morose looking than ever.

Dwight sat curled on his tailbone like a sullen teenager. He'd cut the arms off his T-shirt, and his jeans bore traces of grease stains. Definitely not appropriate for the face of Zydeco. Sparkle sat a few feet away, hiding behind a veil of black hair and making sure to avoid the sunlight coming in through the windows. Estelle sat on the floor near Edie's desk, picking nervously at her frizzy red hair.

Edie came out from behind her desk to fuss over Miss Frankie and shed a few tears. "I'll have someone bring out more chairs," she said when she finally stopped crying. "The meeting will start as soon as everyone's here."

In true southern-gentleman style, Burt shot out of his seat and motioned Miss Frankie toward it. She accepted it with a grateful smile, and I perched on a windowsill near Abe. I silently willed Ox to step up and show Miss Frankie his reliable, trustworthy side, but he didn't move. Maybe he was embarrassed by the fight. Maybe he felt guilty. Maybe he just needed time.

Miss Frankie sat with her back ramrod straight, accepting the whispered condolences of Philippe's employees, but I knew she was wondering if one of them was responsible for yesterday's attack. Was one of them guilty of sabotaging the bakery? Of murder?

I ruled out Estelle, Sparkle, and Isabeau immediately. I didn't think any of them had the physical strength to plunge a knife into Philippe's chest. Abe, Ox, Dwight, and Burt could have, but Burt had been with me. Which left my three old friends as possible suspects. Did I believe one of them was guilty? No. Not really. But I couldn't absolutely rule them out, no matter how much I might want to. Dwight was passionate and emotional. Abe reclusive and secretive. And Ox? Fiercely competitive.

I was still in the middle of sizing up the staff when the front door flew open, and Quinn made a grand entrance in skinny black cigarette pants and a sleeveless cowl-neck tunic made of something so thin and gauzy that it floated around her like a cloud.

I swallowed a groan of dismay.

As if on cue, most of the men in the room rose to their feet and hurried toward her. Burt reached her first and coaxed her gently into the room, settling her in Abe's abandoned chair. Dwight disappeared down the hallway and reappeared a moment later with a cold bottle of water. Abe stopped halfway across the room and hovered uncertainly.

Only Ox remained seated, his face expressionless. Interesting. Did that mean he disliked Quinn? Disapproved of Philippe's choice? I added that to the list of things I wanted to find out.

Isabeau slid forward in her seat and put a reassuring hand on the Drama Queen's arm. "How are you holding up, Quinn? Are you doing okay?" With their blonde heads bent together, they looked enough alike to be twins, except that Isabeau had the "girl next door" look down pat. Quinn looked more like she belonged in an episode of *The Girls Next Door.*

"How could I possibly be okay?" She pouted. "Philippe is dead. Somebody killed him, and they did it right here, in front of all of you!"

The good twin stiffened under the weight of the accusation, while Sparkle, mistress of the dark, shot Quinn a disapproving look from beneath her veil of black bangs. "Back off, Quinn. She's just trying to help." Sparkle was as dark as Isabeau was fair, as sullen as Isabeau was perky, but her loyalty to Isabeau impressed me.

Before I could wrap my mind around their unlikely friendship, Abe muttered something

I couldn't hear and even Burt's friendly expression grew cold and tight. "It was hardly *in front* of us," he pointed out.

Struggling to her feet, Estelle shot him a look and turned to Quinn, oozing sympathy. "I know how you must feel —"

Quinn cut her off. "Do you? Do you really?" She ran a look of distaste over Estelle's round figure. "I hardly think so."

Estelle clamped her mouth shut so hard her double chin jiggled slightly.

Apparently, Sparkle didn't like that either. Her already glum expression grew even grimmer as her lips formed a thin black line on her pale face. "I mean it, Quinn. Back off. They're just trying to be supportive."

Estelle lifted her chins and offered her a little smile. "Thank you, Sparkle."

"Whatever." Sparkle rolled her black-rimmed eyes and went back to looking unconcerned and slightly bored. "Now that Quinn's here," she said to Edie, "how much longer is this attorney jackass going to make us wait?"

She'd never win Miss Congeniality, but Sparkle had shown a kind chink in her goth armor, making it easier for me to under-stand why Philippe had kept her around. Talent alone had never been enough for him. He'd insisted on creating a work environment where everyone had fun.

Edie's answering smile looked pained, but she said, "He's ready for you now," and herded us like sheep up the stairs and into the room where Sullivan had interrogated me the day before. We spent a few minutes sorting ourselves out, and by the time Philippe's attorney strode into the room, we were all settled around the oval conference table, exhibiting various degrees of impatience.

Thaddeus Montgomery, a tall man in his sixties with silver hair and a long face, spent a few minutes chatting softly with Miss Frankie, then introduced himself to the rest of us. I knew his name well. Until now, I'd never met its owner, but I'd seen it on plenty of legal documents in the early stages of my divorce.

He sat beside Miss Frankie at the head of the table and motioned for quiet. "As most of you know," he said, in an accent reminiscent of Kevin Spacey's in *Midnight in the Garden of Good and Evil,* "I've been the Renier family attorney for most of my career. Philippe was not just a client; he was a friend."

A few people nodded, and Thaddeus looked around the table as he continued. "I'm deeply saddened to be here today, as

I'm sure we all are. I'm afraid that the disposition of Philippe's estate may come as something of a shock to some of you, and that's why I wanted everyone here."

A wave of unintelligible murmurs rose up from the group seated at the table. I glanced at Miss Frankie to see how she was holding up. She sat completely still, her eyes locked directly in front of her, her hands tightly clasped on the table.

"I'm aware that Philippe made promises to some of you during his lifetime," Thaddeus went on. "It would be my greatest pleasure to honor those promises now that he's gone. However, the law is the law, and I am bound to uphold it."

Promises? Any worth killing over? Most of the crew looked curious, Ox and Quinn both wore cautious expressions, but nobody looked sinister or secretive.

"The business will be covered by the partnership agreement entered into between Philippe and his mother. Philippe's death leaves Miss Frankie the sole owner of Zydeco. Since he died without a will or other written instruction, the rest of his estate will have to go through probate."

Quinn's head shot up for the first time, and she pinned the attorney to the wall with her gaze. "What does that mean?"

107

Thaddeus smiled patiently. "It means that Philippe's estate will be distributed according to state law."

"And what does *that* mean?"

"The court will appoint a personal representative to administer the estate. He or she will distribute the money — *all* of his liquid assets — along with his other personal property to Philippe's heirs or heirs-at-law."

I wondered just what that entailed, but I didn't ask.

"And those heirs are — ?" With every question, Quinn's voice gathered strength, until she sounded less like a grieving girlfriend and more like a shrewd businesswoman. Surprise, surprise.

"We'll get to that," Thaddeus assured her. He shifted his weight uncomfortably. "I'll file all the necessary paperwork as soon as I can, but you should be aware that absent a court ruling to the contrary, Philippe's estate will go to his next of kin."

Quinn's lips curved as she sat back in her seat. "That's fine, then. I'm sure Miss Frankie will see to it that Philippe's wishes are honored."

Thaddeus cast an uneasy glance in my direction. "Not his mother. At this point, it appears that the estate will go to Philippe's wife, Rita Lucero."

Even though Sullivan had hinted at this outcome, I gasped in shock. Every eye in the room turned on me, and Quinn went straight from benevolent grief to red-faced anger, as if someone had flipped a switch.

Shooting to her feet, she pointed one bony finger at me. "Are you saying that *she* inherits Philippe's money? His house?"

Philippe had a house? Miss Frankie had mentioned that he had his own place, but I'd thought she meant an apartment.

Thaddeus inclined his head slightly. "She does unless the court rules otherwise."

"Are you freaking kidding me?"

Forget Quinn; was he freaking kidding *me?*

"I'm afraid I'm not. The personal estate belongs to Ms. Lucero as Philippe's widow."

I stared at Thaddeus in shock and disbelief, unable to pull my thoughts together or get words out of my mouth.

Apparently, Quinn didn't have the same problem. "You know as well as I do that Philippe and I were going to live in that house together."

"As I said before, Ms. Goddard —"

"I know what you *said,*" Quinn shouted. "But if you think you can give everything Philippe owned to *her,* you're making a huge mistake."

"I'm not giving anything to anyone," Thaddeus said patiently. "I'm merely telling you what the law says. The divorce between Philippe and Ms. Lucero was never finalized."

Quinn shot a venomous look in my direction. "But that was just a technicality! They were divorced in every way except on paper."

I found my voice at last. "I'm sorry," I said to the room at large. "I didn't know . . ."

"You expect us to believe that?" Quinn shrilled. "You expect us to believe that you come to town and Philippe dies, leaving you everything, and it's all just some gigantic coincidence?"

"I'm sorry, Quinn, but yes, that's *exactly* what it is." Quinn was a lost cause. She'd never believe me, so I focused on the jury of my peers, who were all staring at me as if I'd grown three extra heads. I shifted uncomfortably under the weight of their stares.

The attorney cleared his throat in the stony silence that followed. "I know this comes as a surprise to some of you. Ms. Lucero will no doubt want to take some time to think about what she wants to do with Philippe's personal property. But you

110

should also know that Miss Frankie has asked Rita to take over here at Zydeco for the time being."

Now it was Ox's turn to flip out. His face went from curious to furious in a heartbeat. He shot to his feet so fast, his chair toppled over with a *bang!* that made me jump about a foot. "You're putting Rita in charge?"

Miss Frankie turned her head slowly toward him and spoke for the first time. "Do you have a problem with that?"

"Hell yes, I have a problem with that. I've given my heart and soul to this place. I know the business inside and out. If anybody takes over for Philippe, it should be me."

"Don't be an ass," Burt cautioned. "The decision is Miss Frankie's. If she wants Rita —"

"You want the business to crash and burn?" Ox shouted. "Go right ahead and put Rita in charge."

I jerked backward so hard, my own chair rocked onto two legs. "Hey! Wait just a minute —"

Ox went on as if I hadn't spoken. "If you want to continue Philippe's legacy, let me do what I've been trained to do."

He wasn't exactly endearing himself to Miss Frankie. She met his gaze without blinking. "I have no doubt that you're capable of running Zydeco," she said. "But in light of the circumstances, I'm not comfortable handing over the business to you. Rita is my choice. If you can't accept that, you're free to leave."

Leave? Ox? Bad idea. I wasn't the only one shocked by the ultimatum, either. Someone gasped, but I wasn't quick enough to see who it was. Right now, though, my first priority was to keep Ox from doing something foolish.

"Everybody, please calm down," I said, but Ox was out the door before I could say anything else.

I started to follow, but Miss Frankie grabbed my wrist and held on with a strength that surprised me.

"Let him go, Rita."

"But we need him. *I* need him."

"You'll do just fine without him," she said firmly. "If he won't support you, you'll be better off without him."

I sat down at the table and swallowed my guilt over letting my friend walk out the door on his friends, his career, his future. The meeting lasted less than ten minutes after Ox's stormy departure. Not to be outdone, Quinn had also blown out the door behind Ox on another gust of melodrama accompanied by a threat to take me to court. I'm not sure what she objected to most, that I'd been married to Philippe, that we never got around to finalizing the divorce, or that I existed at all.

Thaddeus gave me a key to Philippe's house, got my signature on some legal paperwork, and then offered to drive Miss Frankie home so I could stay and acquaint myself with the business. As the staff filed out of the conference room, Estelle said, "You know, Miss Frankie is right, Rita. Ox has been a complete jerk lately. We'll be fine without him."

"All for one and one for all," Burt put in, flashing teeth and dimples at me.

Isabeau seemed less certain. "Give Ox a break. You know how close he and Philippe were. We all grieve in different ways."

Dwight scratched his beard with the fingers of one hand and eyed the door thoughtfully. "Assuming we're all actually grieving."

That shocked me almost as much as Ox's outburst. "You don't think Ox is grieving?"

Dwight shrugged without looking at me. "I didn't say that."

"No, but you might as well have. What's going on around here, anyway?"

Slowly, Dwight lifted his soulful brown

113

eyes to meet mine. I could see confusion and anger in his expression. "All I know is that Ox took a swing at Philippe yesterday, and half an hour later, Philippe was dead. Do the math."

"You can't seriously believe that Ox killed Philippe?" Edie demanded.

Dwight let out a sharp laugh. "You seriously think he didn't?"

Isabeau's pretty face clouded. "You know he didn't. He would never do something like that."

"Well somebody did," Abe pointed out unnecessarily. "And it was probably one of us."

"He did threaten to kill Philippe," Burt said, half under his breath.

"We're talking about *Ox*," I said. "He's your friend."

"He was a friend of Philippe's, too," Sparkle said, in her trademark monotone. "That didn't turn out so well."

I looked around, seeing the fear, doubt, and mistrust on all their faces. Only Edie and Isabeau seemed ready to believe in Ox. Did the others really suspect him of this horrible thing? I couldn't believe he'd done what they were thinking, but if they didn't trust him, having him around would do more harm than good. I had to let him go

114

for now, but I promised myself I'd find some way to prove that my old friend wasn't a cold-blooded killer.

TEN

I needed to spend some time wrapping my mind around the sudden change in my circumstances. In the blink of an eye, I'd gone from living on a shoestring to owning a home of my own and inheriting what Thaddeus had hinted was a substantial bank account. But I knew that the next few hours at Zydeco were critical. If I didn't get involved now, the staff would never accept me as the voice of authority.

It was a Sunday, but we'd lost most of Saturday to the police investigation and Edie had asked the staff to stick around for a few hours so we could get back on schedule. I urged them to return to whatever projects they had been working on yesterday and assured them that my door was always open. And it would be . . . just as soon as I figured out where it was. As I watched Thaddeus drive off with Miss Frankie, I felt a pang of nervousness. I had never managed an entire staff before, and the idea of stepping into Philippe's shoes was daunting.

I'd always thought that he and I were well matched as partners, partly because of our differences. Philippe was fun loving and gregarious. I was more reserved. He handled the people and drew friends into our lives. I paid the bills and made sure we kept beer on hand for the spontaneous parties he threw together.

I'd have been comfortable finding Philippe's office and locking myself away with spreadsheets and schedules, learning the business from the books outward. But that's not why I was here. My number-one job at Zydeco was getting to know the staff. To learn their strengths and weaknesses. I needed to figure out which of them Miss Frankie could trust and determine whether any of them was skilled enough to take over running the bakery when I left. No doubt about it, I was going to have to step outside my comfort zone while I was here.

I compromised with myself and decided to take a self-guided tour of the building, beginning with a large storage area on the second floor. From there, I moved downstairs to the kitchen and design center.

I wasn't surprised to learn that Abe had

already left the building. He'd always preferred working alone, so his job as head
baker suited him; he worked by himself in
the wee hours of the morning, baking the
cakes the designers would decorate during
normal work hours. It also gave him the best
opportunity of anyone on staff to indulge in
a little sabotage. But how likely was that?
He was too smart to do something so obvious.

In the design center, alternative-rock
music played on a stereo in the corner,
underscoring muted conversations that were
punctuated by bursts of laughter and peri-
ods of silence. The staff worked on half a
dozen projects, ranging from a large pastiage monkey for a child's birthday cake to
gum-paste iris petals that would help cel-
ebrate a schoolteacher's retirement.

I stopped to chat briefly with Estelle as I
passed her workstation. I could tell by
watching her work on the iris petals that
she was highly skilled. She'd tied back her
pouf of red hair and covered it with a lime-
green scarf, and a deep level of concentration had produced a couple more chins. She
was the oldest person on staff by at least
ten years, but she seemed to mesh surprisingly well with the rest of the group.

Dwight had covered his beard with a net

— necessary, but a little odd looking. Sparkle glowered at the world from a corner that kept her out of the sunlight. I made mental notes about each of the projects they were working on. The monkey cake (Sparkle) was due for delivery tomorrow afternoon, the iris-garden cake (Estelle) due the following day, and a four-tier gluten-free Mexican-vanilla wedding cake with buttercream icing (Dwight) the day after that.

As I left Sparkle, I caught Burt sizing me up from his workstation a few feet away. Was he checking me out or taking my measure as a new boss? Sure, I'd been flattered by his apparent interest yesterday, but Philippe's murder had changed everything. Yesterday, I'd been an almost-divorced woman with no social life. Today, I was a rich widow with no social life. Huge difference.

He watched me walk toward him, a smile cutting dimples into his cheeks. "Hello, pretty boss lady."

I smiled but refrained from grinning like a silly schoolgirl. "I think it would be best if you just called me Rita," I said, and then immediately changed the subject. "This is quite an operation. I'm impressed."

Burt glanced around at the controlled chaos and shrugged. If he resented me for not flirting with him, he didn't show it. "This is nothing. Wait until we shift into high gear before a delivery."

"From what I understand, I won't have to wait long." I watched him wrap a narrow strip of pale-blue fondant around a dowel to create a curlicue then asked, "How are things going for you? Any problems I should know about?"

"With me? Nah." He set that dowel aside to dry and grabbed another. "Still in shock about Philippe, but I'm fine. How about you? Have you recovered from this morning's drama?"

I let out a thin laugh. "Which part?"

"Either. Both. Quinn's a real piece of work, but Ox . . . he was harsh."

Burt was direct; I'd give him that. "He's grieving," I said. "I'll give him some time to cool down, and then I'll try to talk with him."

Burt created another curl with a couple of deft twists. "Good idea. Leave him alone for a while. Give him some space to clear his head. He'll come around. He always does."

That surprised me. "He's walked out before?"

One side of Burt's mouth curled into a half smile. "Not like this, but yeah. He and

Philippe went the rounds a few times."

"Over what?"

"This and that. The usual."

I dragged a stool close and perched on it. "There's nothing usual about Philippe and Ox coming to blows. At least not in my world. What's going on around here, anyway?"

Burt lifted one shoulder and didn't even bat an eye. His stubborn silence grated on my nerves. "Don't play games with me, Burt. You weren't even curious enough to step out onto the dock when they started fighting yesterday. You know something. Tell me what it is."

He created another curl and set it with the others, then propped both hands on the table and met my gaze. "What do you want to know?"

"Let's start with how long this thing between Philippe and Ox has been going on."

Something flickered in Burt's eyes, but it was gone before I could read it. "A month or two, I guess. I couldn't say for sure."

Now we were getting somewhere. "How did it start?"

Burt went back to work, curling his last piece of fondant and setting the dowel carefully aside before he answered. "Your guess

121

is as good as mine. Ox was Philippe's right-hand man when I first came here. A couple of months ago, Philippe started handing out Ox's work to other people. It didn't make any sense to me then, and it still doesn't. I'm good at what I do. Ox is brilliant. The graphic-design stuff? He's a master. And I don't know anyone with a steadier hand when it comes to piping work or painting."

Frankly, neither did I. Which is why Philippe's behavior was so confusing. "Do you know why Philippe was bypassing him? Did Ox do something wrong, or did Philippe have a new protégé?"

"Not that I know of. It wasn't like he picked one person and started giving him or her Ox's work. He just . . . avoided Ox."

That made no sense at all. Philippe and Ox had had creative differences in the past, but they'd always worked things out within a couple of hours, usually over a beer or a couple shots of tequila. "How did Ox react to that?"

"About like you'd expect. Philippe and Ox basically opened this place together. When I signed on, Philippe made it clear that Ox was second in command, the go-to guy if Philippe wasn't available. Then one day, it was like Ox got demoted." Burt turned away to pull a container of lime-green fondant from the shelf behind him. "Frankly, I don't blame the guy for resenting the change."

"Do you know what set them off yesterday?"

Burt began kneading the fondant slowly. "Could have been anything. Maybe Ox left the van's gas tank empty. Maybe Philippe put the keys in the wrong place. Who knows?"

If they were actually fighting over such little things, something was really wrong. "The police are calling Ox a person of interest in the case," I said. "Do you think he attacked Philippe?"

Burt shook his head slowly. "No way. I think he and Philippe went at each other, and then he stormed off and took a walk to cool down. That's what he says, anyway."

"And you believe him?"

"Yeah, I do."

So did I. I hoped we were both right. "What about the cake? Any ideas about who trashed it?"

Burt shrugged again. "Not a clue."

I thought about the other incidents Miss Frankie had told me about. Did Burt know about them? "Do you have any ideas about who was responsible for the attack on Philippe?"

Burt shook his head again, took a couple of measurements, and created a swag from the fondant ribbon. "I've been thinking about that since yesterday," he said as he pleated the fondant. "But it just doesn't make any sense, y' know? Don't get me wrong. Philippe was no saint, but he was a good guy and people liked him. No enemies or anything like that."

"Nobody on staff held a grudge?"

Burt looked up from the fondant, his eyes narrowed. "Why does everybody think that somebody from Zydeco killed him? It could have been anybody."

"I don't have any idea who killed him," I said. "I'm just trying to help Miss Frankie figure out who she can trust."

Burt glanced at his coworkers and lowered his voice. "It wasn't one of us."

"Then you think it was a random act of violence?"

"What else could it be?"

"So there's nobody else who might have wanted to settle a score? No former disgruntled employee? No old girlfriend with a grudge?" No current blonde-bimbo girlfriend after Philippe's money?

Burt gave the questions I'd asked aloud some thought before shaking his head again. "As far as I know, he didn't date all that much before Quinn. He worked all the time, trying to get this place up and running and then trying to keep up with all the business he brought in. He was always here or at the Duke."

"What's the Duke?"

Burt jerked his head toward the street. "The Dizzy Duke. It's a neighborhood bar. We all hang out there just about every night after work."

Now *that* sounded more like the Philippe I knew. I should have thought to ask about his after-work habits. Popular as Philippe was, there was always someone he rubbed the wrong way, usually guys with a little less money, an older model car, a less effective bank shot at the pool table. Guys whose girlfriends or wives spent a little too much time checking out Philippe's assets.

I jumped at the possibility that Philippe's killer wasn't one of the staff. "Is there anyone at the Duke who might have had a problem with Philippe?"

"Not that I know of." Burt turned his attention to the other end of the swag and spent a minute or two getting the fondant "fabric" folds just right. "Like I said, he wasn't a saint or anything. He had issues with people, just like anybody else. But nothing serious enough to kill over."

"Apparently, somebody felt differently." I made a mental note to check out the Duke later. That might be the fastest way to ease Miss Frankie's mind about the staff. "What about Ox? Does he hang out there, too?"

Burt looked up from his work and ran a glance over me, this one more curious than flirtatious. "Yeah. Like I said, we all do. Why?"

"Just wondering if he might be there now."

Burt didn't answer. I had a dozen more questions I wanted to ask, but I didn't want to push too hard, so I changed the subject. "So how do you feel about Miss Frankie's decision? Are you going to hate working for me as much as Ox said he would?"

Burt laughed, and those two sharp dimples dipped into his cheeks again. He began rolling the fondant into a large rectangle, a job that made the muscles in his arms and shoulders flex nicely. Not that I was looking. "I'm a pretty easygoing guy. I'm willing to give you a chance. See what you're made of."

My own lips curved in response, and I filed his name in the "Pro Rita" column in my head. I just hoped I was made of sturdy enough stuff to get the job done. "What about the rest of the staff? What can I expect?"

"Isabeau's a team player. She'll be fine. Estelle thinks the world of Miss Frankie. If Miss F wants you here, Estelle will fall in line."

"And Sparkle? How's she going to take the changes?"

Burt laughed softly and stole a glance at his goth coworker. "Sparkle will give you a hard time, but don't take it personally. She hates everybody. Once you get to know her, she's okay. And you know the other guys, right? Edie, Abe, and Dwight? So the only wild card is me."

"As wild cards go, you seem okay." Just then, my cell phone let out a chirp. Burt picked up a couple of trays and carried them toward the industrial-sized refrigerators across the room, making it clear the conversation was over.

I checked the caller ID, saw Uncle Nestor's name on my screen, and immediately felt guilty. I should have called him last night, but by the time Sullivan had followed Quinn out the door, I'd been too exhausted. Today, between the meeting with Thaddeus and Ox's decision to quit, the day had totally gotten away from me. But this wasn't the time or the place for the conversation I needed to have with Uncle Nestor, so I sent him straight to voice mail.

Then I put my phone on silent and slipped it back into my pocket.

I'll call later, I promised him silently. When I had time to explain that I wasn't coming back to Albuquerque right away. But even with eleven hundred miles between us, that was yet another conversation I wasn't looking forward to.

ELEVEN

I finished my getting-to-know-you tour of Zydeco in the front office, where I found Edie sitting at her desk, scowling at a manila file folder. She glanced up as I came into the room, closed the folder, and turned toward her computer. There was nothing unusual about that, but the way her face closed down and the furtive way she slid the folder into a stack of paperwork sparked my curiosity.

What was she trying to hide? I didn't want her to be the saboteur, but Edie did have access to every part of the business. Nobody had a better chance to take the bakery down. But what possible motive could she have? She'd always been intensely loyal to Philippe. I couldn't imagine her doing anything to purposely hurt him.

I crossed to her desk and reached for the folder, mostly to see how she would react. If she did nothing, I'd tell myself that I'd only imagined all that furtive file stashing. My fingers brushed the folder and Edie whipped around in her chair so fast, I jerked backward instinctively.

She snatched the folder away from my hand and stuffed it into a drawer. "Do you mind?"

Okay, so not my imagination. "What's in the folder?"

"Nothing." Edie stared at me without blinking, but the sudden flush of color in her cheeks told another story.

Aunt Yolanda's voice whispered in my head, *Begin as you mean to go on.* It was just one of a hundred pieces of advice she'd given me over the years. I'd rebelled against most of them when I was a deeply unhappy teenager, but today it seemed like a good idea. Be assertive, I told myself, not aggressive. "I'd like to see it."

Her eyes darkened and her lips thinned. "It's nothing important."

"Apparently, it's important enough for you to try hiding it from me. What is it, Edie?"

"Just a client file. No big deal." She started to turn back to her computer, trying to dismiss me and end the conversation.

I hesitated for a heartbeat. I wasn't planning to stay here permanently, so I wondered just how important it was for me to establish my authority. But I *was* here on Miss Frankie's behalf. If Edie was keeping secrets about the business, I needed to know. "I'd like to see it," I said again.

She scowled up at me. "Why?"

I wasn't going to let her put me on the defensive, so I countered with an offensive move of my own. "Maybe you should tell me why you're trying so hard to hide it."

"I'm not trying to hide anything. I'm just doing my job."

"By making it impossible for me to do mine?" I held out a hand and wiggled my fingers. "Just hand it over, Edie. Save us both time."

With a heavy sigh, she tugged open the desk drawer and shoved the folder at me. "Fine. Have it your way. It's no big deal. Just a client who's refusing to pay his bill."

I chalked the moment up as a minor victory. "So why didn't you want me to see it?"

"He's a very wealthy client with an even more wealthy and powerful father."

"Aren't all your clients wealthy?" They had to be, considering the price tags I'd seen on the cakes in the design area.

"Not *this* wealthy," Edie said. "The Hightowers are old money and high society. Julian — the father — has taken the family money and invested it in real estate, businesses, sports teams, entertainment. You name it; they probably own it. Anyway, they're a very big deal, and Philippe was really stoked about getting the contract for J. J. — the son's — wedding."

I sat across from Edie and flipped open the folder. "So what's the issue?"

"It's totally bizarre. The cake was amazing. Exactly what the couple asked for. But the groom," Edie nodded toward the folder, "threw an absolute fit when Philippe delivered it. In front of three hundred guests. So what could have been the greatest boost to Zydeco's reputation yet turned into a complete disaster. Three hundred rich potential clients now think that Zydeco is a half-baked operation. And J. J. Hightower is refusing to pay the balance due, which is a ton of money. It was an incredible cake."

I flipped through the file to acquaint myself with the order. Edie was right. The photos inside showed a stunning cake. Four tiers of milk-chocolate cinnamon cake covered in buttercream of the palest yellow. Sunflowers, also made of buttercream, cascaded from top to bottom, so beautifully sculpted that they appeared real. All for a measly seven thousand dollars. Geez, I could have lived on that for months. "It looks great. What's his problem?"

Edie raked her fingers through her hair. "J. J. claims we made a mistake on the cake. And before you ask, I don't know what he thinks we did wrong. I tried calling him a few minutes ago, but he refuses to discuss it with anyone but Philippe."

My head shot up from the file. "Did you tell him that's not going to be possible?"

"They've been on their honeymoon. Just got back last night and apparently haven't heard the news yet. I tried to explain, but J. J. hung up before I could tell him about Philippe." Edie propped her chin in her hand. "The whole thing is a huge mess. I didn't want Miss Frankie to hear about it until I could fix it. Our reputation has taken a huge hit. We can't afford to take a hit financially, too. I mean, we *could* swallow the loss," she said, "but first of all, I'm not sure that would make J. J. happy. And secondly, if word got out that we let the Hightowers walk without paying, everybody will try to get away with it. That we really can't afford."

I wasn't as worried about the money as I was about the damage to Zydeco's reputation. Delivering a flawed cake, or even one the client just didn't like, to a once-in-a-

133

lifetime event wasn't something we could make better. It wasn't as if we could offer them a replacement wedding cake and undo the damage.

"Do you want me to talk to him?"

Edie squinted up at me, considering my offer. "You're the boss."

Right. "Okay, then. Would you mind setting up an appointment? Maybe Tuesday morning?" At Edie's nod, I held up the folder. "Do you mind if I hang on to this for a couple of days?"

"Go for it." But Edie still looked troubled, and when she spoke again, I realized why. "Listen, Rita, there's something else you should know."

Uh-oh. "Okay. Hit me. What is it?"

"We're supposed to be bidding on a job next week — a grand opening for a high-tech company. Philippe was working on the design right before . . . you know."

"He didn't have time to finish it?"

Edie shook her head. "I don't know. I looked for the design all over Zydeco this morning, but I can't find it. I don't know where it is."

My spirits dived even further. Was this a coincidence or another act of sabotage? "Maybe it's been misplaced," I suggested optimistically. "The police were all over the building yesterday."

"Yeah. Maybe."

I told myself not to assume the worst. Stay calm. Don't panic. There could be a logical explanation. "We'll find it," I said, trying hard to sound as if I believed that. "What's the cutoff date for submitting the bid?"

"The fifteenth."

I glanced at the calendar on the wall. "Next week, right? We should be okay, then. Any idea where he had it last?"

Edie shook her head slowly. "He had it with him the morning he was killed, and now it's gone. That's all I know."

It was ridiculous to wonder if the missing design had something to do with Philippe's murder. Wasn't it? But maybe he'd walked in on the saboteur and caught him stealing the design?

"I thought Ox was in charge of graphic design for Zydeco. Does he have a copy?"

"Not this time. Philippe had decided to work on this cake himself."

Philippe created all of his sketches by hand, and he'd rarely bothered to photocopy or scan his work, at least until he was finished. Ox, on the other hand, was more careful. "So there's no backup."

Shaking her head, Edie reached for a humongous soft-drink cup hidden behind her

135

computer screen. "I'm afraid not. It's not just the sketch, either. I know that Philippe had worked out the time line for building the cake and creating all the pieces for it. He spent hours and hours doing that. Plus, he made a list of all the supplies we'd need."

"That's a lot of work to lose," I agreed. "But it has to be here somewhere. We'll find it."

Edie smiled uncertainly. "I hope so. He worked on that design for days. I feel like it's his legacy or something."

I got to my feet, finally feeling ready to tackle Philippe's office. I'd look for the missing design, too, while I was in there. "I'd like to go over all the outstanding contracts on the books and get a feel for what's coming up in the next few weeks. Can you get me a schedule when you have a few minutes?"

"I post a calendar in the design center at the beginning of every week," Edie said. "I'll make you a copy if you'd like."

"Thanks. That will help, but a week at a time isn't quite enough lead time for me. Can you get me the schedule for the next couple of months? Or tell me where to look, and I'll find it myself."

Edie slowly returned her cup to its position behind the monitor, and I witnessed her inner control freak spark to life. "The next couple of months? I thought you were only going to be here for a few days."

"Probably a week at most. I just want to make sure I have everything lined up for Miss Frankie when I leave."

"Everything is already lined up," Edie said. "I know how to do my job, Rita."

I held up both hands to show that I meant no harm. "I know you do. Philippe wouldn't have hired you if you didn't."

Clearly unimpressed by my backpedaling, Edie rolled her eyes and reached for her computer keyboard. "Whatever."

I hadn't meant to offend her, but I decided to leave well enough alone. Everyone was moody thanks to the murder and the attack on Ox. I had to make allowances. "Thanks Edie," I said to her stiff back. "Let me know when you have the schedule."

She muttered, "I'll have it for you by four."

Pleased with the way I'd handled that, I headed toward Philippe's office. But I had the feeling that dealing with these people was going to be the death of me.

TWELVE

Time alone. That's what I needed. Space to clear my head without somebody wanting or needing anything from me. I reached for the knob on Philippe's office door, but before I could let myself inside, Edie called after me. "Are you going to the memorial tonight?"

I turned back uncertainly. "Memorial?"

"For Philippe. Didn't anybody tell you about it?"

"No. Was someone supposed to?"

Edie looked a little guilty, probably because that someone should've been her. "It's nothing official. Just a thing some of the people at the Duke want to do in Philippe's memory."

"The Dizzy Duke?"

"Yeah. You know it?"

I shook my head. "Burt mentioned it. They're putting on a memorial? It's kind of quick, isn't it?"

Edie nodded. "It's just an informal thing," she said again. "The house band is putting it together. They'll play a few sets, and people can stand up and talk about Philippe if they want. You should come. It's on the corner a couple of blocks down. You can't miss it."

"You can't miss it" is code for "You'll never find it." It's the Murphy's Law of directions. I was already exhausted, and spending the evening in a bar wasn't my idea of a good time, but it would give me a chance to see the staff in a more relaxed atmosphere, and maybe I could find out whether someone at the bar had a beef with Philippe. It was worth a shot, anyway.

"I'd like to be there," I said, "but I can't promise until I see how Miss Frankie's feeling. If she needs me with her, I'll have to skip it."

"Oh. Yeah. Well, sure." Edie's face took on a pinched look. "But it might look weird if you're *not* there, y' know?"

"I'll let you know later," I promised, and let myself into a long, narrow room overlooking the street. The room was pure Philippe, from the cherrywood desk to the flatscreen TV on the wall across from it. The familiar scent of his aftershave rose up from something nearby, causing a giant hand to reach into my chest and squeeze my heart. I could almost feel him watching me, and I wondered if he'd approve of me stepping in for him.

Philippe's desk was nestled in front of a bay created by five tall windows that stretched from floor to ceiling. A couple of built-in shelves held the collection of books that Philippe had relied on when he worked. A file cabinet, paneled in cherry to match the desk, stood in the corner, no doubt holding designs and paperwork from past projects. I made a mental note to check there for the missing cake design, just in case.

But that could wait until later.

I don't know how long I stood there before I realized that I hadn't moved. *Uncertainty never accomplishes anything,* Aunt Yolanda whispered, so I forced my legs to carry me to the desk, where I sat in the heavy leather chair and tucked my purse at my feet.

I'd always loved this chair. In fact, Philippe and I had battled over it more than once. In the early days of our relationship, he'd let me steal it from him. Two years into the marriage, he began showing signs of resentment when he found me in it. And, of course, he got custody when we split up. If

I kept just one thing I'd inherited from Philippe now, it would probably be this chair.

A couple of framed photographs sat on one corner of the desk. They were pictures I knew well: Philippe and his father on their last hunting trip together, Philippe and Miss Frankie dancing at our wedding. A set of three cheap plastic trays took up the other corner, all overflowing with paperwork. The rest of the desk was no better, covered with mounds of invoices and unopened mail, a few advertising circulars, and a dozen or so colored file folders that didn't fit into the stacking trays.

I looked at the clutter, surprised to find myself getting misty over the mess Philippe had always made when he worked. He'd been more concerned with making sure the people around him were having a good time than he'd ever been with documenting his work or organizing his records. That had always been my job, and I fell naturally to the task now. I couldn't turn this office over to someone else in this condition.

Besides, there might be a clue to his murder buried in here somewhere. The police had searched the room already, but they didn't know Philippe. They didn't know how he worked, what he kept, what he routinely threw away. They wouldn't know what belonged in this room and what didn't. Would I? Maybe. It was worth a try, anyway.

As I reached for a stack of junk mail, I felt something jab my thigh through my pocket. I pulled out my cell phone and noted three missed calls from Uncle Nestor along with two voice mails. I still wasn't ready to talk to him, but I might never, technically, be ready. Avoiding him would only make things worse.

I crossed the room and closed the door so Edie wouldn't be able to overhear, then sat in Philippe's big power chair and punched the number on my keypad. My nerves tingled as I waited for my uncle to answer. I didn't know whether to hope that he'd pick up, so I could get the conversation over with, or that he wouldn't, so I could leave a message.

Just as I was about to give up, I heard a familiar voice on the other end of the call. *"Sí?"*

"Uncle Nestor?"

"Sí. Sí. Are you home, *mija?* Do you need someone to pick you up at the airport?" I could hear the kitchen staff working around him, the clang of metal on metal, the sizzle of something on the grill. I could almost smell the cilantro and frijoles, and my

stomach growled at the thought of Uncle Nestor's chiles rellenos covered with bubbling hot *queso blanco.*

"*Mija?* Are you there?" He segued into a string of Spanish, and my fingers grew numb where I gripped the phone. Uncle Nestor's use of profanity and his native Spanish rose and fell with his frustration level. Judging from the diatribe in my ear, I'd called at a very bad time.

"I'm here," I said, resisting the urge to disconnect and claim a bad signal later. "I'm not in Albuquerque. I'm still in New Orleans."

"New Orleans? What are you doing there? You're supposed to be back for the evening shift tonight."

"I know, but . . . There's been some trouble here. I can't leave for a few days."

A loud clang sounded close to the phone, and I guessed that Uncle Nestor had put down a pot with a bit more force than necessary. "What trouble?"

"It's a long story, and I can tell you're busy. Is Aunt Yolanda around? Maybe I could tell her —"

"What happened?" he demanded, cutting me off. "Did that son of a bitch refuse to sign again? *Pendejo.* Stupid, stupid man.

He didn't know a good thing when he had it."

I appreciated my uncle's loyalty, but with Philippe lying on a slab in the morgue, it felt wrong. "It's not like that, *Tío.* Actually, if I could talk with *Tía* Yolanda . . ."

"You don't want to talk to me?"

"It's not that," I lied. "It's just . . ." I took a deep breath and plunged in before he worked himself up any more. "Philippe's dead, *Tío.* He was murdered."

"*Madre de Dios!* How? When? Are you okay?"

"I'm fine. But I'm calling to let you know that I need to stay here for a few more days."

"Why? Are the police keeping you there?" He turned away from the phone and shouted for my cousin Santos. "Bring me some paper! And a pencil! Who's in charge of that investigation? I'll talk to him."

"It's not the police," I said when I could get a word in. "I'm staying to help Miss Frankie with the funeral arrangements." I winced, waiting for the explosion I knew was coming.

Uncle Nestor didn't disappoint. I understood only a few of the words he shouted into the phone until his temper and his vocabulary began to wind down into English again. "You don't need to stay there and help her, *mija*. Those people are not your family anymore."

"I know, but she's all alone now. This has devastated her. I can't turn my back on her." I took a breath and lobbed in my secret weapon. "You didn't raise me to treat anyone that way, *Tío*. I can't walk away from someone who used to be family."

My success rate with that kind of warfare was only about sixty-forty, so I held my breath and prayed for Uncle Nestor's blessing, then quickly continued, "I know you don't approve, but this is something I have to do — for myself. I don't expect you to agree with me, but I do need you to understand. I love you, *Tío*. I'll let you know what's going on when I know more." Before he could let fly with another string of Spanish, I pressed the disconnect button. My heart was hammering against my rib cage as if I'd been running, and my hands trembled as I tossed my cell phone onto the desk. I knew that my uncle Nestor loved me in his own gruff way, but there'd be hell to pay later.

I glanced around the room and allowed myself to fantasize, just for a moment, that this office was really mine. But that only made me feel disloyal, both to Uncle Nestor and Philippe. Not that Philippe deserved

145

my loyalty. Did he?

I shoved the confusion back where it belonged and pushed up my sleeves so I could get to work. The sooner I finished up here, the better it would be for everyone.

THIRTEEN

Putting my conversation with Uncle Nestor out of my mind, I reopened the door to the reception area and sorted through the first pile on the desk, carefully separating trade journals from advertisements, junk mail from envelopes that looked important. Edie had probably already dealt with the bills and invoices, so I made a mental note to go over those with her later. The junk mail I'd toss, and the rest of the unopened mail I'd take to Miss Frankie when I went back to her house that evening.

I found a couple of sketches created in Philippe's bold strokes and put them on the check-with-Edie pile. I didn't think I'd found the missing sketch, but you never knew.

When I finished with the desk, I started on the filing cabinet. Before we separated, I'd been slowly urging Philippe toward the world of computerized record keeping, but he'd put up a fight at every stage. The laptop sitting on top of the filing cabinet made me wonder if someone else had taken over where I left off. The fact that it wasn't on the desk, however, convinced me that Philippe had never embraced the electronic age.

I don't know how long I'd been working when I heard Zydeco's front door open and the sound of heavy footsteps on the hardwood floor. Edie's sharp voice reached me an instant later. "What do *you* want?"

A man with a deep voice answered, "I heard about Philippe. I came to offer my condolences."

I was up to my elbows in files, and I didn't want to be obvious about eavesdropping, but curiosity got the best of me. Leaning back slightly, I peeked into the front office, hoping I'd be able to see Edie's visitor.

Unfortunately, I could only see the side of her face. She sniffed and turned away from the man at her desk. "You should have just dropped a card in the mail."

"Oh, now, Edie, what kind of friend would I be if I did something like that?"

"You're not a friend," she snapped.

Okay, now I *had* to see who she was talking to. Trying not to make noise, I pulled my hands out of the drawer and turned so I could get a better view. I caught a glimpse of dark hair and a white shirt, but that was it.

"You wound me," the man said, but he sounded more amused than injured. "Seriously, Edie, how are you doing?"

"How do you think I'm doing?" I heard a desk drawer slam shut and the slight squeak of the wheels on Edie's chair. "Philippe is dead, and there's a killer wandering around loose, and now you're here. I'm just peachy."

"There's no need to be sarcastic."

"There's no need to be condescending. Just tell me what you want."

Part of me wanted to walk to the door and inject myself into their conversation, but I didn't want to make Edie think I didn't trust her to do her job. If I leaned forward *just so,* I could see a tall man with dark hair, a swarthy complexion, and eyes shielded by sunglasses.

I tried to be inconspicuous, but he spotted me immediately and turned a white-toothed smile in my direction. "Ah, this must be the lovely Ms. Lucero." He advanced on me like a panther after its prey, holding out a hand for me to shake as he closed in. "I heard you were in town."

He oozed charm on the surface, but some internal instinct in me gave off a danger warning. "I see the grapevine is alive and well in New Orleans, Mr. — ?"

He peeled off his sunglasses, revealing clear blue eyes filled with a predatory gleam. "Wolff. Dmitri Wolff."

The name suited him. I wondered if he'd been born with it or if he'd changed it to match his personality.

Edie made a face behind Dmitri's back. "Dmitri owns a cake shop, Gateaux, in the French Quarter." The warning in her dark eyes underscored what I was feeling.

"Ah." Another reason to be careful around the wolf. "So you're Zydeco's competition?"

Dmitri flashed those white teeth again. "That doesn't have to be the case. Besides wanting to offer my condolences, I'm here to put an end to your worries."

Seriously? That was his angle? I folded my arms across my chest and leaned against the door frame. "Is that so? And just how do you intend to do that?"

"I'm here to make an offer for Zydeco — a very generous offer, if I do say so."

Everything inside me recoiled. "You want to buy Zydeco?"

Dmitri held out both hands in a gesture designed to look helpless. "Someone will have to. I don't expect that Miss Frankie will want to run this operation on her own."

"Miss Frankie doesn't have to run this operation on her own," I pointed out. "She has a large, highly trained staff."

He swooped in close and put one hand on my back. He had a light touch, but my skin crawled beneath his fingers. "Well, now," he said, still grinning as if we were talking about nothing more serious than that morning's weather report. "She certainly has a large staff. But highly trained? I'm not so sure about that. I'd put my staff up against this one any day of the week."

I tried to shift away from his touch, but he had me cornered. "Then why do you want the business?"

Dmitri urged me deeper into the office. "It's no secret that I'm interested in expanding my operation into the Garden District."

"It's no secret you want the Zydeco name and reputation," Edie snarled from somewhere just behind me.

Dmitri laughed. "Your reputation? After the fiasco at the Hightower wedding? Hardly."

"We have a perfectly good reputation. That was a fluke," Edie argued. "And we'll prove it to everyone, too."

"Without Philippe's talent?" Dmitri shook his head. "And let's not forget that you've just been victims of a gruesome murder.

Nobody's going to want to spend money here."

"Yet again, you still want Zydeco."

"What can I say? I'm a sentimental guy. I'll take this cursed place off your hands, and I'm even prepared to pay a very good price to boot. I'd bring in my own people to run it, of course. I'd almost have to, considering the talk that's going around on the street. Besides, I hear that Miss Frankie is looking for a buyer."

He was right about one thing. Between the murder, the Hightower wedding fiasco, and Ox storming off (which meant we were down a graphic-design artist), there'd be plenty of talk. Any of those issues alone would be a problem. Together, they left me feeling pretty beat up.

Not wanting Dmitri to sense my insecurities, I squared my shoulders and said, "I believe you heard wrong. As far as I know, Miss Frankie *isn't* thinking about selling. She certainly hasn't made any decisions yet."

Dmitri's smile didn't falter, but his eyes glittered with irritation. "This is a large operation. It would be overwhelming for someone who isn't used to running a business this size."

I removed my arm from his grip and sat

152

behind the desk, a visual reminder that he was — technically, anyway — on my turf. "I'm sure that Miss Frankie will hire someone who knows what they're doing."

Dmitri sat in one of the leather chairs facing me. "Someone like you?"

That predatory energy made me edgy, but the sneer in his voice made me angry. I was tempted to say yes just to mess with him, but I didn't want to make trouble for Miss Frankie down the road. "I'm only here temporarily."

"Of course." He leaned back and made himself comfortable, his arms stretched along the chair, one ankle resting on the opposite knee. "I was curious about you, Ms. Lucero, so I did a little research. There's no doubt you're a talented cake artist, but you have no real business experience."

Jerk! "I'm not the issue," I said. "But for the record, I have as much business experience as Philippe did when he opened Zydeco."

Dmitri didn't even blink. "Of course. I'd forgotten. Although . . . with Zydeco's reputation in the toilet, as we've said, well, that really isn't much of a recommendation, is it?"

"Philippe was a good businessman," I

said. I caught myself and cut off the rest of my argument. Why should I convince him that Zydeco was worth buying?

Dmitri dipped his head, acknowledging my point or at least pretending to. "I shouldn't speak ill of the dead. My apologies. But in light of the circumstances . . ." His gaze traveled around Philippe's office, and I swear he almost licked his chops in anticipation. "I would like to make your life, and Miss Frankie's, a little easier."

By swallowing Philippe's life's work? Not by the hair of his chinny-chin-chin. "I suspect you're really here to make *your* life easier."

Dmitri's smile wavered ever so slightly. "That's harsh."

"So is swooping in and trying to get your hands on Zydeco before Philippe's body is even cold. Now, if you'll excuse me, I have a lot to do. I'm sure you understand." I stood to indicate that our conversation was over.

Dmitri's eyes narrowed, and I caught a glimpse of the danger I'd only sensed before then. With a show of reluctance, he got to his feet and gazed around Philippe's office one more time. "I understand this is all very sudden, so take your time. Think about my offer. You'll regret it if you don't." He turned toward the door, tossing one last thing over his shoulder. "I'll be in touch."

I watched him leave, barely repressing a shudder. He was a thoroughly unlikable man. The only question I had was whether he'd just issued a warning or a threat.

At eight that evening, I parked Miss Frankie's car in a small lot between two saggy old buildings and walked half a block to the Dizzy Duke, an ancient redbrick building two blocks east of Zydeco. The neighborhood had definitely seen better days. As I walked past one rundown store after another, I wondered whether I was looking at damage from Katrina or the passing of years. I'd nipped back to Miss Frankie's for a couple of hours after work to make sure she was doing okay. If she had asked me to stay, I would have skipped the memorial entirely, but she'd practically begged me to go and represent her to Philippe's colleagues and friends.

I couldn't say no. Even though I'd wanted to.

I stepped into the dimly lit interior and paused for a moment to let my eyes adjust. A polished wood bar stretched across one end of a long, narrow room. Round tables filled with people surrounded a small dance

155

floor, and at the far end of the room, a small raised platform held an array of musical instruments, just waiting for the band to take the stage.

A pungent musty smell rose up beneath the overlying odors of cigarette smoke and sweat. Laughter and conversation ebbed and flowed from all around me, and jazz music blared from speakers positioned around the room.

After a minute, I spotted Sparkle and Isabeau at a table in the corner. Isabeau noticed me at the same time and bounced out of her seat to wave me over. Sparkle looked less enthusiastic, but I was getting used to her gloomy outlook.

Amazed that smoking indoors was still allowed anywhere on the planet, I hitched my purse onto my shoulder and plunged into the smoky room. I slid between crowded tables and inched between chairs. It seemed to take forever, but I finally wedged myself into an empty chair in the corner.

Isabeau grinned up at me. "You came!" She had to shout to make herself heard.

As my nose grew accustomed to the mustiness, I picked up the aroma of seafood and spice — shrimp, sausage, and cayenne pepper if I wasn't mistaken. Jambalaya. My mouth watered just thinking about the possibility. "Edie told me about the memorial," I shouted back. "I hope I'm not intruding."

Sparkle rolled her black-lined eyes in my direction. "Whatever makes you happy," she shouted.

Wow. I felt all warm and fuzzy now. "Where's everybody else?"

"They'll be here," Isabeau assured me. She spotted an overworked cocktail waitress and bounced up again, trying to get her attention. Either the woman didn't see her or she pretended not to.

Isabeau scowled at the woman's rapidly retreating back, but her irritation didn't last long. With a perky toss of her pale-blonde ponytail, she turned back to me. "Sorry about that. You may want to go to the bar to order. It could be a long wait."

What I wanted was to try the jambalaya, but I was in no hurry to make the long trip back through all those tables. So I settled in, stashing my bag under my chair and taking in the aged brick and weathered wood of the place. Jazz posters and neon lights. Wooden tables and chairs that looked as if they'd been here for at least fifty years and a huge mirror behind the bar that reflected an impressive inventory of bottled courage.

Sparkle downed a straight shot, grimaced, and reached for a wedge of lemon. Tequila.

Interesting choice. I'd have put my money on absinthe. She'd already lost interest in me, and her gaze was firmly locked on the four or five people who had stepped onto the small bandstand and were in the process of picking up and strapping on their instruments.

Within minutes, the guitar player stepped up to a microphone center stage and began talking — but that's when he lost me. Between the dull roar coming from the crowd, the echo caused by bad acoustics, and his unintelligible accent, I didn't understand a single word.

The jukebox went silent, and the band launched into a high-spirited tune. I recognized the style. Philippe had loved zydeco music — that was why he'd named his bakery after the New Orleans sound — and hearing it played in his honor made my heart twist painfully. "So this was Philippe's regular hangout?" I shouted at Isabeau.

She nodded and pulled her half-empty strawberry daiquiri closer. "We came here every night after work. Our home away from home, I guess you could say. Oh! Look! There they are!" She waved one hand over her head, and I craned to see past Sparkle.

Burt and Dwight were squeezing between chairs on their way to our table. Dwight had changed into a clean T-shirt and jeans without holes. He paused now and then to shake someone's hand or touch a shoulder. Burt swaggered from female to female, offering comfort to teary-eyed women of all ages, shapes, and sizes. As I watched him, I felt a little foolish for having let that smile get to me, even momentarily.

We shifted seats to make room, and Burt dragged an empty table over to extend our claim. He sat next to me and scooted his chair close enough to make himself heard over the music. Dwight acknowledged me with a nod and leaned his chair back against the wall on two legs.

"I'm surprised you're here," Burt said. "If I'd known you were interested, I'd have told you about this myself."

"No problem," I assured him. "Edie told me. She thought I should be here." I scoured the room again, taking a mental inventory of the Zydeco family. "Where is she anyway? Have you seen her?"

Burt shrugged, clearly unconcerned. "Probably still at the bakery. You know how she is."

"Not really, not anymore." I smiled, hoping I looked curious, not suspicious. "How is she?"

Burt slid a look at me, and his charm

159

slipped a bit. "She's dedicated, okay? Is that a problem?"

I shook my head quickly. "Not at all. I'm just trying to get a feel for people, that's all. Have you seen Estelle?"

Burt nodded toward a table on the far side of the room where a tearful Estelle was hugging a woman about half her size. "She's over there."

That left Abe and Ox unaccounted for, but under the circumstances, I didn't really expect to see either of them. Abe was notoriously people-shy, and Ox was probably still steaming.

Burt caught a woman's eye and moved onto the dance floor. I watched him go, imagining Philippe in this bar, picturing him moving through the crowd with the same ease that Burt possessed. I wondered if Philippe had seen something of himself in Burt. I certainly did. My throat constricted, and a heavy sadness settled over me. I missed him. I couldn't deny it.

As I turned back to the table, I spotted a tall man with a shaved head walking toward the bar, and my plans changed abruptly. Apparently, I'd been wrong to think that Ox wouldn't show up tonight. I shot out of my seat and began the tortuous process of moving through the crowd again. I could check out the rest of the staff later. I might not get another chance to talk with Ox.

FOURTEEN

Ox bellied up to the bar and exchanged greetings with a bartender, a good-looking guy with a lazy shank of dark hair falling onto his forehead, a lopsided smile, and — I noticed when he called a comment to a passing cocktail waitress — a sexy Cajun accent.

Two seconds later, guilt hit me like a rogue wave. What kind of person was I, scoping out the hot bartender while at a memorial for my ex-husband? Really!

I shook myself and focused on getting to Ox. The bar was lined with people ordering drinks the waitresses didn't have time to deliver, which kept the bartenders racing to make everyone happy. On one side of Ox, a woman in shorts and a tank top flirted outrageously with the bartenders. On the other, a sour-faced man of about forty sucked down one beer and belched as he ordered another. The woman moved away first, and I slid onto the stool she'd been blocking.

Ox didn't look up, but I could tell he knew I was there. I decided to give him some space, which he used to ignore me for a few minutes. Rude and very un-Ox-like, but I didn't let that deter me.

While I waited for a bartender, I breathed in the intoxicating scent of homemade jambalaya and tapped my fingers on the bar in time to the music. I've never been a fan of the accordion, but the energetic beat and lilting melodies brought back fond memories of Philippe and wore down my resistance.

After a while, Ox cut a glance at me and growled, "What do you want?"

The bitter anger in his voice put my bravado to the test. I scanned the surrounding area for sharp knives and hated myself for doing it at the same time. I told myself not to let him intimidate me. This was Ox. My friend. "What do you think I want?" I snapped. "You were a jerk to me today. You walked out on the bakery. What's going on with you?"

The belcher leaned up to look at me. I put him at around forty. Shaggy haired with a leathery face he hadn't shaved in a few days. Probably wrestled alligators in his spare time. "Hey, little lady," he snarled. "Why don't you leave the guy alone?"

Little lady? Was he serious? I leaned up to glare back at him. "Hey, jerk," I said, matching his tone exactly. "Why don't you butt out? This doesn't concern you."

The band switched to another fast-paced song, and in the lull I heard Ox say, "It's all right. She's a friend."

The jerk took a long pull on the bottle he held and reluctantly removed his bulbous nose from our conversation.

Slowly, Ox turned to me, giving me a look that was far from friendly in my opinion. "I'm surprised, Rita. Do you really have to ask what's bothering me?"

I tried to act as if a giant bubble of animosity wasn't sucking the oxygen from the space between us. "I kind of picked up on the fact that you think you should be running Zydeco. You were pretty subtle about it, though. I'm not sure anybody else got it."

My effort to inject a little humor into the conversation fell flat. Ox scowled at me from beneath his thick black eyebrows. "You think this is funny?"

The half smile I'd been wearing slid from my face. "No. I don't."

The alligator wrestler muttered something

I couldn't make out. Before I could politely offer another suggestion that he mind his own business, he turned his attention to the harried cocktail waitress I'd noticed earlier. Fine with me. Maybe she could keep him occupied.

"I'm just confused," I said to Ox. "This isn't like you. What's going on?"

"What's not like me? Being pissed that Philippe sold me out? That Miss Frankie is handing you the keys to Zydeco when they should be mine?"

"She's handing me the keys temporarily," I reminded him. "I'll be here a few days at most. But while we're on that subject, what the hell was that crack you made about the business imploding if I'm running things?"

He looked away. "This isn't your deal, Rita. Zydeco was mine and Philippe's. I was on the fast-track to partnership. Then, all of a sudden, I'm lower than dirt on a snake's belly."

"I can't believe that," I said. "Philippe wouldn't turn on you like that. Maybe you misunderstood what he was doing."

He lifted the bottle to his lips, but stopped short of drinking. "There was no misunderstanding. Believe me."

"Good grief, Ox! No wonder the police are calling you a person of interest in the murder. You're making yourself sound guilty as hell."

He reared back as if I'd sucker punched him. "You think I killed Philippe?"

I shook my head and scooted my stool closer so we wouldn't have to yell at each other. "No, I don't. But I'm definitely one of a very small minority. Look, this thing with me and Zydeco? It's not permanent. If that's what your arrangement with Philippe was, I'm sure Miss Frankie will honor it. She's just freaked out right now, you know? Give her a few days. I think I can manage to keep Zydeco afloat that long."

He snorted a laugh and finally took a drink, but he didn't say anything.

I took the laugh as a hopeful sign. "So what's going on at Zydeco? What were you and Philippe fighting over yesterday?"

Ox lowered the bottle to the bar and shrugged. "It's complicated."

I was losing patience with his evasive answers. "So tell me about it. What did he do to make you that angry?"

He picked at the bottle's label for a moment. "What makes you think I'm the one who started it?"

I stared at him, shocked by the implication. "Philippe started the fight?"

With the cocktail waitress gone again, the

alligator wrestler turned toward me and muttered something that sounded like "couldn't put the fish dime."

I ignored that helpful remark and silently willed him to find someone else to annoy. "Why?" I asked Ox. "What did you do?"

"I didn't do anything, but he wouldn't believe that."

"Okay, then, what did he think you did? Come on, Ox, *talk* to me."

He gave me a long look out of the corner of his eye. "Why, Rita? What would be the point?"

"The point," I said, "would be to convince the police you're innocent and then help me convince Miss Frankie that you should be in charge at Zydeco. Isn't that what you want?"

He shifted in his chair so he could look at me straight on. "You really think you can do that?"

"I think I have a shot at it, but only if you'll quit acting like such a jerk."

"Jerk," the alligator wrestler agreed. He leaned up and caught my eye so he could wink at me. "Total jerk."

Yeah. Thanks. "So what did you and Philippe fight about?" I asked for what felt like the millionth time.

"What else?" Ox said. "Zydeco."

I rolled my eyes in exasperation and looked around for one of the bartenders so I could take the edge off my increasingly irritated mood. No such luck. They were all helping other customers. "Come on, Ox."

He shook his head and took a long pull on his beer. "It was no big deal."

"You guys fought. Philippe was found dead just a few minutes later," I reminded him as gently as I could. "A lot of people might think it was a big deal, including the police."

Ox smirked. "I didn't do anything wrong. The police can't prove I did. As for them?" He gestured toward the staff's table. "What do I care what they think? They've already shown me their true colors." He slid from his bar stool, as if he intended to walk away.

I wasn't finished with him yet, so I grabbed his arm. "What's that supposed to mean?"

"Nothing you need to worry about."

"That's where you're wrong. Miss Frankie has asked me to figure out what's going on at Zydeco, and I intend to do that. So what do you know about the accidents that have been happening around the bakery?"

The smirk on his lips evaporated. "I know that somebody's been causing trouble. Why?"

"Who do you think is behind it?"

Ox's smile turned nasty, and he slapped a bill on the bar. "You haven't figured it out yet? Ask any one of the crew. They'll tell you that Philippe was convinced I did it. And if Philippe believed that, you can bet Miss Frankie does, too." He looked as if he wanted to say something else but changed his mind. "This was a mistake," he growled. "I never should have come here." And before I could stop him, he pushed through the crowd, leaving me gaping after him like a fish on land.

As Ox walked away, the alligator wrestler sent me a knowing look. "That guy was a real son of a bitch."

"Ox is under a lot of pressure," I said automatically. I watched him disappear through the front door and wondered if I'd made the right decision to let him go. As if I could have stopped him.

"I'm not talking about Ox," my new friend said. "I'm talking about the other one."

The air left my lungs in a whoosh. I could only stare as I tried to figure out if I'd understood him correctly. "What other one?"

He waved an arm to encompass the crowd and the bar, and the stench of body odor hit me in the face. Charming. "I'm talking about Pretty Boy. The one all this bullshit is for."

"Philippe?" Of course that's who he meant. Who else could it be? "You think *he* was a jerk?"

Alligator man lifted one shoulder. "Like I says, couldn't push the fish dime that son of a bitch started trouble."

This time, I tried translating his heavily accented mumble and finally realized he was saying, "Wouldn't be the first time . . ." but Philippe had never been the type to start trouble.

"What do you mean by that?" I asked, but a young man staggered between us and leaned heavily on the bar for support, diverting the alligator wrestler's attention away from me.

The older man belched and elbowed the kid beside me. "You seen my old lady? I need some money."

"Wait!" I tried to use my own elbow to get around the kid, but he wasn't moving. "Mister! Wait! What did you mean by that?"

If he heard me, he pretended not to. I slid from my stool, determined to continue our conversation. Before I could move, Isabeau bounced into the space between us with a swish of blonde hair. Her big blue eyes were wide open and brimming with worry.

170

"Got a minute?" she asked me.

"Actually, no. I just need to talk to —" To my dismay, I spotted the alligator wrestler moving away from the bar. "Wait!" I shouted, but my voice was swallowed by the noise all around us.

"Please, Rita? It's important," Isabeau continued.

The alligator wrestler stopped to say something to the cocktail waitress. She scowled but pulled a couple of bills from her pocket and passed them over.

In spite of Isabeau's obvious impatience, I considered going after him, but what would I say? What if *he* was a knife-wielding murderer? Did I really want to follow him into a dark alley?

Letting the rational side of my brain take over, I sank back onto the stool and tried again to catch the attention of a bartender. No sense being *too* rational. Isabeau tapped me on the shoulder.

"Seriously, Rita? I need your help."

With a sigh, I turned back to her. "Sure. What's up?"

"I saw you talking to Ox. Did he tell you anything?"

The question wasn't what I'd been expecting. I gave up on the bartenders and took a closer look at her. "About what?"

"Anything." She inched closer and shouted in my ear. "I'm worried about him. I was hoping he'd talk to you. He sure isn't talking to me."

Her blue eyes were clouded and I saw something in them that sparked a realization. "Are you and Ox . . . a thing?"

Blushing like a schoolgirl, Isabeau swept that pale-blonde lock of hair from her shoulder and nodded miserably. "Yeah, but we haven't said anything to the rest of the crew, so keep it under wraps for now, okay?"

I had news for her. Shouting it to me in a crowded bar was hardly the way to keep their relationship secret. At least now I understood why she was so eager to defend him. "Why don't you want the others to know?"

Isabeau stared at me as if I'd lost my mind. "It's not that. It's just that the age difference and everything . . . I mean, why rock the boat before we know whether it's going to last?"

I wondered whose idea that was but decided not to ask. A woman holding two daiquiris turned away, and Isabeau claimed the bar stool Ox had been sitting on. "So did he? Talk to you, I mean?"

I hesitated over my answer. She seemed genuinely worried, and I hadn't picked up any weird vibes from her. Ox hadn't said anything useful, but she might be able to answer a few questions for me. No telling what she'd learned from pillow talk.

I shook my head. "He didn't say much. He's in a foul mood, that's for sure. Do *you* know what went wrong between him and Philippe?"

"Me?" She squeaked a little and one hand flew to her chest.

"Did Ox confide in you?"

She glanced over both shoulders to make sure nobody was paying attention, then leaned in close. "Ox never said anything, but if you want my opinion, I think it's her."

"Her who?"

"You know . . . Quinn."

My heart gave a little skip. "You think she was responsible for what happened between Philippe and Ox?"

Isabeau made a face. "Maybe. Maybe not. I don't have any proof. But things didn't start going bad between them until she came on the scene."

She had my full attention now. "You think Quinn was intentionally stirring up trouble between them?"

"Intentionally?" Isabeau shook her head thoughtfully. "I wouldn't go that far, but Philippe was so wrapped up in her, he couldn't see anything else."

My breath caught, and a sharp pain shot through my chest to hear about Philippe's infatuation, but it only lasted a second. Was I surprised? Not really. Disappointed? A little. Knowing that he'd left me and taken up with someone like Quinn was a blow to my ego. I told myself I'd have felt better if he'd traded up, picked someone more intelligent or more talented than me. Or if I'd found out he was gay. Okay, maybe not. But knowing that he'd lowered his standards for someone like Quinn was downright insulting.

"He didn't do it," Isabeau said, jerking me back to the moment. I must have looked blank because she clarified. "Ox. He didn't kill Philippe, you know."

"I know," I assured her. At the moment, my money was on Dmitri Wolff. Or Quinn. I wouldn't put anything past her. I was also curious to know just why the alligator wrestler seemed so hostile toward Philippe. Was it just the alcohol talking, or was there something more sinister afoot?

"But Ox is so stubborn," Isabeau said, dragging my attention back to our conversation. "He's making things worse for himself, not better."

I nodded agreement. "You need to talk

him into telling the police what happened between him and Philippe."

Isabeau laughed, but she wasn't amused. "Are you kidding? The mood he's in, I couldn't talk him into brushing his teeth. That's why I wanted to talk to you."

"Why me?"

"Because Ox has told me about you, about how you and he and Philippe were such good friends. About how you were always the smart one." Isabeau gripped my hands and squeezed. "Please, Rita. He's going to end up in prison if he's not careful. Can't you talk to him again? Make him tell you what happened that morning."

I tried to pry my hands away from hers, but she wouldn't let go. "Weren't you paying attention in the meeting this morning?" I said. "He's not exactly thrilled with me right now."

"He's angry and hurt," she said, "but he'll listen to you. I know he will."

The rational side of my brain told me to just say no. But Isabeau looked so worried I had trouble getting the word out. I could hear Aunt Yolanda warning me to keep my nose out of other people's business, but I ignored her just as I always had. I wanted to help Ox, and I was really curious about what had come between these two men who'd once been so close.

And I really wanted to know who *had* killed Philippe.

"I'll try," I told Isabeau, "but I'm not making any promises."

Tears shimmered in her eyes. "Oh, thank you! If I can ever help you with anything, just let me know."

"You could start by letting go of my hands."

She let out a self-conscious laugh and loosened her grip. "I'm sorry. I'm just . . . Well, you know."

Actually, I think I did.

She lifted her hand, and two bartenders made a beeline for our section of the bar. There were a lot of things about New Orleans that made me feel oddly out of place, but some things are the same wherever you go: if you're twenty-two, blonde, and curvy, the world's yours for the asking. Add ten years, mousy-brown hair, and twenty pounds, and you can wait all night for someone to notice you.

I looked around the rest of the bar, and as I did, my gaze lit on an unexpected face. Unlike me, Detective Sullivan seemed right at home inside the bar. I didn't know why he'd showed up for Philippe's memorial, but I was pretty sure he wasn't here as a mourner.

I didn't object to him doing his job, but I didn't want him ruining the memorial for Philippe's friends who *weren't* guilty of murder.

It felt like it took forever to work my way through that raucous crowd. A few more people had drifted onto the dance floor, but most were gathered at tables, huddled deep in conversations I couldn't make out over the music.

When I finally drew up to Detective Sullivan, he was leaning against the wall by the front door, arms folded, one leg crossed over the other in a pose I was beginning to recognize. He greeted me with a jerk of his chin and a lazily drawled, "Evenin', Miss Rita."

"Good evening, Detective. What brings you here? Following a suspect, or looking for one?"

He uncrossed his feet and straightened slightly. "Maybe a little of both. How's it going so far?"

I flicked a glance at the chaos behind me. "Loud. Other than that, I'm not sure."

"How's your mother-in-law?"

I probably should have argued with him over technicalities, but I was too tired. Besides, it was nice of him to ask. "Miss

Frankie is hanging in there; thanks for asking. How's the investigation going?"

He shrugged and pushed away from the wall with one shoulder. "Slow. There's not a lot of physical evidence to go on, and nobody on your staff is interested in talking with us."

Disappointment landed hard inside my chest. "There's *no* physical evidence?"

He stepped out of the way to let a heavyset man come inside. "Seems odd, doesn't it?" he said as the man moved past us. "It's almost enough to make me officially rule out a crime of passion."

"You really think someone planned to kill Philippe?"

"It's looking more and more that way."

Before I could stop myself, I glanced at Zydeco's table and found everyone at it watching me and Detective Sullivan. Edie had joined the others while I wasn't looking, and she glared at me as if I'd turned traitor.

The band ended one song and started another, and more people came inside, bringing with them a blast of hot, moist air from outside. How did people live like this? All this warm, moist air made me feel like a mousse in a bain-marie. I swiped perspiration from the back of my neck, but the noise, the people, and the music were beginning to wear on me. A dull throb started up in the back of my head. "For what it's worth, I don't think it was anyone from Zydeco," I told Sullivan. "In fact, I may have a lead for you. But I don't want to talk about it here." Just in case Dmitri Wolff had spies at the bar.

The smile slid from Sullivan's face. "You know something?"

I shook my head quickly. "I don't *know* anything, but there is something I'd like to talk to you about. It may or may not mean anything." I stole another look at my temporary comrades and asked, "Could we talk tomorrow? I really don't want to ruin this for Philippe's friends."

Sullivan gave that some thought, but finally dipped his head. "You want me to come to you, or do you want to talk at the station?"

I didn't like either option. I didn't want to talk at Zydeco, and I wasn't excited about the idea of going down to the station. "Can we meet at Miss Frankie's? Say, eight o'clock?"

"You got it." Sullivan jerked his chin toward the table. "Looks like your friends are wondering what you're doing." Which I

179

figured was copspeak for, "We're through here."

"Right. Tomorrow." I inched my way back to the bar. I expected Sullivan to leave, but as I caught my reflection in that massive mirror, I saw him claim a recently vacated table, where the last group's empty glasses hadn't yet been cleared away.

I dragged my eyes away from him and finally found a narrow opening in the crowd in front of the bar. Hot Cajun slid a beer onto a coaster, took an order from the cocktail waitress, and then made his way toward me. He settled a frankly assessing look on my face. "What'll it be?"

I tried not to let his look make me self-conscious, but I felt myself shifting uncomfortably under its weight. "I'm not sure. What do you suggest?"

He shrugged and flicked at the lock of hair that insisted on drooping over one eye. "That depends. You a beer drinker, or are you interested in something stronger?"

"I'm not really a drinker at all, but tonight seems to call for something."

"Ah. You're here for the memorial."

I nodded.

"You were a friend?"

"You could say that. Philippe was my ex-husband."

The bartender pulled back slightly. "You're Rita?"

Okay, *that* was awkward. "He told you about me?"

"Not exactly." He offered me a hand to shake. "Gabriel Broussard."

His hand was warm and hard, his handshake as bold as the look in his eye. "You were a friend of Philippe's?" I asked.

"Not exactly. So, about that drink . . ."

"Can you make a blended margarita?"

"The best in New Orleans. Salt?"

"Of course. Do you have any of that delicious-smelling jambalaya left?"

"Sorry. We ran out about ten minutes ago."

She who hesitates, starves. "Another time, maybe." A couple of young women abandoned their bar stools, and I hitched myself onto the closest one to wait. The band stopped playing, and in the abrupt silence, several conversations stilled. The band's lead singer, an aging man with a shaggy Fu Manchu moustache and long graying hair pulled back in a ponytail, shifted his guitar so that it hung at his side. "Y'all know why we're here," he said, his voice deep and surprisingly gruff. "Philippe was a good friend. A great guy. The kind of guy who'd give you the shirt off his back and buy you a beer to go with it."

Murmurs of agreement rose up from all around the bar, and that lump that was never far away these days landed in my throat again.

"It's a helluva thing that's happened, and we're holdin' Philippe's mama and all y'all in our hearts." Fu Manchu mopped at his eyes with his sleeve and cleared his throat a couple of times. "The mike's yours if anybody wants to say a few words."

A handful of people rushed to the stage, and I wondered if the staff would expect me to say something. I wanted to honor Philippe in some way, but in front of two hundred strangers?

I'd rather crumb coat a thirty-tier cake with nothing but a butter knife.

FIFTEEN

Gabriel returned with my margarita a minute later. I took a sip and sighed with appreciation. The perfect blend of tequila and triple sec. Just the right ratio of salt to glass on the rim. It was love at first taste. I slid a ten onto the bar and began the laborious process of squeezing through the crowd to rejoin the staff. I hadn't gone far when Quinn blew into the bar in a wild-eyed, overly emotional whirlwind that caught everyone's attention. Did she always have to make a grand entrance? I was in no mood for another confrontation with her, so I scooted back into the crowd and settled in at the bar for the duration.

Quinn found a seat at Zydeco's table and cried on every shoulder she could reach, moving from Edie to Burt to Dwight and on around the circle, soaking up sympathy and attention like sponge cake.

What *had* Philippe seen in her?

"How are you doing?" Gabriel asked as he passed from one end of the bar to the other. "Ready for another?"

I shook my head and reluctantly pushed my nearly empty glass away. "Probably not a good idea."

"No? Why not?"

I jerked a thumb toward Zydeco's table and the blonde bombshell holding court at its center. "I don't need my inhibitions lowered right now."

"Ah. The new girlfriend." Gabriel leaned on the bar and shook his head slowly. "I never did understand that relationship."

I whipped around to look at him, delighted to find someone else who didn't seem hypnotized by Quinn. "I know, right?"

His warm brown eyes traveled over my face. "So what's the story with you and Philippe? You're the ex, but you're here for the memorial? That's unusual, isn't it?"

"It's complicated."

"You must have had a pretty good relationship."

A shrill cry erupted before I could respond, and I glanced behind me to see Quinn staggering toward the stage.

"This ought to be interesting," Gabriel said with a grin. "Sure you don't want another margarita?"

I hesitated, torn between the desire to numb myself and the more sensible desire to remain rational. This night wasn't about me, and I didn't want to do anything that might ruin it for Philippe's friends. On the other hand, the margarita was delicious, and another round of tequila might ease the tension I was feeling. "Okay. One more. Thanks."

Quinn stumbled on the short step to the stage and lunged for the microphone once she maneuvered the difficult climb successfully. *Please,* I begged any higher power that might be paying attention, *don't let her do something stupid.*

Apparently, the higher powers were busy because Quinn stumbled backward and lowered the microphone in front of a large black speaker, resulting in an earsplitting screech that drew groans from most of the crowd.

I took the second drink from Gabriel and swallowed enough to give me a brain freeze. Fu Manchu grabbed Quinn's hand and helped her move the microphone away from the speaker. If he'd stopped there, we might have been okay. But then he made the disastrous mistake of putting the mike in front of her mouth. I could only guess that he'd never met her before.

"Philippe Renier was my boyfriend," she said, her voice high and tight.

I swallowed another mouthful of frozen tequila slush.

"But he was a real son of a bitch. He told me he loved me, but that was a lie. He was still married, but he never told me." She swayed slightly, then zeroed in on something, which turned out to be me. "Married to . . . *that.*"

Every head in the place turned to see who she was pointing at, even the people who already knew the answer. Some people in the crowd looked curious. Some amused. But most of Philippe's friends looked outraged. My face burned with embarrassment, and I'd have given anything for a shovel so I could dig a hole and crawl into it.

"I thought you said he was your *ex,*" Gabriel said, in the silence that followed.

"I told you it was complicated," I shot back. With every eye in the place on me, I tried desperately to think of a way to salvage the moment. Lifting my chin, I got to my feet, but the room tilted precariously beneath me. Apparently, two margaritas was one too many. I gave up on the idea of walking to the stage and held onto my bar stool for support. "It's not what it sounds like," I said. "Philippe and I were separated. If he hadn't . . . died, our divorce would have been final by the end of the month."

Quinn let out a sharp laugh, and the crowd turned to her like spectators at a tennis match. "Yeah. So *you* say." She appealed to the crowd. "Don't you think it's a little too convenient that he died while they were still married so she gets everything? All his money. His house? She's even managed to talk Miss Frankie into letting her run the business —"

"Miss Frankie *asked* me to take over for a few days."

Thankfully, Dwight saved me from further embarrassment by jumping onto the stage and taking the microphone away from the airhead. The band launched into a song, and little by little, conversations struck up at tables around the bar. But the damage had been done. I could see several of Philippe's friends eyeing me with suspicion. Worst of all, the memorial had been ruined, all because one stupid woman couldn't keep her mouth shut.

I could only think of one thing as I stood with my face burning and ears ringing. *Get out.* But my purse was still beneath the chair at Zydeco's table. That meant I had a choice: abandon my purse and everything in it, including my car keys, or go back to that table and get my stuff. It wasn't an easy choice to make.

To buy myself some time, I ordered a third margarita, told Gabriel that I'd be right back, and went outside to clear my head and catch my breath. The temperature had dropped a few degrees, but the air was still heavy with humidity, and my clothes felt damp as I walked from the bar toward the corner, where a signal light flashed its red light on and off.

Zydeco music followed me out of the bar, its sharp accordion notes muted by distance. At first, I thought I was alone, but when a few desultory notes sounded on a trumpet, I realized that someone was sitting on a bench, partially hidden by a tree.

I moved closer out of curiosity and saw a man of indeterminate age, his dark face smooth and unlined, his body softly rounded. Even in the darkness, he wore sunglasses, and he tilted his head at the sound of my footsteps in a way that made me suspect he couldn't see me.

I started to move on past him, but he stopped playing and turned his head in my direction. "You da wife?"

His question surprised me, and I hesitated, uncertain how to answer. "You were inside?"

"I was. I have friends in the band. I sit in wid dem sometimes." He lowered his trumpet, clasped in both hands, between his knees. "You're hurtin', no?"

I laughed softly, surprised by how much he could tell without seeing my face. "I'm hurting, yes."

"I can feel it. It come out of you like a cloud."

His observations left me feeling raw and exposed. I folded my arms across my chest, as if I could keep him from reading me. "It's strange," I said, with a smile he couldn't see. "We weren't together anymore. I was over him, and he was definitely over me. But since he died, I . . ." I broke off, annoyed with myself for spilling my guts to a perfect stranger.

"Dese things, dey make you feel like to die for a while, but it get better wid time. You'll see. Old Dog Leg, he know what he talking 'bout."

"Dog Leg?"

"You heard of me mebbe? Dog Leg Magee?"

He sounded so hopeful that I hated to say no. "I'm new around here," I reminded him. "I haven't heard of anybody."

Dog Leg laughed and patted the seat beside him. "I like you, wife."

After enduring the hostile stares of the people inside the bar, his friendliness was hard to resist, but I didn't move. "You knew Philippe?"

The smile on Dog Leg's face faded. "I knew him, all right. Long time. Dis t'ing that happened . . . it shouldn't have."

"That's an understatement." I glanced up and down the street, trying to decide whether to sit and talk with him or to keep walking.

"You don't have to worry, *chérie.* You're safe wid me. Come. Sit. Tell me how's his mama?"

"You know her?"

"Sure do. Miss Frankie's a mighty fine woman. If I were twenty years younger . . ."

I couldn't resist moving closer to get a better look. If he was too old for Miss Frankie, that would make him —

"Seventy-eight on my next birthday. Too old to be much good anymore."

Seventy-eight and blind. Probably not much of a threat. I sat on the bench and waved a hand in front of my face in a vain attempt to create a breeze. "I doubt that's true," I said. "Seventy-eight's not all that old."

He let out a gravelly laugh and shook his head. "Not all dat young either. You helpin' Miss Frankie out down the bakery?"

"For a few days. Until the funeral's over and she can figure out what to do next."

"It gonna take her more'n a few days to get past this." He mopped his face with a handkerchief and stuffed it into his pocket with a shake of his head. "What do the police say? Dey got any idea who done this?"

"Not yet," I admitted. "But they'll figure it out."

"You got more faith than I do. 'Round here the po-lice got their hands full. Dey don't solve a case in a day or two, somethin' else comes to take its place. I wouldn't count on dem catchin' the killer."

I didn't like hearing that, but it was probably true. Dog Leg put his trumpet to his mouth and played a few bars of a song that sounded vaguely familiar. I watched a man stagger from the front door of the Duke, stop to relieve himself on the wall of a nearby shop, and then disappear around the corner. Charming.

I fanned the front of my shirt, still trying to cool off. "I hope they do catch this one," I said as his tune trailed off again. "For Miss Frankie's sake."

"You 'n' me both, wife. You 'n' me both."

I smiled and set the record straight. "It's Rita, not wife."

"Ah. Lovely Rita, meter maid." He played the opening riff of the old Beatles song, the notes clear and sweet. "Dat girl in dere. She don't know what she talking about. You not the kind to kill a man just to get your hands on his money."

I laughed softly. "I could kiss you for saying that."

He leaned toward me, presenting his cheek. "What you waitin' for den?"

I brushed a brief kiss to his full cheek and felt myself relax a little more. "I wish I knew more about Philippe's life," I said as I sat back on the bench again. "I don't have a clue who might have wanted to hurt him."

"Mebbe the girlfriend."

"Quinn? Do you know something I don't?"

"She foun' out he was married. Hell hath no fury —"

"Like a woman scorned," I finished for him. "But I don't think she knew that before he died."

"You don't *t'ink.*"

He had a point. So far, I'd taken everybody at their word, but what if Quinn had found out that Philippe wasn't free before he died? I shook that idea off almost as soon as it formed. Philippe could have been free within weeks. He *would* have been if someone hadn't murdered him.

Unless . . .

I thought about the message he'd left for me. Had he changed his mind about ending our marriage? Had he told Quinn that their relationship was over?

"Was their relationship in trouble?"

Dog Leg shook his head. "Don' know 'bout that, but there was some kinda trouble. Dat I do know."

My heart skipped a beat. "What kind of trouble?"

"Somethin' Philippe wasn't talking about. I don't know more'n that. But something was bothering him those last couple a days. I could tell."

"Have you told the police?"

Mopping his face again, Dog Leg frowned as if I'd asked a stupid question. "You t'ink the po-lice gonna believe an old man like me? I don' see nothin'. I don' hear nothin'. I just know."

"Well, then, tell me. How do you know?"

"Because Philippe was distracted. He was here two, maybe three days in a row, but he couldn't hardly carry on a conversation. His mind was somewhere else."

My nerves buzzed, and my heart beat a

little faster. "Do you have any idea what kind of trouble? Was it something about work? About Quinn?"

His face scrunched, and for the first time since I sat down beside him, Dog Leg looked like an old man. He shook his head slowly, his disappointment palpable. "Wish I knew, Miss Rita. I truly do."

"It's all right," I assured him. "That's more than I knew five minutes ago. Can you think of anyone else who might know what was bothering him?"

"Not offhand. He wasn't the kind of guy to air his dirty laundry."

No, he hadn't been. He'd lived in the "Don't Worry, Be Happy" camp. I put a hand on Dog Leg's arm and gave it a reassuring squeeze. "Thank you. If you think of anything else, please let me know. I'll be at Zydeco during the days." I took a deep breath and made a promise I hoped I didn't regret. "And maybe I'll come here in the evenings while I'm in town."

A slow smile curved his old face. "You gonna step in where Philippe left off mebbe? Learn to play wid us?"

"Did Philippe play?" He'd toyed around with the guitar when we were married. It wouldn't have surprised me to learn that he'd jammed with the band here.

Dog Leg nodded slowly. "Sometimes."

"Was he any good?"

"Sometimes," Dog Leg said with a grin. "He was tryin'. I'll say that much for him. So how 'bout it?"

I laughed and shook my head. "Music's not my thing, I'm afraid. I can barely carry a tune."

"Ah, well, can't blame an old man for tryin'." He got to his feet, groaning as he did so. "I tell you who you could ask 'bout Philippe," he said, jerking his head toward the Duke's front door. "Talk to Rikki. She knows just 'bout everything goes on inside that place."

I perked up at that. "Who's Rikki?"

"Young lady servin' da drinks."

I glanced at the building behind us. "I just talked to some guy who had a few bad things to say about Philippe. Any idea who he is or why he's so angry?"

Dog Leg shrugged. "That's probably Guy LeBeau. Nasty piece a work, you ask me."

"What's his problem with Philippe?"

"Same problem he got with de rest of de worl' I bet. He don' like nobody. But if dere somethin' to know, Rikki can tell you."

"Is she in there now?"

"Could be. Just be careful, Miss Rita. You ask the wrong person, you might stir up

195

trouble you don't want."

An icy finger traced a line up my spine, but I couldn't just sit back and do nothing. "How will I know her?"

"Nice lady. Whiskey voice. Smells like roses." He gave a crisp nod and ran his handkerchief across the back of his neck. "Ask her."

Oh good. All I had to do was chase down every harried woman carrying a tray of drinks until I found one who sounded like she drank too much and smelled like my grandmother's garden. Piece of cake.

I watched Dog Leg shuffle away, amazed that he could navigate the narrow sidewalk without help. As I gazed after him, I gave some thought to his advice. Should I talk to Rikki and find out what she knew, or should I tell Detective Sullivan about my conversation with Dog Leg and let him question her?

I vacillated for a minute or two, but in the end, I decided not to bother Sullivan until I knew whether Rikki actually had information that might help with the investigation. I couldn't see any reason to bother a busy cop unnecessarily.

At least, that's what I told myself.

SIXTEEN

Dog Leg disappeared from sight, making me acutely aware that I was standing outside, alone, late at night, in a strange city. In spite of the heat, a breeze came out of nowhere, stirring the tops of the trees, and a shiver racked my body. I turned back toward the bar eagerly.

Inside, Edie had just taken the stage, and an expectant hush fell over the crowd as she launched into a speech that made Philippe sound like a candidate for sainthood. I worked my way back to the bar, where a fresh margarita waited for me.

I spotted Detective Sullivan, still sitting at his table and watching the reactions of the crowd as Edie spoke. Quinn was sobbing uncontrollably. Most of the other women dabbed at their eyes and blew their noses softly. A few of the men did the same, while others sat ramrod straight, trying not to show emotion.

"You going to say something?" Gabriel asked on his way past with half a dozen long-neck bottles in his hands.

I shook my head and licked salt from the rim of my glass. "Are you kidding? These people don't want to hear from me."

He grinned. "You don't know that. *I'm* kind of curious to hear what you have to say."

"That makes you a minority of one." I licked again, once more appreciating Gabriel's perfect salt-to-glass ratio. While I rated him on his margarita-making skills, Edie gave up the mike to Burt, who shared a story about Philippe that drew a few laughs and put smiles on most of the faces in the room.

Burt passed off to Isabeau, who thanked Philippe for hiring her, after which a young woman staggered up to the stage from a table near the bar and told everyone how Philippe had loaned her the money to fix her car a few months earlier.

I wanted to listen to all of the stories, but Dog Leg's warning kept interfering, and I found myself watching the cocktail waitresses closely. I counted three of them on duty, any one of which might be Rikki.

Candidate number one was the woman who'd ignored me when I first arrived, a young-looking woman with long brown hair and a smile that revealed a row of teeth too small for her face. Number two: a woman barely out of her teens with spiky burgundy hair and a hip-to-hip walk that attracted a lot of male attention. Number three was a tired-looking woman about my age whose dirty-blonde hair had been seriously over-processed.

While I waited for a chance to strike up a conversation with any one of them, I sucked down my third margarita. How hard could it be to find Rikki? All three women looked friendly enough, if a bit stressed and impatient. The more I drank, the less daunting the task in front of me became. That prompted me to order a fourth drink. Which may not have been the smartest decision I made that night.

I turned on my stool to place my order and found Gabriel watching me as he poured scotch over ice for a thin man at the end of the bar. The look in his eye brought on a little flush of pleasure that was probably heightened by the high blood-alcohol level coursing through my veins.

I tossed him a jaunty smile — at least I hoped it looked jaunty. After three margaritas, I couldn't be sure. While I was at it, I tried to get a look at his ring finger. Just in case. A woman needs to know what she's working with.

The finger was bare, which made me happy. I blame the tequila for that, too. When he came closer, I decided to find out a little more about him. It seemed like the logical thing to do if he was going to keep looking at me like that.

I lobbed the best conversation starter I could come up with onto the bar between us. "Have you worked here long?" Tequila, remember? Working with diminished capacity.

His lips quirked as if I'd said something funny. "Since college."

"How long is that?"

"I'm thirty-two, if that's what you're asking." He swiped at the bar with a towel and stuffed tip money someone had left on the bar into his pocket. "And no, I'm not married."

My face flamed, and somehow I lost my balance on the bar stool. I tilted like a Mad Hatter cake and grabbed for the bar in front of me. "I wasn't asking," I said, trying to regain a little dignity.

"No, but you were wondering."

"I was not."

He held up his left hand and wiggled his

fingers in front of my face. "You could have asked."

The fire in my face grew even hotter. I pushed my glass away and decided I'd had enough. "Okay. So I looked. That doesn't mean anything. For the record, I'm not interested. I'm not going to be around long enough to care."

His grin grew a little broader. "Right."

I looked away in embarrassment and noticed that Sullivan was watching us both. He turned in his chair and faced the bar, giving him a straight-on view of me blushing and Gabriel smiling. I wasn't doing anything wrong, but I didn't want the cop investigating Philippe's murder to think that I was on the make less than forty-eight hours after my ex-husband's brutal murder. I pushed the drink farther away, gathered what was left of my pride around me, and stood. "I think you have the wrong impression."

Gabriel threw back his head and laughed. It was a great laugh, and under different circumstances, I might have liked the sound. Right then, it made me want to hit him with something. "You're pretty full of yourself, aren't you?" I said.

"You say that as if it's a bad thing."

"Where I come from, it is."

Still grinning, he leaned in so close I could feel his breath on my neck. "Far as I'm concerned, there's nothing wrong with confidence. In fact, I think it's kind of sexy."

Out of the corner of my eye, I spotted Detective Sullivan scowling at me, and I pulled away from Gabriel. But I moved too quickly, and the stool tilted beneath me. For real. I grabbed for the bar, but I wasn't quick enough. The stool, the margarita, and I all fell over in what felt like slow motion.

I heard a woman's voice swearing as I continued toward the floor, and I found myself looking up into the very angry eyes of Possible Rikki number one. She'd looked about twenty-five from a distance, but now that I was closer, I realized she hadn't seen her twenties in at least a decade — maybe longer.

"Son of a —" she shouted, and jumped back in a vain attempt to escape the slush flying out of my glass. I watched in horror as the mixture hit her in the neck and then slid down, down, down, into her substantial cleavage.

She glared at me for what felt like eternity then turned a vicious stare on Gabriel. "I've had it. I can't do this tonight. I'm out of here."

"You can't go! We're already short-handed."

"Bite me."

She stepped over me and snagged her purse from behind the bar, then pushed out into the night.

Gabriel muttered something under his breath and shouted for the other two waitresses, but I no longer cared about them. In the angry waitress's wake, she'd left the unmistakable scent of roses.

"Need a ride?"

The familiar voice sounded right in my ear as I struggled to my feet. I turned to find Detective Sullivan standing behind me. His blue eyes crinkled at the corners, but that was the only indication that he found my situation amusing.

He was one up on me. I didn't find it at all funny. I brushed pieces of dirt from my jeans and shook my head. "No. Thank you. I'll be fine."

"You're not driving, are you?"

I tugged my blouse back into position and made a point of looking sober and in control. "I'll call a cab. I repeat, I'll be fine."

He put a hand on my arm. "I'll drive you home."

Now he was just making me mad. "I'll be fine," I said for the third time. "My

203

purse . . . it's over at the table. I'll just go grab it." I was perfectly capable of crossing the room on my own — at least I thought I was — but I made it a point not to make eye contact with anyone as I did. I'd embarrassed myself enough for one night.

Sullivan was still there when I came back, and he jerked his head toward the front door. I headed for it like a puppy with its tail between its legs.

He didn't say another word until we were outside and next to his car, but then he took my arm again, pulling me around to face him. There was no force in the action. No anger or irritation, either. In fact, the look on his face was almost friendly. "You're really okay?"

I nodded up at him, determinedly ignoring the sudden rolling of my stomach. "I had a couple of drinks. I'm not drunk."

"Four," he said. "You had four. Including the one that spilled. And you're at sea level. That can make a difference in how your body reacts to alcohol."

I ignored 99 percent of what he said and zeroed in on the part that struck me as odd. "You were counting how many drinks I had?"

He shrugged. "I was concerned."

"About me? Why?"

"You need to ask? Have you had anything to eat lately?"

I shook my head reluctantly. "Not since breakfast."

"Figures." He started walking slowly to the driver's side. "And you wonder why I was concerned."

Beads of sweat popped up on my nose and forehead — not odd, since it was about two hundred degrees outside. I ignored them and opened the passenger-side door. "Well, yeah. Actually. I do. I was fine in there."

"Except for the part where you fell over."

"That was an accident," I informed him.

"And the part where Quinn called you out."

"Yeah. Well there was that. But she's wrong, you know. I didn't come here to get my hands on Philippe's stuff."

He slid a grin at me as he started up the car. "So you've said, more than once."

"Because it's true! And I'll keep saying it until you believe that I didn't kill Philippe."

"Well, then, you can stop. Unless you have some kind of superpowers, I don't think you *could* have killed him. You were with Edie when the fight broke out, and within eyesight of at least one other person until about three minutes before you found the body. Philippe hadn't been dead long, but the absence of blood spatter on your clothes makes a pretty strong argument in your favor."

The weight that lifted off my shoulders made me a little dizzy. "Really? You believe I'm innocent? Thank God."

He dipped his head once and turned his gaze to the street in front of us. "You weren't sitting with the folks from Zydeco in there. Any special reason?"

I made a face. "Yeah, a big-busted blonde one."

"You don't care for your ex-husband's new girlfriend?"

"She's just a bit over the top for my taste." I decided to change the subject to something less personal. "What about you? Did you learn anything useful in there?"

"Not really, but you have to look at everything in an investigation like this one. Turn it over and see what shakes out."

Both Miss Frankie and Old Dog Leg had expressed doubt over the outcome of the investigation, but I wasn't ready to give up on New Orleans' finest. "How often do you find the answers?"

Sullivan shook his head. "Not often enough. Sometimes you catch a case with an easy solution, but too many cases are like this one. No obvious solutions. No easy answers."

"So what do you think the chances are of actually finding Philippe's murderer?"

"You want the stock answer, or the truth?"

"The truth, please."

"I think we have a good chance. I'm sure going to give it hell. I figure somebody must have seen something that morning." He checked for oncoming traffic and pulled away from the curb. "The trick will be finding that person and then praying that he or she will be brave enough to speak up."

"You pray?"

He looked away from the street just long enough to grin at me again. "That surprises you?"

"A little, I guess. I didn't realize that cops and God could coexist."

"Guess that depends on the cop. My father is a Pentecostal pastor, and my mother taught me that there's eternal hellfire in store for disobedient kids. God and I have been on speaking terms since I was a small boy."

I laughed and leaned my head against the seat. The slight breeze I'd noticed outside the Duke had gained strength, and a few drops of rain splattered the windshield. But the swaying of the car wasn't helping my stomach or my head. I felt around for the controls on my door panel and rolled down the window, hoping for a breath of cool, fresh air. What can I say? Where I come from, rain cools things down. Apparently, that's not how it works in Louisiana. I got a blast of greenhouse-quality air: hot, wet, and stale. My stomach pitched dangerously.

I closed my eyes and tried to remember what we were talking about. Right. God. Who was probably making notes in my permanent record that very minute. "So you're a believer," I said, inching open one eye. "Does that mean he helps you solve cases?"

His eyebrow winged upward. "Are you mocking?"

I held up both hands to ward off the suggestion. "Raised by a Catholic aunt. I wouldn't dare."

He actually chuckled. "Still want to meet tomorrow, or do you want to tell me what's on your mind right now?"

I'd have preferred waiting until my head was clear, but I didn't want to admit just how cloudy it was. "Now's fine," I said, and gave him a brief rundown on Dmitri Wolff's visit to Zydeco. "If you haven't already," I said when I finished, "you might want to find out where he was yesterday morning."

"I'll do that," Detective Sullivan said, and

we fell into a silence that might have felt companionable if I hadn't been hanging my head out the window and battling the urge to toss all four margaritas onto the city streets. I'm not sure how far we drove, but suddenly, without warning, the rain that had been sprinkling my face every few seconds gathered into a full-scale rainstorm. A deluge fell on me as if someone had overturned a bucket, washing away the last few shreds of my dignity.

Could this night get any worse? I was afraid to ask.

Gasping in shock, I pulled my head inside and fumbled to roll up the window while torrents of rain pelted both me and the passenger side of Sullivan's car. Water dripped from my hair onto my face, and to my horror, tight little ringlets formed with every drop. I don't let anybody see me in my natural state, so I used the hem of my blouse to wipe hair and rainwater out of my eyes. "Holy Mother of God, what just happened?"

"Rain."

If Sullivan hadn't been wearing a gun, I might have slugged him. "I got that much. Where did it come from?"

"Usually clouds."

I pondered how much jail time assaulting

an officer might get me as I squeezed water from my hair. "Is this normal?"

"It rains here. A lot. But we could have done without this storm."

If this was just a harmless rainstorm, I didn't want to know what a hurricane was like.

He turned onto Miss Frankie's street and squinted to see through the sheets of running water. "If there was any evidence in the garden we missed the first time through, it'll be gone now."

"I thought you said there wasn't any physical evidence."

"None that we found at the time. I haven't given up hope that we'll find something somewhere."

I forgot about my hair for a moment. "Are you looking for anything in particular?"

"Footprints would be nice. An eyewitness would also be good."

"What about Ox? Did he see anything?"

Sullivan shook his head. "He says whoever it was hit him from behind. He didn't see a thing."

And here I was freaking out over a little uncontrolled frizz in my precious hair. I needed to get my priorities straight. "The sooner you can find the person who did this,

210

the better."

Sullivan took his eyes from the road for a split second and settled them on my face. "We'll find him, Rita."

As he pulled into Miss Frankie's driveway, a rogue wave of nausea tore through me, and all four margaritas rose up in my throat. I was powerless to control them. Sullivan stopped at the bottom of the drive behind a dark-colored car partially hidden by the shadows. I paid scant attention, assuming it was Miss Frankie's car. Memory loss brought on by tequila. Very common.

Rain pounded on the car so loudly, I could barely hear my own groan of horror. I searched frantically for the door handle, running both hands over the door like a crazy woman.

Sullivan leaned across me to open it, and I tumbled out of the car, right into the small lake that had already formed at the end of the driveway. I scrambled to my knees and crawled blindly toward a flowerbed I re-membered edging the street. It was a bad choice and I knew it, but I wasn't going to cough up the contents of my stomach right there in front of Sullivan.

Apparently, he had other plans because between hacks, I heard the sound of his boots on the pavement. He waited patiently for me to finish, then reached down and helped me to my feet. My stomach hurt, and my pride had taken another severe beating, but at least the cold sweats and nausea had passed.

He held me with one hand and brushed hair from my face with the other. "You okay?"

"Yes. No." I sagged against him, grateful for his strong arms and solid body. "I'm sorry. I don't know what happened."

"Tequila, and lots of it. I think your new friend Gabriel poured generously when he mixed your drinks."

I groaned again. "You think he tried to get me drunk?"

"I think it's a distinct possibility."

"But why?"

"If you don't know the answer to that, you're not as smart as I thought." He turned me around before I could react. "Go inside. Take a hot shower and get into bed. You'll feel better in the morning."

"Sullivan, I —"

"Don't worry about it." He paused at the car door and grinned at me. He looked good wet. "And after what we've been through together, you might as well call me Liam."

SEVENTEEN

When I say I'm not much of a drinker, I mean I'm not much of a drinker *anymore.* I wouldn't say that I was wild in high school, but I attended my fair share of parties. I honed my skills in college, and by the time I met Philippe, I could slug back a few shots with the best of 'em. But it had been a while since those days. When I woke up the next morning, I learned another useful tidbit: holding one's liquor is a skill that deteriorates if not properly maintained.

I'm not sure how I made it upstairs and into bed, but I must've managed it somehow, because that's where I woke up. My wet clothes were lying on the floor in a soggy mound, and when I moved my face, I realized that my pillow had soaked up some of the water from my hair.

Aunt Yolanda would be so proud.

Moving slowly and carefully, I hauled myself to the shower and spent a while trying to wash away the bar stench of stale cigarette smoke and recycled alcohol. And I thought. A lot. About why I was in New Orleans in the first place, about my marriage and its failure. In the bright light of morning, much of last night became a blur, but I clearly remembered flirting with the bartender and the look on the detective's face as we stood in the rain. Which was odd behavior for me, at least the me I'd been since the divorce. Flirting with two different men at my not-quite-ex-husband's memorial service? Who did that?

Things had gotten complicated and painful before Philippe and I split up, and I'd shut down after he left. Oh, sure, I'd had the occasional fleeting romantic thought, but I hadn't been feeling any particular longing to hook up with anyone. Yet somehow, stepping off the plane in New Orleans seemed to have flipped a switch on my libido.

The timing couldn't have been worse.

I swallowed some ibuprofen that I found in the medicine cabinet and pulled on some clean clothes, then lifted my head as high as I could and marched down the stairs to face Miss Frankie. She hadn't come out of her room as I stumbled up the stairs last night, but I was pretty sure she'd heard me come in.

Not my finest hour.

I found her in the kitchen with a pot of fresh, strong coffee and a plate of eggs and toast, which she put down in front of me.

The smell made my stomach revolt, so I pushed the plate away. Subtly, so as not to insult her.

She moved it right back and shook her finger in my face. "Eat. The protein will help the hangover."

So much for avoiding the large pink elephant in the room. My face turned the same shade as the pachyderm, and I mumbled, "I guess you heard me come in."

"Well, I guess so." She smiled and sat across from me. "It's been a while, but I remember what pickled sounds like."

I tried to hide my burning face behind my napkin. "I'll take a taxi to pick up your car. If anything happened to it overnight, I'll pay for the damages."

Miss Frankie pushed at the air between us. "Oh, pish. I'm not worried about that, sugar. We can pick it up later. The important thing is that you didn't try to drive when you were three sheets to the wind."

"Yeah. Well." Thank God for Sullivan.

"That reminds me," Miss Frankie said as she reached into her pocket and pulled out a key. "This is yours."

I took it from her and let the key chain dangle on my finger. "What's it for?"

"Philippe's Mercedes. The police brought it back last night. It's yours now."

A Mercedes? Was she kidding? I shook my head and tried to give the key back to her. "I don't need it. It should be yours."

"Don't be silly. I have a perfectly good car of my own." She pushed the key back in my direction. "At least use it while you're here."

Oh. Sure. "I should spend some time at Zydeco after we get your car," I said, then realized that Miss Frankie's hair was teased and sprayed and her face made up as if she had somewhere to go. "What's on your agenda today?"

Miss Frankie spent a minute pouring coffee, first cracking open a new can of condensed milk and splashing a little into each cup before adding the freshly brewed chicory coffee. She put together a plate for herself and carried everything to the table. "I suppose I'll have to talk with the funeral director at some point."

I'd forked up a bit of the egg, but I stopped with it halfway to my mouth. "Do you want me to go with you?"

"I'd love you forever if you did." Changing the subject, she scowled at the uneaten

216

egg on my fork. "Go on. Eat. It'll help." Her scowl deepened, and she got to her feet. "Maybe I should grab that bottle of bourbon. Put a dash in your coffee. A little hair of the dog that bit you might do the trick."

"No!" I detest the taste and smell of bourbon, and just the thought of it made my stomach pitch and roll. I slipped a bite into my mouth to prove that I was on the road to recovery. "I'm fine. Really I am."

Miss Frankie watched me chew and swallow before she resumed her seat. "So, did that detective tell you anything last night? Are they any closer to figuring out who killed my boy?"

To my surprise, the food was helping me feel better. I slathered Miss Frankie's signature strawberry freezer jam, still slightly frozen the way I liked it best, on the toast and took a little bite of heaven. Fresh strawberry flavor exploded on my tongue, and the sensation of still-cold jam on the warm toast swept me back to childhood for a moment. Back when the world was safe and nothing bad ever happened. But bad things were happening now. I shook my head slowly. I didn't want to discourage her, but I didn't want to offer false hope, either. "Not yet, but he seems to think they'll find the killer eventually."

"Eventually." Miss Frankie let out a heavy sigh. "I'd give anything to be able to help the police solve this case. Philippe didn't have any enemies that I knew of, but *someone* certainly seems to have hated him."

"You could help the police, you know," I said around another mouthful of egg. "Tell them everything you know and point them in the right direction."

"But that's the hell of it, sugar. I don't really know anything."

"You know about the accidents at Zydeco," I said to Miss Frankie. "Start there."

"If I thought for one minute the two things were connected, I'd run to the police."

I had my doubts, but I knew the stubborn expression on her face. The harder I pushed, the more determined she'd become. "You might be right," I said, shelving the sabotage angle for the moment. "What do you know about a man named Dmitri Wolff? Have you ever heard of him?"

Miss Frankie shook her head slowly. "Should I know him?"

"He stopped by Zydeco yesterday. Apparently he also owns a cake shop, in the French Quarter."

Miss Frankie's expression grew cold. "Gateaux?"

"I think so. He's interested in buying Zydeco."

"Over my dead body!" The minute the words slipped out, she looked horrified. "That was a horrible thing to say. How could I have said that?"

I reached across the table and put my hand on hers. "It's okay."

"It most certainly is not!" She jerked her hand away and covered her face. "It's too much. It's just all too much. The bakery. Some awful person trying to take it away. And Philippe. I swear, if I knew anything that might help the police, I'd tell them. But Philippe never said a word to me about his life."

If that was true, then something had been seriously wrong. If anyone should have known what was going on in Philippe's life when he died, it ought to have been Miss Frankie.

I braved a sip of coffee, and closed my eyes in bliss. I'd learned to appreciate chicory in my coffee while Philippe and I were married, and his mother could brew a heavenly cup to rival anything at Café Du Monde. "So who *did* he confide in?"

"I have no idea. Someone at work, maybe." She shifted in her seat, and her expression grew grim. "Or that woman."

"Quinn?"

Miss Frankie shrugged. "Maybe. Oh, don't get me wrong. She's a lovely girl, and she has the face of an angel. But there were times when I wondered if maybe she wasn't a little too interested in Philippe's money, if you know what I mean."

Did I ever! "You don't think she was really in love with him?"

"No, I don't."

I shouldn't have felt so pleased by that, but that didn't stop me from gloating or from wondering again if Quinn could have wielded the knife that killed Philippe. "I guess that means you didn't like her?"

Miss Frankie made a face. "Let's just say that I was surprised when Philippe brought her around. She didn't seem like his type at all. You wouldn't think they had a thing in common."

"*We* didn't have much in common outside of the kitchen," I reminded his mother.

"That was different. Your differences didn't bother you."

That wasn't exactly true. It was our differences that had driven us apart in the end. I'd loved to read; Philippe had preferred spending his leisure time with a gun or a fishing pole. I'd loved movies and the theater; Philippe had liked fast cars and

220

motorcycles.

"There's no law that says you have to like every little thing the other one does," Miss Frankie said, as if she could read my mind. "Robert and I were as different as can be, but we spent thirty wonderful years together. The differences between Philippe and Quinn were deeper. Spend five minutes with her, and you'll see what I mean."

I reached for the strawberry jam and a second piece of toast. "I already have, remember?"

"Then you know she's nothing like you."

That was quite possibly the nicest thing she'd ever said to me.

"No, but a lot of people think she seems genuinely distraught over Philippe's death."

"Distraught over losing his bank account, you mean." Miss Frankie sat back with a tight smile. "I've thought about this a lot in the past couple of days, and I think something wasn't right between them. I saw them the night before Philippe . . . was killed. We had dinner together at Napoleon House." She stopped speaking for a moment, remembering.

I munched toast and waited for her to go on.

"They tried to act as if nothing was wrong," she said at last, "but the tension between them was as thick as pea soup. I wish now that I'd asked Philippe what was going on, but I didn't. I just pretended not to notice."

The curiosity I'd been battling since yesterday stirred to life again. Aunt Yolanda had spent a lifetime warning me about poking my nose where it didn't belong, but the advice had never stuck. Philippe's relationship with Quinn definitely fell into the "none of your business" category, but that only made me wonder about it more. "Have you told the police about that? I mean, if there was something going on between them, the police should know."

Miss Frankie fumbled with a handkerchief for a moment, dabbing tears from her eyes, before letting out a weary sigh. "What is there to tell? Neither of them actually said or did anything unusual. If there was some kind of trouble between them, Quinn is the only one who knows what it was, and she's not going to admit anything that might make her look bad."

"But the police will know how to interrogate her," I pointed out.

"And what? She'll lie, and they'll believe her."

"They won't take her word over yours," I assured her.

"You don't know that. She's convincing. Look how she got to Philippe."

"You think she lied to him?"

"I'm almost certain of it. I just can't prove it. But things changed between Philippe and me after she came along. That's all I know."

"The police need to know that, too," I said again.

"No. I refuse to drag Philippe's memory through the mud when he isn't here to defend himself."

Her refusal made no sense to me, but I tried once more to change her mind. "But you *have* to tell them everything. They need to know so they can pursue every angle."

Miss Frankie put her cup down on the table with a soft *bang*. Her mouth was set in a thin, hard line. "I don't have to do any such thing. Family is family."

"Exactly! That's why we should do everything we can to bring Philippe's killer to justice. I'm not saying Quinn did it," I pointed out, "but what if the murder is somehow related to what happened between them?"

Miss Frankie folded her hands together in her lap and fixed me with a look. "And what if it's not? What if I tell them what I *think* was going on, and I'm wrong?"

I sighed with frustration, but clearly Miss

Frankie wasn't going to budge. I could tell Sullivan — *Liam* — what she'd just told me, but would that be enough? Or would he just chalk my suspicions up to jealousy? "Okay, let's forget about Quinn for a minute. Did Philippe ever mention having trouble with anyone from the Dizzy Duke?"

Miss Frankie looked up suddenly. "As a matter of fact, he did. I can't believe I forgot about that."

"Can you tell me?"

"I don't know the details, but he mentioned something about a man bothering one of the girls there. Things got heated. Philippe stepped in. You know how he was."

"Yeah. I do. Do you know the woman's name?"

"I don't think he mentioned it. The only reason he said anything at all was because his shirt was ripped when he stopped by to bring me a cake for my book club."

"Does the name Guy LeBeau ring any bells?"

Miss Frankie shook her head. "No."

"How about Rikki?"

"Not that I recall. Should they?"

"I don't know for sure," I admitted, "but I'll try to find out if they were involved with the incident you mentioned."

"You see why you have to run Zydeco for

me," Miss Frankie said with a satisfied nod. "You've already made progress. What about the sabotage? Anything new on that front?"

"Nothing yet, except that apparently Philippe thought Ox was responsible."

Miss Frankie's mouth pinched so tightly, little lines fanned out from her lips. "Like I said, you're the only person I can trust. Just promise me you'll stay and keep Philippe's dream alive. I'll make you a partner. We can have the same agreement that Philippe and I had."

That offer of a partnership dangled in front of me like a piece of carrot cake. Oh so tempting. "Zydeco was Philippe's dream, not mine." But even as I said it, I knew that was a lie. Philippe's shop was my dream store in almost every particular.

Miss Frankie knew it, too. "But now it can be yours. It doesn't make sense to turn your back on such an opportunity. How can you let the business fail because of foolish pride? Besides, you're family," she said stubbornly, leaning forward and grabbing both of my hands the same way Isabeau had at the Dizzy Duke. "There's no time to search for someone else with the insight, talent, and business acumen to take over. Zydeco is doing very well right now, but if Edie has to cancel all of the bakery's contracts while I

225

try to find someone to take over and then we waste more time bringing someone new up to speed, the business will never recover. And that man will get his hands on it after all. Philippe would be mortified if I let that happen."

A dozen different emotions warred inside me. The temptation to accept her offer was hard to resist, but how could I stay in New Orleans? What would Uncle Nestor say, and how much of it would I be able to understand?

On the other hand, what if the business began to falter? *Would* Dmitri get his Wolff paws on it? I didn't like that possibility at all. Especially since I was 75 percent convinced that he'd murdered Philippe to get the business in the first place.

I couldn't make the decision now. I needed to get rid of my hangover and think about it. I offered Miss Frankie a reassuring smile and a compromise. "I promise I'll think about it."

Her eyelids fluttered shut, and she loosened her grip on my hands. "I'll have to be content with that, I suppose."

Guilt washed over me like a wave for offering Miss Frankie false hope, for even thinking about turning my back on Uncle Nestor and Aunt Yolanda, and for allowing the very sweet idea of being a partner in Zydeco to tempt me, even for a moment.

Eighteen

I hurried outside half an hour later carrying a travel mug filled with Miss Frankie's excellent coffee. Thanks to the rain, I hadn't really noticed the car parked in the driveway last night, but it was hard to miss it this morning. Sleek, black, and sporty. A convertible built for two. The kind of car I'd never have let myself dream about. I stared at it for a long time, unable to make myself move toward it.

Eventually, the sun — already bright and hot — pulled me out of my stupor, and I stepped over a puddle on the driveway, left from last night's storm.

Which reminded me . . .

I put the coffee and my bag in Philippe's Mercedes and dragged the garden hose from its neat coil at the side of the garage toward the flowerbed where I'd tossed the margaritas last night. The rain seemed to have washed away all evidence of my bleak moment, but I turned the spray on the flowerbed anyway, just to be sure.

As I was about to finish the job, a flash of sunlight reflected off something shiny on the far side of the lawn, and I spotted a woman watching me from behind a low hedge.

Great. Nosy neighbors. Just what I needed.

The woman straightened when she realized that I'd noticed her and shielded her eyes with one hand to get a better look. She was medium height with a plump figure and a halo of white hair, the perfect picture of a cookie-baking grandmother. Had she also been watching last night as I crawled around on the driveway? Is that why she was staring at me this morning?

I ignored her as I hurried back to the Mercedes.

"Hello?" she called.

Drat! I considered pretending that I hadn't heard her, but she'd already reached the end of the driveway, and I could see her waddling toward me holding a pair of hedge clippers. Unless I ran over her, there was no way to avoid her.

"Excuse me? Hello?"

I turned to face her and pasted on a smile. "Can I help you?"

She was huffing a little by the time she reached me, and I could see grass stains on the knees of her linen slacks. The cost of staking out the neighbors, I guess. "I'm Bernice Dudley. From next door? You're staying with Francis Mae, am I right?"

Francis Mae? I hadn't heard Miss Frankie's real name in a while, and I couldn't help but wonder if she approved of Bernice using it. "I'm Rita," I said. "I'll be here for a few days."

"Well, thank the good Lord for that." Bernice huffed as she battled to catch her breath. "I heard what happened, of course. We all did. And I want you to know that I'm utterly devastated."

"Thanks." I think. "It's been difficult."

"Difficult? Goodness! That's an understatement, isn't it?" She swatted at a mosquito with her free hand and scowled. "I can't even imagine how Francis Mae is handling it."

Was she offering condolences or pumping for information? I couldn't be sure. I tried to offer a response that fell in safe ground. "She's hanging in there."

"Well, I am so glad to hear that," Bernice said with a sigh of relief. "It's not natural, a woman losing her only son. I was afraid this would destroy her."

"She's devastated," I admitted, "but she's a strong woman. It won't be easy, but she'll get through it."

"Well, of course she will." Bernice pulled a handkerchief from a pocket and mopped sweat from the back of her neck. "I've been thinking of bringing over a covered dish for supper, but I wasn't sure when would be a good time. When I saw you out here, I decided that now was the time to ask. Can I bring something over tonight?"

I remembered neighbors rushing to our door with meals after my parents died. I'd been too young to appreciate their offerings at the time, but age and experience had helped me learn to appreciate the tradition. In a time when family was too shell-shocked to care about food, having meals already prepared helped in a very practical way.

"That's very generous," I said. "But we'll be out this evening."

"Tomorrow then?"

"Maybe," I said uncertainly. "Maybe you could just call her later and see how she's feeling."

"Of course. Of course." Bernice squinted at the house and let out another heavy sigh. "Francis Mae and I have been neighbors more than twenty years, but I don't have the faintest idea how to deal with this. It's just so awful."

"Yes," I agreed. "It is." The air was still and hot this morning, the calm after the storm, I guess. In addition to the humidity I was breathing, hot moist air rose up from the saturated ground, giving New Orleans a double-shot of misery. Imagine enduring this without clean water or electricity. Just the thought made me weak in the knees. I looked longingly at the Mercedes — specifically at its air-conditioner controls — and wondered how long good manners required me to stand in the broiling sun.

"I've been so worried since I heard," Bernice prattled on. "But, then, my husband said he thought she had family with her. You *are* family?"

The truth was too complicated for this conversation, so I hedged, "I'm a friend of the family."

Bernice smiled up at me as if I'd introduced myself as Mother Teresa. "Well isn't that sweet of you? You don't often see that kind of devotion these days, do you?"

I didn't know what to say to that, so I mumbled vaguely and moved closer to the car door. "It's very nice to meet you, Bernice. I appreciate your concern about Miss Frankie."

"Well, she's a wonderful woman," Bernice

said, with a nod that set her chins wobbling. "An absolute gem of a woman. But I'm sure you know that, or you wouldn't be here."

"A gem," I agreed, and started to slide behind the steering wheel.

Apparently Bernice was just getting warmed up. "What do the police say? Do they know who killed Philippe?"

I stopped sliding and shook my head. "Not yet, but they're working on it."

"Terrible. Terrible." Bernice noticed a smudge of dirt on one pant leg and took a moment to brush it off. "He was such a nice man. So devoted to his mother. And so sweet with that young lady he was seeing."

Gack. Mentions of Quinn on an already sour stomach? Not a good way to start the day. "Well, that was Philippe," I said, trying to keep the smile from sliding off my face. "Considerate to a fault."

Bernice dropped the hand she'd been using as a sun filter. "Isn't that the truth? I don't like to speak ill of people. I really don't. But that girl wasn't half good enough for him. I never did understand what Philippe saw in her."

All of a sudden, I felt myself warming to Miss Frankie's neighbor. "You know Quinn?"

"The little blonde?" Bernice shook her

head. "Not exactly. We met once or twice. In passing. You know how it is. But I saw them together quite often. Here. There. Sometimes in town . . ." Her lips compressed in a thin line, and she glanced toward Miss Frankie's door almost guiltily. "I never said anything to Francis Mae, but I don't think that girl was good for Philippe."

Obviously a woman of intelligence. "What makes you say that?"

Bernice put a hand on her ample bosom and sighed heavily. "I shouldn't say. I don't like speaking ill of anyone."

"No, of course not," I said in my most sympathetic tone. "But if there's some reason you feel that way, I think it would be a kindness to let Miss Frankie know. After I leave, it will be just her and Quinn." Which, now that I thought about it, didn't comfort me much.

Bernice glanced down at her hedge clippers for a moment. "I don't think she was faithful, if you know what I mean."

My mouth fell open in surprise. "You think she was cheating on him?"

"I'm almost certain of it. I saw her with another man. More than once."

I knew it. I *knew* it. "Do you know who he was?"

"No. He was a good-looking guy, though.

234

That much I can tell you."

"And you're sure they were together romantically?"

Bernice's eyes flashed scorn. "They were sitting close together every time. Whispering. All cozied up. What else could it be?"

What else, indeed? "Do you remember when you saw her with this other guy?"

Bernice scrunched up her round face and thought about that. "The first time was probably a couple of months ago. Right after I met her, as a matter of fact. I saw her at a little coffee shop while I was out shopping. I started over to say hello. You know, because I'd met her just a few days earlier and it was the polite thing to do."

"Of course."

"But then I realized she wasn't alone." Bernice's frown deepened as she relived the memory. "What is it with the young women these days? In my day, that kind of behavior was unheard of."

I pretended to believe that to keep her talking. "You said you saw them together more than once?"

"Two or three times," she said, with a knowing look. "And every time it was the same thing. Sitting close together. Whispering things they didn't want anyone else to hear. I never said a word to Francis Mae, of course. I didn't want to worry her."

Keeping such a secret must have been difficult for Bernice. Unless she hadn't actually kept it a secret. "Did you ever mention what you saw to Philippe?"

Bernice's eyes grew huge. "You don't think — ?"

"You did tell him?"

She nodded slowly. "I mentioned it about a week ago. After I saw them together the last time. Philippe was a good boy. I've known him since he was a teenager. I didn't want her to take advantage of him." Her chins wobbled, and she looked as if she was ready to cry. "You don't think that had anything to do with what happened?"

Bernice looked so heartbroken, I couldn't leave her believing she'd unwittingly brought on Philippe's death, even as I wondered it myself. "I'm sure it didn't," I lied, and because she hadn't answered me the first time, I asked again. "You don't know who the man was, by any chance?"

She shook her head and bit her bottom lip. "I don't. I'm sorry. He was tall, dark, and handsome. That's all I know."

That wasn't much to go on, but it was something. I was convinced that Philippe had confronted Quinn about cheating on him. Even if he hadn't ended their relationship then, she would have seen the writing on the wall. She might be an airhead, but she wasn't stupid. She would have sensed that she was about to lose the future she'd been planning for herself.

I put a reassuring hand on Bernice's shoulder. "Please don't worry. You did the right thing."

Bernice gazed up at me, her eyes full of hope. "You're a sweet thing, you know that?"

I laughed softly. "It's nice of you to say so."

She looked as if she wanted to say more, but just then the front door opened and Miss Frankie came onto the porch. Bernice let out a little cry and forgot all about me. "Francis Mae, how are you, dear? I've been beside myself with worry since I heard about poor Philippe."

I watched her hurry up the sidewalk and wrap Miss Frankie in a warm hug. Bernice had passed the litmus test as far as I was concerned, and I felt better knowing that Miss Frankie had friends nearby. But I couldn't stop thinking about Quinn and her secret man-friend. Who was he, and what had Philippe done when he found out that Quinn was cheating?

NINETEEN

Steering my thoughts away from last night's fiasco and onto the issues facing Zydeco, I parked in the employee lot and let myself in through the back door. With the bid deadline coming up next week, I had to spend some time searching for that missing design, but then I wanted to get to work on something artistic and constructive.

We had three cakes scheduled for delivery today. The first was the monkey cake that Sparkle had been working on yesterday. The second, a sweet-sixteen birthday cake, was a three-tier whimsical stack covered in colorful fondant stripes and dots, topped off with a huge fondant bow. It would be challenging in several ways, not the least of which would be controlling the weight of each tier and making each layer perfectly even so the cake would look as if it were about to topple over without actually doing so.

The third cake on the agenda was a

sculpted cake that the client wanted to look like a crab boil, complete with fondant painted to look like newsprint covering the sheetcake base, cobs of corn, crab claws, and mallets — all sculpted out of modeling chocolate.

Not only was I anxious to do the work I loved, but spending time with the staff would allow me to assess their strengths and weaknesses so I could offer Miss Frankie suggestions for how to go on from here. And it would give me an opening to ask about the other strange things that had been happening without pulling them off task. And with Ox out of the picture, someone had to make sure the operation ran smoothly. All in all, it was a bad day for a hangover.

After stowing my gear in Philippe's office, Edie and I arranged for a couple of staff members to retrieve Miss Frankie's car from the Dizzy Duke and return it to her, while we spent some time hunting for the missing cake design in her office, the supply closet, and the break room. We gave Philippe's office one more toss and turned the conference room inside out before moving on to the design room. The staff, minus Ox, were all present and accounted for, with everyone working on some aspect of the cakes. I felt reassured, knowing the group was all professional enough to do the work without someone cracking the whip every second.

Dwight, who was covered in white from the net covering his shaggy hair to the beard restraint on his chin, finished prepping the base for the whimsical birthday cake, while Burt applied edible paint to the crab claws with an airbrush. Across the room, I spotted Estelle cutting geometric shapes from a sheet of fondant and Sparkle at the table next to her using a veining tool to create lifelike kernels on a corncob made of modeling chocolate.

Burt spotted Edie and me as we came through the door and put down the piece he'd been spraying. He turned off the sprayer and turned on the charm, flashing a dimpled grin as I walked toward him.

"This was Ox's project," he said to me. "Do you want to take over now?"

I waved away the offer. "You're doing fine. Right now, I'm worried about finding the design that's gone missing. Have you seen it lying around anywhere?"

"The one for the bid on the fifteenth?" Burt glanced uncertainly at Dwight. "Not me. What about you?"

The part of Dwight's face I could see looked annoyed at the interruption. He inserted a dowel into the bottom tier of cake and stepped back to make sure he'd centered it correctly. "I came in early and took this room apart this morning. No sign of it in here."

My head was still pounding after last night's binge, so I pulled a stool to his table and made myself comfortable. "I just don't understand how it could disappear so completely."

Dwight pulled out a measuring tape and stretched over the next tier to measure width, height, and circumference. "That's no mystery," he said when he had the figures he needed. "Somebody took it."

It was looking more and more like he was right, but I wanted to exhaust every other possibility before I went down that road. "You don't think maybe Philippe left it somewhere?"

Dwight smiled as if I'd said something funny. "You knew Philippe better than anyone. You know how he was about things like that."

"I thought I knew him once, but I'm not so sure anymore."

"He didn't change that much," Dwight assured me.

I found that strangely comforting. "Okay, so who took the design, and why? Any guesses?"

He raised one eyebrow. "You want the whole list?"

"The whole list," I said.

Dwight stopped working and leaned against the table, crossing one foot over the other. "Okay, start with Dmitri Wolff. He's a competitor, and he's bidding on the same project. He's the most likely suspect, if you ask me."

"He's got my vote," I said, "except for the fact that nobody saw him around that morning, so I don't know how he could have taken it."

"That doesn't mean anything. He could have come in through the back gate. It's usually locked, but it wouldn't be that hard to get around."

"The one by the rose garden? It was locked that morning. I saw it myself. You think he attacked Ox, killed Philippe, stole the design, *and* got away without anyone spotting him?"

Dwight shrugged. "Maybe. Or not. It doesn't seem very likely though, does it?"

"Not really. So who else is on your list?"

Dwight didn't even hesitate with his next suspect. "Ox. He's been acting weird for weeks."

"But why would he take the design? What could he possibly have to gain?"

Dwight used his shoulder to adjust his beard shield. "It's no secret that he's been unhappy for the past few weeks."

"That's what everyone keeps saying, but nobody will tell me why. What could possibly have come between Philippe and Ox?"

"Two things," Dwight said. "Quinn for one. Dmitri Wolff for the other."

The first name didn't surprise me. The more I learned about Quinn, the more I thought she'd brought about some big changes in my ex. But the second name was a bit of a shock. "Dmitri came between Philippe and Ox? How so?"

Dwight spent a minute stacking the second tier on the cake before he answered. "Dmitri's been trying to drive Zydeco out of business since the day we first opened our doors. I think he's talked to just about everybody on staff about jumping ship, but as far as I know Ox is the only one who listened."

I couldn't have been more stunned if he'd thrown the cake to the floor at my feet. "Ox was thinking about going to work for Dmitri? Are you sure about that?" Dwight gave me a tight-lipped nod, but I just couldn't believe it. "He *told* you that?"

Dwight sized up the work he'd done and clipped three more dowels to size. "Things got rough for Ox after Quinn started hanging around," he said. "She had issues with how close he and Philippe were — probably thought Ox was going to get the business, but she had her heart set on keeping it where she could get her hands on it eventually."

"So she tried to destroy their friendship?"

Dwight locked eyes with me. "She didn't just try."

"But I don't understand. Why did Philippe listen to her?"

"He was head over heels for her, Rita. She had him wrapped around her little finger. When she said 'jump,' he asked how high."

I felt a little flash of hurt, but I pushed it aside. "So Ox considered accepting Dmitri's offer because of Quinn?"

Dwight's gaze darted to mine for a heartbeat. "He said he could see the writing on the wall. She wanted him out, and he was pretty sure she'd get her way in the end. He tried to fight it for a while, but he finally realized it was a losing battle."

I felt a little sick to my stomach hearing that. "Then why didn't he just leave? Why stick around and fight a losing battle?"

"I'll give you three guesses."

The look on Dwight's face made it easy to figure out what he meant. "You think he stayed around to sabotage the business and get back at Philippe."

Dwight picked up a ruler, took a measurement or two and carefully shaved a millimeter-thin slice of cake from the bottom of the tier. "I think that's exactly what he did."

"After everything they'd been through together?"

"*Because* of everything they'd been through together. They both thought the other one was stabbing them in the back. So maybe Ox decided to take things a step further."

"So you think Ox is responsible for all the accidents, the broken and missing equipment? And you think he killed Philippe?"

Dwight looked around the room with another shrug. "I think it's possible."

"Maybe," I admitted reluctantly. "So who else is on your list? Is there anyone else around here who'd want to sabotage Philippe?"

Dwight smoothed the jagged ends of the dowels he'd just clipped. "You think the saboteur and the murderer are two different people?"

"Maybe," I said again. "The police are working on the murder. I'm just trying to help Miss Frankie figure out who was trying to hurt Zydeco. Whoever's sabotaging the company, it has to be someone with access to the building, right? So who has keys? Maybe we can narrow it down that way."

"Nice try, but we all have keys to this area," Dwight said. "You know how it goes in this business. If your part of a project takes longer than you expected or something goes wrong, you might have to pull an all-nighter."

And Philippe had never been one to babysit his coworkers. That at least hadn't changed. "Did all of the accidents happen in this part of the bakery?"

Dwight nodded again. "Pretty much."

"Who has keys to the front offices?"

"Edie. Ox. Philippe. That's it as far as I know."

I felt a faint glimmer of hope. "Then maybe it wasn't Ox. He could have done anything, anywhere, but the accidents were all confined to this area."

"Ox isn't stupid," Dwight said. "He wouldn't leave that kind of calling card."

He was probably right, but the "evidence" against Ox was circumstantial, at best. "So Ox is the only person at Zydeco who had an issue with Philippe?"

Dwight didn't answer immediately, and that was enough for me. "Who else?"

"It's probably nothing," he said as he lowered the second tier back to the table.

"Who else?"

He met my gaze, but only for an instant. "It's crazy. I know that. But you know how protective she's always been of Philippe."

"Edie?" The name squeaked out too loud. I lowered my voice and asked, "You think *Edie's* been sabotaging Zydeco?"

"I know, right? Crazy. But you asked."

"Maybe you should fill me in on what's been going on with Edie and Philippe."

"You know that Edie had a thing for Philippe back in pastry school. Everybody knew it."

I'd always suspected as much, but I'd never let it bother me. But what if I'd been wrong? What if Edie's feelings had run deeper than I suspected? I forced myself to ask, "Did he have feelings for her, too?"

"Not that I know of. It was a one-sided deal as far as I know." Dwight fell silent while he lowered the second tier onto the first. Satisfied with the way it looked, he leaned against the counter and eyed me for a minute. "Does that bother you?"

I shook my head quickly. "Not really. I suspected her feelings for him in pastry school, but I never took it seriously, and I always thought she'd gotten over him."

"Edie doesn't get over things," Dwight said. "She doesn't forget or forgive."

The hair on my neck stood up. "You know that from experience?"

Dwight carefully inserted dowels through both tiers before he answered me. Had I made him nervous, or was he just focused on the work? Hard to tell. "I guess there's no harm in telling you," he said at last. His voice was so low I could barely hear him. "She and I had a thing back in pastry school. Nothing serious — at least not in my book. We went out for a few weeks, but I decided she was too intense for me. I wasn't interested in settling down and tying myself to one person."

I tried not to look shocked, but I had as much trouble picturing Dwight and Edie dating as I'd had visualizing Ox and Isabeau together. "I'm guessing she didn't feel the same way."

"Not even close. After our second week together, she was already reading bride magazines and talking about names for our kids."

"So you ended it."

"As gently as I could. We went our separate ways after pastry school, and I never saw her again until I came here." He swiped at his forehead with the sleeve of his jacket.

"Let's just say she wasn't happy to see me."

"What did she do?"

"She tried to convince Philippe to get rid of me. When that didn't work, she tried to drive me away. It was just little things at first — something missing from the kitchen, my keys disappearing for most of one day — minor annoyances, really. Nothing serious."

"Did you tell Philippe?"

Dwight nodded. "I didn't run to him and snitch, if that's what you're asking. But I did tell him about it later, after she gave up trying to drive me away."

"What did he do?"

"What could he do? I didn't have any real proof, but I knew it was her."

"And you think she's pulling the same kind of stunt now." It was possible, and my own suspicions about her just added weight to his. "I have to admit that I've wondered for a while if she was diverting my messages to Philippe," I said. "But it doesn't really make sense. If she had a thing for Philippe, why would she stand in the way of our divorce? And she seems pretty loyal to Zydeco, so why would she do something that would destroy her career and put Philippe's legacy at risk?"

Dwight circled one finger around an ear

in the international sign for crazy. "It may have escaped your notice, but Edie's not exactly rational. You weren't a threat to her anymore. If Philippe divorced you, he'd have been free to marry Quinn, and she *was* a threat."

A big part of me wanted to agree with him, but I just couldn't. Edie might not be my favorite person at Zydeco, but I couldn't deny that she was good at her job, and I didn't think she could be so successful at what she did if she was some kind of fruitcake.

"She seems to have a handle on things," I said in her defense.

"She's a control freak," Dwight said. "I'd keep an eye on her if I were you."

"Yeah. Of course. So I'm guessing that Philippe's relationship with Quinn made her angry?"

Dwight looked around for the third tier. "She tried everything to break them up in the beginning. Poor thing. I mean, don't get me wrong. I want nothing to do with Edie, but even I feel a little sorry for her. She was so desperate to get Philippe to look at her, but he just wasn't interested."

"Come on," I said. "You're making Philippe sound like a complete doormat. Ox was sabotaging him, but Philippe just sat back and took it. Edie was trying to break up his new relationship, and he did nothing about it. That doesn't sound like Philippe at all."

"He didn't like what Edie was doing," Dwight said, "but he didn't do anything to stop her. He didn't want to get romantically involved with her, but he always had a soft spot for her. Don't ask me why."

I made a mental note to check into Edie and tried to steer him toward what I considered a more likely scenario. "So . . . Quinn. Have you ever heard any rumors about her? Is there any chance she was cheating on Philippe?"

Dwight laughed through his nose. "Quinn? I doubt it. She was nuts about him."

"Are you sure? Someone told me this morning that she'd been seeing someone else."

Dwight's expression grew serious. "I don't believe it."

"This person saw Quinn with another guy more than once," I said.

Dwight stopped working and shook his head firmly. "Not in this lifetime, Rita. Say what you will about Quinn, she really loved Philippe. And he loved her. But if you don't believe me, talk to Estelle or Sparkle. They'd probably know more than I do."

Good idea. I mumbled something about not wanting to keep him from his work and returned the stool I'd been sitting on. But I couldn't stop wondering why Dwight was trying to paint Edie as a complete whack job. Was she really crazy, or was he trying to hide something by making her sound that way?

Maybe he was the one who took the missing design. I had no idea why he would, but that was just one in a long string of things I didn't understand.

I crossed the room to the corner where Estelle was working on fondant pieces for the whimsical cake. That mop of bright red hair was pulled up in a clip that appeared strained almost to the breaking point. Ditto for her chef's jacket. Next to her, Sparkle's black-lined eyes were focused on a gum-paste bottle of hot sauce that would become part of the crab-boil cake.

Estelle beamed at me as I approached. "Feeling better this morning?"

My face burned, but I managed to laugh at myself. "Anything would be better than what I was feeling last night. I'm sorry if I ruined the memorial."

Sparkle's tarantula-lashed eyes lifted to my face, but her only response was a soft snort of derision.

252

"Don't let it bother you," Estelle said, with a pointed look at Sparkle. "It was at a bar. I'll bet most of the people there were feeling the same way."

That was kind of her to say, but no one else had dumped a drink and landed on the floor. At least not while I was there. I glanced around quickly. "Where's Isabeau?"

"Delivering the monkey cake with Abe. They should be back in an hour or two."

"Great." I motioned at the work in front of her. "Can I help?"

"Sure, if you want to." Estelle spent a few minutes showing me what she was doing with the various size cutters and explaining Ox's original vision for the cake. Within minutes, we settled into a rhythm. "I saw you talking to Ox last night," she said. "Is there any chance he's going to come back?"

"I hope so. I'm going to try to convince him to, but he didn't have a lot to say to me last night, I'm afraid."

"Don't take it personally," Estelle said. "He's been in a foul mood for weeks. Just stay out of his way until he calms down."

Unfortunately, staying out of his way wouldn't solve any of my current problems. "So what's your take on what's wrong with him?"

Sparkle glanced away from the hot-sauce

bottle, her brush poised and ready to resume its work, her black-painted lips pursed. I realized right then and there that I wouldn't want to meet her in a dark alley. It was freaky enough being around her in a brightly lit room. "I don't think you should be talking about that, Estelle," she warned in that low monotone of hers. "It's nobody else's business."

Estelle carefully peeled a two-inch circle from the nonstick baking mat in front of her. "I think Rita ought to know. She's in charge now. She needs to know what's been going on around here."

I stopped pondering the likelihood that Sparkle would cast an evil spell on me and swallowed a little bubble of excitement. *Finally, someone who was eager to talk!* My head buzzed, and not just from the hangover. "Thanks, Estelle. So, what do you think is going on around here?"

Estelle shook her head so hard I thought her clip would finally lose its battle. "Stuff going missing. Equipment breaking down. People refusing to pay for the work we've done. It's been one thing after another for the past few months."

Sparkle sent her the evil eye, so I hurried to set the record straight. "Don't worry. I've heard about your string of bad luck already."

Estelle rolled her eyes and cut a series of diamond shapes. "I wouldn't worry if it were only bad luck. I think somebody's trying to shut us down."

"That's what I'm afraid of, too," I admitted. "Any guesses about who it might be?"

Estelle slid a glance in Sparkle's direction but stopped short of making eye contact. "I don't know," she said, lowering her voice to avoid being overheard, "but Philippe thought he did."

"Do you know who he suspected?"

"Isn't that obvious?" Sparkle asked. "He was pretty sure Ox was behind all the weird stuff."

"Is that what Ox and Philippe argued about the morning of the murder?"

Estelle took up where Sparkle left off. "*Somebody* destroyed the paddle-wheel cake that day. Philippe thought that Ox did it."

"So I've been told. But why?"

Sparkle went back to work on the bottle of hot sauce. "I don't think anybody really *knows* why." For all her scary demeanor, she was a seriously talented artist. The bottle looked remarkably realistic.

"She's right." One curly red lock sprang loose from Estelle's poor overworked clip. "Philippe wasn't talking, and neither was

Ox. It got real ugly there toward the end, and then, when that cake got ruined . . . Well, that's when everything blew up."

"I still don't understand that," I admitted. "It was hot that day. Really hot. But the cake had to be outside, unattended, for a while to give someone time to destroy it. I can't imagine Philippe leaving a cake out in the heat like that."

"He wouldn't," Estelle agreed. "That's why he was so convinced that Ox trashed it. And you have to admit, it looks bad. Ox was out there with the cake. The cake was destroyed. One plus one equals Ox with a grudge of some kind."

I looked toward Ox's empty workstation. The only explanation that made sense was the one Dwight had just offered me, but I still had trouble believing that Ox was planning to defect to Dmitri's bakery. "Ox told me that Philippe had started giving his work to other people. Do you know why he did that?"

"You tell us, and we'll all know," Sparkle mumbled. "Nobody can figure out what was going on with him toward the end."

"Do *you* think Ox has been sabotaging the business?"

Estelle looked down at the fondant she was kneading. When she looked up at me again, I could see the confusion in her eyes. "I don't *want* to think that it's Ox, but I don't want to think it's anyone else here, either."

"What about Dmitri Wolff?"

Estelle's hands stilled. "Do you think he did this?"

"I don't know. Just trying to make sense out of the confusion. Did either of you see him that day?"

Estelle shook her head. "I haven't seen him in a couple of months."

"He was here yesterday," I told her. "But I guess you wouldn't see someone arriving from back here, would you?"

"We don't see anything from back here," Sparkle mumbled. "Somebody could walk out the front door with the safe, and we'd never know about it."

I glanced out the window to see just how much the staff could observe from here. I could see one corner of the employee parking lot, but the loading dock itself was obscured from view. I could see bits and pieces of the garden paths, but the trees were so thick in places most of the gardens were obscured from view. "What about the day of the murder? Did either of you notice Philippe or anyone else in the garden?"

Sparkle curled her black-coated lip at me.

"We've both given statements to the police. But no. I didn't see anything."

"Neither did I," Estelle said, barely suppressing a shudder. "I wish I had. I wish I could help the police figure out who killed Philippe. I'd like to see whoever it was locked up forever."

"You and me both," I told her. "Can I ask the two of you about something else?"

Estelle gave me a friendly smile. "Anything. Ask away."

"Someone I talked to this morning suggested that Quinn might have been seeing someone else on the side. Do either of you know anything about that?"

To my surprise, Sparkle's nostrils flared. "I wouldn't put it past her."

But Estelle gave her head a firm shake. "I don't think that could possibly be true. She seemed so devoted to Philippe."

"She was seen with some other guy," I said. "More than once."

"Well, there must be a perfectly logical explanation," Estelle insisted. "She owed Philippe too much. She never would have betrayed him."

"She owed him?" I said. "For what?"

"Oh, honey, she was just a nobody when the two of them met. He lifted her *way* up the social ladder. And she knew it wouldn't last without him. No, she wouldn't have turned her back on that. Believe me. Being where she is now means too much to her."

I felt a rush of something warm and fuzzy inside. I'd been so sure that Quinn belonged to a social status I could only read about, but she didn't belong with the moneyed set anymore than I did. It's the little things, y'know?

Sparkle rolled her black eyes. "She loved what Philippe could do for her. I'm not so sure she loved him."

So far, the staff seemed evenly split on that question. "Why do you say that?" I asked. "What did she do . . . or not do?"

"I don't know," Sparkle said. "I can't put my finger on it. But there's something wrong there. I can feel it."

So could I, but I needed specifics. I needed proof. "One more thing," I said. "Do either of you know about some trouble Philippe had with a man named Guy Le-Beau at the Duke?"

Sparkle's mouth pursed and Estelle gasped softly. "I know who you're talking about," Estelle said. "He's mean as an old snake."

"Someone told me that he and Philippe had some kind of argument," I said, giving them a verbal nudge. "Is that true?"

Sparkle's frown deepened. "Everybody who knows Guy LeBeau has trouble," she said. "That man *is* trouble."

"I'm told it had something to do with Guy bothering some woman?"

"Rikki's the only woman I know dumb enough to give Guy the time of day," Estelle said. "And he just treats her like yesterday's leftovers."

I'd seen him bugging her for money. Sweet. "Did Philippe ever do anything about that?"

"It wouldn't surprise me," Sparkle said. "He'd have been the first one to jump in. But did I ever see it? No."

The conversation died away after that, and we spent the rest of the morning working. While Estelle applied the geometric shapes we'd created to the cake, I fashioned a hot-pink bow out of fondant. Under normal circumstances, making that fondant bow would have been child's play for me. That morning, with my head still pounding from an excess of tequila and my thoughts racing around the things I'd heard from nosy neighbor Bernice and the staff at Zydeco, it was more of a challenge than I'd expected. Knowing that the staff was sizing me up added another layer of stress. Temporary or not, I wanted to show them that I had what it took to help Zydeco sift through its current troubles.

TWENTY

A little after noon, I escaped for lunch. My hangover had let up slightly, but my brain was still feeling overloaded, between getting used to a new work environment, the strain of trying to decide whether someone on staff at Zydeco was responsible for the string of bad luck, and the ever-present worrying over who killed Philippe. I was no closer to handing Miss Frankie a list of trustworthy employees, no more ready to recommend someone to run Zydeco for her, but at least the sweet-sixteen cake was out the door, and the crab-boil cake wasn't far behind.

I walked half a block to a small market I'd noticed on the corner that advertised New Orleans' best muffuletta sandwich. Philippe had insisted I try the one at Central Grocery, the store that had made them famous, but that was my only basis for comparison, and I was eager to test out this place's claim. The muffuletta came into existence in the early 1900s, when the farmers' market was located close to Central Grocery in the French Quarter. Most of the farmers who lugged their produce to the farmers' market were Sicilian, and nearly every day they'd visit the grocery during their lunch breaks, where they'd wolf down salami, ham, olive salad, cheese, and bread all served separately — until one day the grocery's proprietor suggested combining the ingredients to make a sandwich. And the rest was history.

In the muggy heat, even half a block was enough to work up a sweat, and I ducked into the small building praying its air conditioner was in good working order. A bell over the door tinkled to signal my arrival, and a bouquet of tantalizing aromas lured me deeper inside. I tried to sort out the different scents as I closed the door behind me. I picked up the smokiness of cured meats, the tang of yeast, the earthiness of oregano mixed with onion, pepper, and lemon. My appetite ramped up a few notches before I even spotted the menu on the wall.

Two women in jeans and tank tops sat at a small round table in front of the window. An old man wearing a greasy mechanic's uniform stood at the counter, behind which

263

a pleasant-faced woman with short-cropped salt-and-pepper hair, and a figure almost as wide as it was tall, slapped a giant sandwich together. A young woman with milk-chocolate skin and what looked like hundreds of tiny braids all adorned with brightly colored beads sat on a stool, slowly turning the pages in a library book.

A muffuletta sandwich is typically made on a round loaf of bread roughly eight inches in diameter and two inches thick. I've been told that the key to a good muffuletta is the olive mix — traditionally olives, peppers, pimentos, capers, onions, herbs, and olive oil — so most sandwiches are made in advance to give all that olivey, oily goodness a chance to soak into the bread.

Put all of that on a whole loaf of bread, and you have enough food to feed a family. When it was my turn, I ordered a mere quarter of a sandwich and a Coke and waited as patiently as I could for the clerk to wrap it up for me.

Through the shop's front windows, I could see the corner of Zydeco's property. I wondered if either of the women behind the counter had noticed anything unusual at Zydeco over the past few days. That led me to a thirty-second argument with myself, but in the end, it wasn't me who made the decision. It was Uncle Nestor and Miss Frankie who sat firmly on opposite shoulders, one urging me to come home right away, the other pleading for my help. I had to help Miss Frankie or I'd be here forever.

Pasting on a big, friendly smile, I turned to the older of the two women. "Everything smells wonderful," I told her. "Are you the owner?"

She laughed and shook her head. "Me? Laws, no. I just come in three afternoons a week while the grandkids are in school. But I'll be sure to pass along the compliment." She handed me a tall paper cup filled with ice and Coke and urged me to find a table while I waited.

I stayed where I was, gulping the Coke greedily and coming up for air only when the carbonation took my breath away.

"You're not from around here, are you?" she asked, smiling.

I shook my head and tried to ignore the siren song of that ice-cold cola. "What gave me away?"

"You don't sound like New Orleans, honey. Dead giveaway. Where you from?"

"Albuquerque."

"That's a ways away." She reached for the door to the refrigerator. "What brings you here? Vacation?"

"Not exactly. My ex-husband owned the cake shop four doors down."

"Zydeco?" She forgot all about my sandwich and treated me instead to a look of sympathy laced with a healthy dose of curiosity. "The poor man that got himself killed was your ex? And you came here for the funeral? Well, isn't that sweet."

"It's not exactly like that," I said. "I came to see him about something else, so I was here when he died."

"Oh!" One hand flew to the name tag on her chest. Lorena. Her eyes widened slightly. "Well, that's just terrible, honey. You have my deepest sympathies — if that's the right thing to say under the circumstances."

"Thanks. It's been harder than I would have imagined." I took a breath before launching into my questions — which was a mistake. Now that she was wound up, Lorena showed no signs of slowing down.

"Oh, honey, don't I know it. My ex passed on a few years back, and I like to cry myself silly for the first few weeks. Here I thought I hated that man, but when he passed . . ." She shot a glance at the window and sighed heavily. "Well, my prayers'll be with you, that's for sure."

She seemed friendly enough and obviously willing to talk, even to a perfect stranger.

Curiosity kept me right where I was. "I don't suppose you noticed anything unusual that day?"

"The whole thing's unusual, if you ask me. I've been jumpier than a cat in a room full of rocking chairs since it happened. It's bad enough having somebody murdered right under your nose, but in broad daylight!" She glanced at the young woman with the book and rolled her eyes. "I used to feel safe around here, but no more. Not after what happened down your way. I told Felix that, too. Told him I wouldn't work alone anymore, at least not until they get the killer locked up behind bars. I thought he'd get all huffy about it, but he just said to me, he said, 'Lorena, I wouldn't dream of putting you at risk.' Isn't that just the sweetest thing? So now Kenya and I are here during the days together."

"That must be a comfort," I said, though I had my doubts that Kenya would even notice if Lorena needed saving.

"Do they know who did it yet?" she asked as she pulled a paper plate and napkins from containers on the counter. "Because I don't know that I'll sleep until they do. I'm exhausted. Really and truly exhausted. Why, just look at my eyes. They're bloodshot from lack of sleep."

"I don't know —"

"Oh, no, of course they don't. I tell you, there's so much crime around this city, it'll make your head spin." Lorena waved a knife in my general direction. "You watch your back, y' hear? There's no tellin' what could happen to a pretty young girl alone in this city. Why, you're probably not even safe walkin' from here back to the cake shop. Doesn't what happened the other day prove that?"

"About that —"

Lorena didn't seem to need my contribution to the conversation. "It's a shame, that's what it is. A downright shame. Nice young man like him. Friendly guy, too. Always helping folks when they needed it."

I'd shed so many tears, I refused to cry today. "Did he come in here often?"

"Sure. Several times a week."

"Did he get along with the others in the area?"

Lorena expertly sliced bread. "He got along with everyone. Friendliest guy you'd ever want to meet."

Kenya glanced up from her book as if Lorena's answer surprised her.

"I'll tell you who I don't like from over there," Lorena said, without pausing for air. "I don't like that little girlfriend of his.

What's her name, Kenya?"

"Quinn."

"Why don't you like her?" I asked.

The stream of words stopped abruptly, and Lorena's eyes widened in horror. "Oh, listen to me, babbling on like an old fool. Boring you to tears."

"I'm not bored," I assured her. "Why don't you like Quinn?"

Lorena pulled a thick sandwich from the refrigerator and placed it on the cutting board. I could see the meat mounded on top of a thick layer of olive salad, and my mouth watered just thinking about eating it. "She's rude, that's why," Lorena said. "Not an ounce of manners." She stopped working to scowl out the window. "She acts all high and mighty all the time, coming in here barking orders at everyone and acting like she owns the place. And it's not just in here — she almost ran me down a few days ago. I was walking home, and she came tearing out of the parking lot over there like somebody set her tail on fire."

I dragged my gaze away from the sandwich and asked, "When was that?"

"A week ago or so? Had to be a day I was on shift, so Monday, Wednesday, or Thursday. She didn't even slow down or say sorry."

That wasn't surprising, but what really grabbed my attention was Lorena's schedule.

"You don't work Saturdays?" Lorena sliced the sandwich in two, then cut one of the halves again and shook her head. "Not me," she said as she wrapped my portion. "I have the grandkids that day."

"So you weren't here the day of the murder?"

"No, and thank the good Lord I wasn't!"

"What about you, Kenya?" I leaned forward, trying to get my face in the girl's field of vision.

She glanced up and locked eyes with me, letting me know that she wasn't as bored as she appeared. "I was here, but I didn't see anything, and I don't want trouble."

"No. Of course not." I picked up my cup and tried to look casual in spite of the fact that my heart was beating with the speed of hummingbird wings. "You know what's bothering me? That morning, before the attack, somebody destroyed a cake that was sitting in the van on the loading dock. I just can't figure out how somebody slipped back there, hacked up the cake, and then got away without anybody seeing a thing."

Lorena's mouth formed a little O, and her eyes skipped back and forth between Kenya and me. "Seriously? Oh, I wish I'd been here. I mean, not that I wish I'd been here, but . . . well, you know what I mean. I'd do anything to help put the killer behind bars."

Sighing with exaggerated patience, Kenya marked her place with one finger and scowled up at me. "I didn't see anything. I didn't see anybody. Just Ox. That's all."

Was that good news or bad? "You saw Ox?"

"Yeah. So? He's around here every day. Ask me when I *don't* see Ox. That's probably a better question."

"Okay, when don't you see Ox?"

"Never. He's here every day. Just like clockwork."

"When you saw him that day, what was he doing?"

"Walking."

"Where?"

"Down the street." She jerked a thumb toward the Dizzy Duke. "That way."

"Did you notice what time it was?"

She rolled her eyes. "No, and I also didn't see him carrying a knife or wiping blood off his clothes. Now, do you mind?" She held up her book and gave it an impatient wiggle. "I'm trying to study here."

Lorena put my lunch into a bag and handed it to me over the counter. "Don't mind her," she said, her voice hushed. "We're all a little nervous after what happened down your way."

I wasn't finished with Kenya, but before I could ask her another question, the bell over the door tinkled to announce another customer. Reluctantly, I paid for my lunch and turned toward the door. I still didn't know what Philippe and Ox had fought about, but unless I missed my guess, I'd just helped my old friend establish an alibi. That made me happy.

My happiness lasted only about three seconds. When I looked up to see who'd entered the shop, I saw Dmitri and his wolfish smile standing in front of me, and my mood sank again.

"Ah, if it isn't the lovely Rita." He reached for my free hand and bowed over it.

I jerked away and glowered at him. "What are you doing here?"

"The same thing as you, I imagine." He glanced at the bag and cup in my hand. "Are the sandwiches here as good as they say?"

"I wouldn't know. I've never been here before." I tried to walk around him, but he was blocking my escape route and made no effort to move out of my way.

"I'm glad I ran into you," he said. "I've

been meaning to check in and see how things are going."

"Things are just fine," I said. "Now, if you'll excuse me, I really need to get back . . ."

"They're keeping you so busy you can't even take a break for lunch?"

I wasn't about to confide in him about Zydeco's problems, so I met his gaze squarely. "Zydeco's got so many orders, we're all working overtime."

He had the nerve to chuckle as if he found me amusing. He looked past me to Lorena. "I'll have the same thing she's having." She turned away to work on his order, and he turned his attention back to me. "And your dear mother-in-law? Is she any closer to accepting my offer?"

"You haven't actually *made* an offer," I reminded him. "But don't bother. She's not going to sell."

"Ah, but I have. I had it delivered to Mrs. Renier yesterday. She didn't tell you about it?"

"I don't believe you."

"You should." He handed me a business card. "Talk to her about it. Give me a call when you've both come to your senses."

I glanced at the card, shuddered at the sight of Dmitri grinning wolfishly from a small picture in the corner, and shoved it into my bag. "Don't hold your breath."

"Don't wait too long. Zydeco's value is dropping by the day. I heard you've had some trouble with your bid for the Carleton Technologies project. That's too bad. Whoever wins the bid also wins a full spread in *Extreme Cakes Magazine.* I'm sorry Zydeco won't get a chance at that."

I was tempted to use my muffuletta sandwich to wipe the smirk off his face, but there were more important things to think about. "Who did you hear that from?"

"That's not important, is it? What *is* important is that you aren't going to be able to bid against me for this job. That's too bad. I was looking forward to the competition."

Liar. He was thrilled. I could see it in his eyes. "Well, don't let it get you down," I said. "We're not out of the running yet."

He laughed out loud at that. "You're determined. I like that."

"Oh good. That's what I live for." He'd relaxed enough to let me slip past him, so I did.

"Ask Miss Frankie about that offer," he called after me. "Talk some sense into her. I'd hate to see her get in over her head after you leave."

274

I ignored him and kept going, straight out the door and onto the sidewalk. I was both irritated and a little frightened. Not only did we have a saboteur at Zydeco, but we apparently had a leak, too. Is that why Dmitri was wandering around this neighborhood? I was convinced that he'd followed me into the market, and that made me nervous. Why follow me? I couldn't do anything for him.

I was back out in the afternoon heat, but for once, I barely noticed it. I had too many questions racing through my head. I looked around for a place to eat and spotted a couple of sagging picnic tables in the shade, so I carried my lunch toward them.

I'd have been more comfortable in the air-conditioned lunchroom at Zydeco, but I'd spent so much time with other people lately I needed a little solitude and a chance to regroup. Besides, maybe Dmitri hadn't met with his informant yet. Maybe I could watch and figure out who was selling Zydeco down the river.

Dmitri Wolff's offer to buy Zydeco and Miss Frankie's suspicions about Quinn and the staff kept skewering me whenever I let my mind wander. Someone who knew about the missing design had leaked the information to Dmitri, but I was having trouble believing that any of the staff could have done it.

Quinn? I could believe anything of her, but she hadn't known about the missing design — had she? And I still couldn't come up with a motive for her. It seemed to me that she lost more than she would have gained by Philippe's death.

I again considered the possibility that Philippe had been the victim of a random act of violence. But that missing cake design, the sabotage, and now the leak of information made that seem doubtful. No, I was convinced the killer must've been someone Philippe knew — but who?

Frustrated by my lack of answers, I turned my attention to the sandwich. The bread was perfect, crusty on the outside, soft on the inside. It had soaked up the flavors of the olive spread so that every bite filled my mouth with earthy flavors. Capers and olives provided texture, and the smoky mortadella, ham, and Genoa salami added robust flavors and complexity. The creaminess of the mozzarella and provolone pulled everything together so that it was pure heaven in every bite. I polished the whole thing off and slurped down the rest of my Coke while I waited. A few minutes after I sat, I saw Dmitri scurry out of the market, walk half a block in the opposite direction from Zydeco, and roar off in a small black car.

Well, damn. So much for my grand master plan to catch the saboteur red-handed.

TWENTY-ONE

My conversation with Dmitri nibbled at the back of my mind for the rest of the afternoon. Since we couldn't find the missing design, I spent a couple of hours working on a new design for the bid. Maybe I could come up with something good enough to win. Maybe not. I only knew that I couldn't just sit back and let Dmitri walk away with the job.

Unfortunately, my design skills were rusty, and I spent most of the time second-guessing myself. As a result, I was in a sour mood by the time I got back to Miss Frankie's. She'd asked me to meet her at the house at three, to accompany her to the funeral parlor. The fact that she hadn't told me about Dmitri's offer to buy Zydeco rankled. I hate being blindsided, and I resented her for allowing Dmitri to get the drop on me. She should have told me about the offer — and if she trusted me, she would have.

I told myself to swallow my feelings at least until we'd finished at the funeral parlor. No matter what she'd done, this wasn't the right time to start an argument.

I parked in the driveway and let myself in through the kitchen door, where I found Miss Frankie and Bernice at the kitchen table on either side of a pitcher of sweet tea.

Miss Frankie looked perfectly put together. Every hair was in place and held there with a heavy application of Aqua Net. She wore a linen pantsuit in a shade of olive drab only she could pull off, and I was pretty sure the sensible white sandals on her feet had been serving time since the Nixon era.

Bernice smiled up at me. "She's all ready to go," she said, with a nod toward Miss Frankie. "I thought she could use a little company, considering what she's fixin' to do today."

"That was very thoughtful," I said, forcing a smile I didn't feel. To Miss Frankie I said, "I hope I didn't keep you waiting."

That's when I realized that appearances can be deceiving. Miss Frankie stood unsteadily and offered me a thin-lipped smile. "Don't you worry for a minute, sugar.

Bernice and I have been reliving a few memories." She headed for the door, wobbling a little as we walked out to the driveway. Beneath the floral scent of her perfume, I caught a whiff of something decidedly *unflowery*. If I didn't know better, I might have guessed that she'd been nipping at the bourbon in the butler's pantry. Bernice seemed to be suffering from the same affliction.

As I followed them out the back door, I worried a little about how to keep Miss Frankie from getting behind the wheel. As it turned out, I didn't have to worry. She dropped into the passenger's seat of her car and turned a half smile up at me as she passed over the keys. "I'm not in any mood to deal with traffic today, sugar. You'll drive, won't you? I just want to ride along as a passenger."

"Absolutely."

"Bernice has agreed to come along as moral support. You don't mind, do you?"

I served up a smile as Bernice slid into the backseat. "Of course not. Whatever you want."

Miss Frankie leaned her head against the seat with a deep, resigned sigh, and I decided not to concern myself with her level of sobriety — which may have been my first big mistake of the afternoon. But the woman was grieving. Her husband was gone, and her only child had just been murdered. Difficult as this situation was for me, I couldn't imagine what she must be feeling. Few things in this world are as unnatural as having to bury your own child. We were on our way to pick out his coffin and discuss funeral arrangements. If she needed a little liquid courage to help her get through the next couple of hours, who could blame her? After the day I'd had already, I was tempted to join her.

Miss Frankie directed me into traffic, and Bernice pointed out items of interest as I drove. I found myself constantly surprised by the differences between the arid landscape of New Mexico and the lush green of New Orleans. Even the sky felt different here. The sun beat down on the city from high overhead, but instead of the clear dark blue I was used to, the sky here was pale and languid, its color muted by the moisture in the air.

We drove past old cemeteries filled with seemingly endless rows of aboveground tombs and mausoleums and sped past thick stands of trees and dense green undergrowth that blotted out the city for a moment before giving way to civilization again.

Coming from a place where water is an import, I was fascinated by the fact that a new body of water shimmered around every curve in the road even though I imagined half-buried alligator eyes peering at me from almost all of them.

We passed neighborhoods still bearing the scars of Katrina and others that looked as if they'd relocated somewhere safe during the storm. After a while, Miss Frankie pointed out the funeral home, and I pulled into a large parking lot in front of a spacious building. It was set well back from the street behind a neatly trimmed lawn, looking like an oasis of calm in the middle of the busy city, until I spotted a hearse parked next to a side door, and reality whacked me like a two-by-four. I could tell from the look on Miss Frankie's face that it had taken a swing at her, too.

I turned off the engine, and Bernice climbed out of the backseat, but Miss Frankie didn't move. She sat with her hands clasped tightly in her lap and a look on her face that almost tore me in two. I sat with her until the heat became unbearable inside the car — roughly two and a half minutes — then said, "Miss Frankie, I know this is going to be difficult. I can't even think about how hard this must be for you. But we can't sit out here in the car or we're going to expire ourselves. This can't be healthy."

Her gaze flickered up to mine and her lips curved sadly. "Oh, sugar, of course you're right. I'd just give anything not to have to do this." Tears filled her eyes and dropped onto her cheeks. She sighed — a sound filled with such sadness it put a huge, painful lump in my throat.

With a flick of her wrist, she pulled a snowy-white handkerchief from the pocket of her pantsuit and dabbed at her eyes and cheeks gently, effectively removing the evidence that she'd ever been anything but cool and pulled together. Which only proved how she's made of something I'm not. Once I start crying, it's not a pretty picture, which is why I try to avoid doing it. A white handkerchief would never be able to keep up with me, and there's no dainty removal of the tears, either.

I rounded the front of the car, and Bernice offered Miss Frankie a hand as she stepped out into the heat. My hair had turned into a giant Brillo pad, and sweat poured down my face. Neither Miss Frankie nor Bernice seemed to even notice the humidity.

I urged both women toward the air-conditioned building, eager to get inside before I melted. The glass door swung open as we approached, and a short, middle-aged man with a bad comb-over and even worse teeth bent slightly at the waist as we walked past him. He introduced himself as Sawyer Biggs and asked if he could be of assistance; I deferred to Miss Frankie. After all, Philippe was her son. But she didn't answer, so I glanced her way and found her putting the handkerchief to work again.

"I'm Rita Lucero," I said, shaking the hand Biggs offered. "My mother-in-law and I need to make some funeral arrangements for my . . ." I hesitated for a moment and then took the path that would require the least explanation. "For my husband."

"Yes. Of course." Biggs ushered all three of us into a bland office filled with bland furniture and spent a few minutes offering condolences and pulling out the forms required to lay Philippe to rest. When he deemed us adequately consoled, he dug a pen from a drawer and got down to business. "Let's start with the basics. What was your husband's name?"

I shot another look at Miss Frankie, but she seemed perfectly content to let me keep going. Taking a steadying breath, I answered his question, and we moved on to date of death and other information he needed to make the proper arrangements.

As Biggs and I went over the details, Bernice whispered softly to Miss Frankie, who stared straight ahead, occasionally lifting the handkerchief to blot away a tear, but otherwise remaining uninvolved and almost catatonic. I felt a little uncomfortable being left to sort through the details of Philippe's funeral, and that only added to the irritation I felt with her for keeping secrets from me. But for a while at least I'd known Philippe better than almost anyone else, so I swallowed my irritation and answered every question Biggs asked.

Occasionally, after some elderly relative or acquaintance passed away, Philippe and I had talked about the things we'd want the other to arrange when the inevitable day arrived for us. I'd put in an order for pink roses, a silver urn, and Aunt Yolanda's *arroz con leche* served to friends and family when they gathered afterward to eat. Philippe had expressed a preference for cherrywood, a traditional burial, and "Smoke on the Water" playing as the pallbearers carried him from the church.

I didn't know how Miss Frankie or Sawyer Biggs would feel about Deep Purple, but I did my best to make choices I thought Philippe would have liked. We agreed that Miss

Frankie and I would write the obituary later that evening, and I'd drop it by the mortuary the next day. Sawyer promised to forward our preferences to the florist and take care of a few other details so we wouldn't have to worry about them. With Miss Frankie on autopilot, I was relieved to let him take over.

Eventually, the only thing left was picking out the casket. I should point out that I hate coffins. I've hated them ever since I saw the bodies that once belonged to my parents lying inside a couple of them. I was only twelve when Aunt Yolanda made me stand in front of those horrible boxes to say goodbye. She'd encouraged me to kiss my parents on the cheek, believing that I'd regret it later if I didn't. But I knew my parents weren't in those boxes. They'd flown away somewhere beautiful. The image of my mother running through some heavenly meadow into the arms of my handsome father had sustained me for years. I hated anything that reminded me that their bodies had been buried in the cold, hard ground.

Once again, we rose to our feet, and once again, Miss Frankie swayed slightly. Bernice hurried to her side, keeping up the soothing monologue as she steered Miss Frankie back into the foyer. Miss Frankie looked pale and wan and fragile, and she leaned on Bernice as we walked, but she smiled at me with both gratitude and affection.

So you can see why I wasn't worried about anything but getting out of that room as quickly as possible. And, of course, making sure Miss Frankie didn't collapse. I was still concerned about her emotional state, and when I got close enough, I could still smell bourbon on her breath.

We followed Sawyer Biggs up a wide, curving staircase to a large room filled with several different models of caskets. The sight of them made it hard for me to breathe, and I worried that Miss Frankie was going to collapse on the spot.

Sawyer began his spiel, pointing out the various types of wood and metal and citing the benefits of bronze fittings versus those made of steel or plastic. I didn't want a sales pitch. I just wanted to find a cherrywood coffin, hand over Miss Frankie's credit card, and get out of there before my memories could catch up with me.

"This here is a lovely model," Sawyer said, gesturing toward a black coffin with stainless steel handles. "And fairly reasonable in price. We call this one the Captain. That one over there is slightly more expensive.

You're still looking at stainless steel handles, though, which keeps the cost down. You'd never know it, would you? Looks just like brass." He did a little Vanna White thing with his hands, directing our attention to a coffin labeled "The Admiral."

"And, of course, we have a large selection of head panels." Sawyer gestured toward a wall where a handful of quilted and embroidered pieces hung above a catalog that I assumed contained other options. "Was your loved one in the military?"

I shook my head and stifled a hysterical giggle at the thought of Philippe in the armed forces. He'd never been a rule follower unless the rule was one of his mama's.

"He'd have been a handsome soldier," Bernice said, with a little sigh. "But that wasn't his way, was it?"

"In that case, might I suggest one of these selections?" Sawyer put one hand on the catalog and curved his lips in the perfect semblance of a smile. "I'm partial to the praying hands myself. They're a lovely touch. Although 'Going Home' is a popular choice." He indicated a velvet panel sporting three doves flying in formation while a fourth peeled away from the others, right over the tastefully embroidered "Going Home" motto.

Ummmm . . . no.

The smell of funeral flowers, that odd mix of carnation and rose, came at me from somewhere, and I felt my head begin to swim. "Cherry," I choked out. "He wanted cherry."

"Cherry is a lovely choice," Sawyer agreed. "We have the Commander over there. Or, if the dearly departed was ecofriendly, you might want to consider one of our green models. Perhaps you'd be interested in our polished-bamboo version, or this one here, made entirely of extra thick cardboard. Durable. Comes with these handy die-cut handles."

I think I gasped. Or maybe I choked. I'm not sure.

Sawyer Biggs didn't seem to notice. Miss Frankie made a sound, and I turned toward her just in time to see her shake off whatever had been keeping her quiet since our arrival. Her eyes flared to life, and color flamed in her cheeks. "Stop right there, Mr. Biggs. I will not be laying my only son to rest in a *cardboard* coffin, like some family pet in a shoebox."

The ever-supportive Bernice glared down at him, too. "What in heaven's name is wrong with you?" she hissed.

Sawyer's eyes widened in horror at the

thought he'd insulted a prospective customer, and he hurried to undo the damage. "Naturally. Of course. I only mentioned these other options because so many people these days are worried about the environment. It's a perfectly acceptable option. Not an indicator of income or social status at all." He held out a hand, both to placate her and to steer her back toward the other end of the room. "Some people are unnecessarily worried, if you ask me. It's all well and good to recycle your newspapers, but a person ought to be buried in a proper coffin."

Apparently mollified, Miss Frankie walked on slowly, taking in the obvious benefits of the most expensive products — here an ornate brass fitting, there a satin interior — and finally stopped walking in front of a coffin I thought Philippe might have liked. Solid cherrywood. White velvet interior. Even an eternal rest adjustable bed. The Commander in all its glory.

"It's really lovely," I said, trying to hide the fact that the whole topic was increasingly creeping me out. "In fact, I think it's perfect."

"It's beautiful," Bernice said almost reverently. "Just beautiful."

Miss Frankie turned toward me, her eyes

shimmering with hope. "I do think he'd like this one, don't you?"

Sawyer Biggs must have smelled a tidy profit coming his way because his nose twitched as he moved in to seal the deal. "These sculpted corners are a nice touch. And you'll notice inside there's a matching pillow and throw made of the same white velvet. Would you like to feel it?"

I backed a step away, but Miss Frankie surged forward, eager to touch the fabric that would go into eternity with her baby boy. "Very nice," she agreed. "Looks like a good quality, as well. But I don't know. What do you think, Bernice?"

Bernice ran her fingers over the velvet throw and gave a businesslike nod. "I think it's perfect."

Miss Frankie pulled her fingers away from the velvet throw and turned to me. "It doesn't look big enough, and I worry about that adjustable bed. Will that hold up?"

Sawyer assured her that it would, and I refrained from pointing out that Philippe wasn't going to be moving around much once he got inside.

But she still wasn't convinced. "I'd feel so much better if I knew that it would be the right size."

"Unless the dearly departed is unusually

large —" Sawyer began.

But Miss Frankie wasn't listening. "I think you should try it," she said to me. "Just so we'll know for sure that it's roomy enough."

I gaped at her. "You think I should do *what?*"

"Try it." She gave me a gentle nudge. "I just can't spend that much money without knowing for sure that Philippe is going to fit and be comfortable for all eternity."

"Of course he'll fit," I told her. "He's not even six feet tall, and he probably didn't weigh more than one-eighty-five. He'll be fine."

"I think it's a good idea," Bernice said, once again stepping up to support her friend. "It's best not to leave important details to chance."

I stared at her in disbelief. Despite my best efforts, the irritation I'd been trying to ignore surged to the surface. "He'll be *fine,*" I insisted. I could tell by the look on Miss Frankie's face that she heard the sharpness in my voice.

Her eyes flashed, and she lifted her stubborn little chin, sure signs that we were in for a showdown. "I don't want him to be fine. I want him to have the best."

"But he can't *feel* it. He can't see the praying hands or appreciate the delicate quilting on the velvet pillow. That's all for you. He's not going to care."

"You don't know that," Bernice said.

"Yeah, I *do*."

Sawyer Biggs shifted around on his feet as we talked and finally muttered something about leaving us alone to discuss matters before disappearing entirely. Chicken.

I rubbed my forehead with one hand and tried again. "I know you're upset, Miss Frankie. I am, too. But let's try to remain rational."

"I'm being perfectly rational," she insisted. "They're going to put my boy inside one of those boxes. I see nothing wrong with making sure it's acceptable before I write out the check."

Bernice glared at me. "Surely you aren't going to let a little pride stand in the way of Miss Frankie's peace of mind. She has enough to worry about."

"It's not a matter of pride," I reasoned. "It's common sense. And I'm trying to make things easier for her, not worse. Do whatever you want to make sure it's acceptable. But I am *not* climbing into that casket."

Miss Frankie looked at me as if I'd betrayed her. "I'm not asking you to be buried in it, Rita. I'm merely asking that you lie down for a minute to see how it feels. Is that too much to ask?"

"It's *way* too much to ask," I said. "I'm not going to do it."

Bernice patted Miss Frankie's shoulder gently and served me another disapproving scowl at the same time. "I'm so sorry, dear. Really. I'm sure she's not trying to be difficult. She just doesn't understand. Why don't I check it out?"

Miss Frankie clucked at her friend. "With your knees? Don't you even think about it." She turned back to me. "Please, Rita."

"My climbing into that coffin won't change anything for Philippe," I said. "Now, can we please just move on?"

Giving a sniff of dissatisfaction, Miss Frankie put down her purse and mumbled something. I couldn't hear all of it, but I thought I heard Quinn's name — which should have been a clue. "If you won't do this for Philippe," she said as she straightened up, "I will."

I didn't believe her. I truly thought she was bluffing when she took hold of a nearby chair and began dragging it toward the coffin stand.

"Miss Frankie —"

She positioned the chair carefully and put both hands on the open coffin. "At least be so kind as to give me a hand."

294

"I'm not going to help you climb in there," I whispered, glancing over my shoulder to see if Sawyer Biggs was on his way back. "It's not safe. Bernice, please. Help me talk sense into her."

Miss Frankie ignored me and lifted one leg, swinging it easily into the open box. But it was just enough to throw off her already precarious balance. She and the chair began to wobble. I reached for her and tried to prevent the disaster I saw coming, but I wasn't fast enough.

I watched in horror as Miss Frankie and the chair tilted toward me. The next thing I knew, I landed on my back with a thump hard enough to knock the wind out of me. I gasped for air, but Miss Frankie and the chair came crashing down on top of me before I could catch my breath, and the coffin tilted unsteadily above us. Showing remarkable agility, Bernice threw herself in front of the heavy wooden casket and managed to keep it upright.

I lay there in stunned disbelief, reluctantly acknowledging that Miss Frankie was much closer to the edge than I'd previously thought. Could I really just go back to Albuquerque and leave her alone in this state? What would happen to Zydeco if I did?

TWENTY-TWO

An hour later, over dinner, Miss Frankie and Bernice chitchatted as if we were enjoying a normal meal on a normal day. As if Miss Frankie hadn't created serious doubts in my head about her mental state. As if the thought of leaving her to run Zydeco on her own hadn't just become a little frightening.

I wrapped my worries in a creamy crawfish pie baked inside a flaky puff pastry followed by a crisp salad covered with perfectly breaded catfish and pecans roasted to perfection and laced with lemon and butter. I wasn't sure I could eat another bite, but when the next course arrived, I gave it my best. Miss Frankie suggested that we share the "Cajun Sampler," which included cool, creamy coleslaw; Cajun meat pies; and a chicken gumbo so perfectly seasoned I could have lived off it for a week.

We ate alligator sausage — more tender than I'd expected — shrimp etouffée, jambalaya, and red beans and rice with an-douille. By the time dessert arrived — peaches Foster in a brown sugar–cinnamon sauce served over rich, creamy vanilla-bean ice cream — I'd almost forgotten about the visit to the funeral parlor.

Miss Frankie told me that the restaurant we were dining at had been a famous brothel before what she termed the "War of Northern Aggression." Bernice raved over the menu — *The best gumbo this side of heaven!* — and the two of them gossiped about mutual acquaintances — *I swear, sugar, that woman could make a preacher cuss.* After a while, the conversation hit a lull, and I thought surely they'd simmer down. But Miss Frankie turned up the heat.

"I suppose there's no sense putting it off any longer, sugar. We're going to have to decide when we're going to the house."

I swallowed wrong, so it took me a few minutes to answer. "The house?"

"Philippe's house. Your house now. It's a beautiful place, and I can't bear the thought of it standing there empty. Abandoned. All of Philippe's things . . ." Miss Frankie medicated a sob with half a glass of wine. "I'm going to need your help to sort through his clothes and things. I don't think I can do it on my own."

The pleasant food buzz I'd picked up over dinner fizzled out with an almost audible pop. Sorting through Philippe's personal belongings was just about the last thing I wanted to do, but how could I say no?

Besides, I was curious about the house even though I still hadn't wrapped my head around the facts that, one, Philippe had owned a house at all, and two, that house was technically now mine.

I held back a sigh and gave in to the inevitable. "When do you want to go?"

"Tomorrow? Or the next day. I'd like to take one of Philippe's suits to the mortuary and find a particular pair of Italian leather loafers he picked up a few months ago. Lord, he loved those shoes."

I smiled softly. "I'm sure he did."

She blinked at me, and I watched the reality settle heavily on her once again. She drained her glass of wine, then covered her mouth with her hands and caught back a sob. "I can't do this, Rita. I just can't. How am I supposed to just go on?"

I reached across the table and put a hand on her arm. A weak gesture, but it was all I had. "You're going to take it one day at a time. One minute at a time if that's what gets you through."

"I can't believe —" She glanced around

to see if anyone was paying attention to her and lowered her voice just in case. "I can't believe that this is what it all comes down to. Everything he worked for, everything he loved. It's all so meaningless."

"I know it feels overwhelming," I said. "And worrying about Zydeco must make it even more difficult." I took a deep breath and put the idea that had been nagging at me since we left the mortuary on the table between us. "You know, there's no reason to hang on to the bakery if it's too much. Maybe you should consider letting it go."

Miss Frankie jerked backward as if I'd slapped her. "Never in a million years!"

Bernice looked at me as if I'd suggested we all run through the restaurant naked. "I can't believe you said that," she hissed at me. "You ought to be ashamed."

"It was just a suggestion," I assured them both. "I'm still no closer to figuring out who's been causing the accidents at the bakery, and I can't stay here forever."

Miss Frankie's lips quivered. "But I need you."

After the episode at the mortuary, I couldn't argue with that. Tears brimmed in her eyes, and I felt guilty for upsetting her. I reached for my bag, hoping to find a tissue

I could offer her. As I lifted it to the table, the strap caught on the back of my chair and the purse jerked out of my hand. I had enough momentum going to make the whole thing flip over onto the floor, spilling keys, wallet, lip gloss, and a dozen other things as it fell.

Could this evening get any worse?

Swearing under my breath, I began gathering my stuff. The ever-helpful Bernice leapt out of her chair and came around to my side of the table to help. "Don't worry," I told her. "I've got it."

She scooped up a couple of receipts and my keys and shoved them into my hands. "It's okay. I'm happy to help." She reached for something under Miss Frankie's chair, but instead of handing it to me, she stared at it with her mouth open. "This is the man," she cried, holding up the business card Dmitri had given me earlier. "The one I told you about the other day."

Dmitri Wolff was the man Bernice had seen canoodling with Quinn? "Are you sure?"

Miss Frankie's gaze darted back and forth between us. "What man? What are you talking about?"

Bernice's excitement faded, and a sheepish look took its place. "Oh, honey, I'm sorry I didn't tell you. I just didn't want you to worry."

Miss Frankie's brows beetled together, forming a little worry ridge over her nose. "Tell me what? What are you talking about?"

"This man. And Philippe's girlfriend." Bernice handed her the card. "I've seen them together more than once. I told Rita about it this morning."

Miss Frankie snatched the card out of Bernice's hand and glanced at it briefly before turning a furious glare on me. "Quinn and Dmitri Wolff? You knew about this and you didn't tell me?"

I squirmed a little under the force of her anger. "Bernice told me that she thought Quinn was seeing someone else. I didn't know who until now."

Miss Frankie turned on her best friend. "You *knew* she was seeing someone else and you didn't tell me?"

"Don't be angry with her," I said. "She was just trying to keep you from being hurt." I kept my voice low and my tone soothing. The last thing I wanted was another scene. "And I think it might be best if we talk about this later, don't you?"

Miss Frankie glanced around as if she'd forgotten where we were. "I think it would be best to discuss it now." She rose to her

301

feet, her back stiff and her anger palpable. "Please take me home."

While Bernice kindly offered to take care of the bill, I trailed Miss Frankie to the car, feeling like a child headed for time-out. Once we were all settled in the car, I tried again to explain. "I'm sorry I didn't tell you," I said. "I wanted to be sure before I gave you something else to worry about."

Miss Frankie didn't even look at me.

"It's not as if you have any right to be angry," I went on. "After all, you haven't been entirely truthful with me either."

That brought her head around with a snap. "What are you talking about?"

"Dmitri's offer to buy Zydeco. I had to find out about that from him."

She looked away again and stared at the road in front of us. "That's hardly the same thing, Rita. After all, you've made it very clear that you don't intend to stay."

"But I'm here now," I argued. "I can't help you figure out who's trustworthy and who's not if I don't know what's going on."

But the damage had been done. We drove the rest of the way in silence. Bernice set off across the lawn, and Miss Frankie disappeared into her room without so much as a good-night. I climbed the stairs, swallowed three ibuprofen tablets, and vowed to put the whole mess out of my mind for a few hours.

I awoke the next morning to the insistent beeping of my cell-phone alarm and a downpour, complete with flashes of lightning and peals of thunder deep enough to shake the entire house. I managed to hit snooze on the phone and collapsed back on my pillow with a shudder. Groaning, I leaned up on one elbow and looked out the window. The sky was a dismal gray, which matched my mood perfectly.

After the day I'd had yesterday, all I wanted to do was pull the covers over my head and go back to sleep. Not only did every inch of my body hurt from the incident at the mortuary, but my pride had taken a beating over the past couple of days, as well. The ache in my head and the stiffness in my joints warned that it was going to be a long day.

Another boom of thunder shook the house, and I silenced the alarm on my cell phone. Rolling onto my side, I reached for the window and inched open the curtains so I could watch the storm for a few minutes. But even that small movement made me groan in protest. I felt as if I'd been beaten with a rolling pin — twice.

After a while, I dragged myself out of bed and padded down the hall to the bathroom. I swallowed another dose of pain relievers and hit the shower, then limped back to the guest room and tried to put together an outfit from the meager contents of my suitcase.

I wanted to find Quinn and demand a few answers from her, but it would be smarter to tell Detective Sullivan about the latest development and let him handle it. Besides, Edie had scheduled a meeting for me with J. J. Hightower and his lovely bride for this morning. I had to be across town in an hour to talk about the bill they still refused to pay.

I wanted to look professional and put-together for our meeting, not an easy task considering that I'd packed to stay in New Orleans just a couple of days and nothing I'd brought was particularly businesslike.

After shaking the wrinkles out of my black pants, I dug through the guest-room closet and found a peach-colored sweater-set that I thought might work. The sweater was a bit too tight for me and too warm for summer in Louisiana, but it would have to do.

After making a mental note to find an inexpensive clothing store where I could pick up a few items, like . . . oh, some more underwear and an extra bra, I hurried downstairs. To my surprise, the kitchen was empty. No coffee. No breakfast. No Miss Frankie. Either she was sleeping off yesterday's bourbon or she was avoiding me. Maybe both.

I hesitated for a few minutes over whether to knock on Miss Frankie's door or leave her alone, but I decided that it would be irresponsible and rude to walk out the door without at least checking to make sure she was okay.

I could hear her moving around behind her bedroom door, but she made me wait for a while before her muffled voice responded to my knock. "Yes?"

I took a page from her book and tried pretending that yesterday had never happened. "I'm getting ready to leave," I called out in my most chipper voice. "Is there anything I can do for you before I go?"

"No. Thank you." Another bit of shuffling reached me, followed by a weak sounding, "I'm fine."

If she was fine, I was Miss America. "Why don't I make you some breakfast?" I suggested. "I can have it ready in half an hour at the most."

"Don't bother. I don't have much of an appetite."

"I have to eat, too," I said. "And some protein may make you feel better." Yes, it was a bit snarky of me to throw her own words back at her, but I reasoned that if a good meal had worked for me yesterday, it should work for her today.

She didn't respond, so I decided to stop pretending and go for the direct approach. "Listen, about last night —"

The door flew open, startling me and revealing Miss Frankie as I'd never seen her before. Her short chestnut hair was spiked from sleep, and her face was bare of makeup. Exhaustion and grief etched deep lines into her face, and she looked every minute of her true age — whatever that was. "If you don't mind, I would prefer not to discuss yesterday's unfortunate incident. I have no doubt that sad little man is already spreading rumors to anyone who cares to listen."

"I'm sure he's not," I said, wincing at the memory of the tongue-lashing she'd given poor Sawyer Biggs after we'd tumbled to the floor. I didn't point out that he didn't have to resort to rumor. The truth was juicy-enough gossip.

Apparently, she was going to pretend that the rest of the evening had never happened, and I wasn't going to force the issue. "We never did work on the obituary," I reminded her. "I can come home early if you'd like, and we can do it this afternoon."

Her rigid expression softened slightly, and one hand fluttered to her chest like a wounded bird. "Yes. Thank you. That would be nice." She started to shut the door, but I stopped her.

"Are you feeling all right, Miss Frankie?"

She worked up a thin smile, but the effort seemed to cost her. "I'm a little tired, that's all. I'll be better by this afternoon." She shut the door between us as if the conversation was over. And I guess it was.

I made a mental note to check up on her partway through the day and whipped up a light breakfast for two of scrambled eggs, bacon, and fruit. I ate my share, then rinsed the dishes, loaded them into the dishwasher, and left a note about breakfast for Miss Frankie on the table.

Outside, I fired up the Mercedes, plugging the address Edie had given me for the Hightowers into the GPS. The directions took me to an upscale apartment building overlooking the Mississippi River.

I checked my reflection in the rearview mirror and strolled toward the apartment building — slowly, so I wouldn't work up a sweat. No such luck. The sweater was sticking to my back by the time I reached the front door, and the hair at the nape of my neck was dripping. So much for making a good impression.

Inside the gleaming glass doors, I stopped to get my bearings and found myself in a lobby that sported a massive fireplace on one wall and a handful of conversation areas with the illusion of privacy thanks to skillful furniture placement and a few towering flower arrangements. Everything — from the artwork on the walls to the rugs scattered across the hardwood floors — made it clear that the residents here weren't living from paycheck to paycheck. Which meant that the Hightowers certainly ought to be able to pay their bills.

I gave my name to a uniformed doorman who presided over the lobby from behind an antique desk, then rode the elevator to the twelfth floor. J. J. Hightower, a twenty-something kid with spiky sun-bleached hair, opened the door when I knocked. He rolled his eyes over me once, dismissing me as beneath him with the curl of his lip.

I was struck by two things: how young he was and how arrogant he was. I thanked him for agreeing to meet with me and offered him a hand to shake. He turned away, ignoring my hand and speaking over his shoulder as he walked away from me. "Well, come on. Don't just stand there."

I followed him into a spacious living room filled with sleek, modern furniture and a breathtaking view of the broad, brown Mississippi.

A young woman with thin, straight hair and a pallid complexion, presumably the new Mrs. Charlotte Hightower, sat on one of two couches that resembled twin slabs in a mortuary. She looked surprised to see someone walking into the room with her husband, and I wondered if he'd neglected to mention that I was coming.

"I don't know what you think this is going to accomplish," J. J. grumbled as he sat beside her. "You can't undo the damage your people did at our wedding."

Charlotte did a double take. "Are you from Zydeco?"

"Rita Lucero," I said, and proffered my hand to her before perching on the other slab.

She held out a limp hand for me to shake, and I spotted bones protruding from places I don't think bones belong. Proof that you *can* be too thin. "I don't think we've met before."

"I haven't been at Zydeco long, but I worked with Philippe for several years in

Chicago, so I'm familiar with his business, his style, and his artistry. I'm hoping we can come to an understanding."

J. J. put an arm around his wife. Protective or possessive? Hard to tell. "That's highly doubtful. You people destroyed our wedding, didn't they, darling?"

"It was awful," Charlotte agreed. "I've never seen J. J. that upset."

"So what do you want to know?" J. J. demanded. "And make it quick. I have a meeting in half an hour."

I resisted the urge to tell him he could leave. I didn't want to talk to him anyway. Pegging Charlotte as the more reasonable of the pair, I addressed my statements to her. "Let's start at the beginning, if you don't mind. I'd like to make sure I have all the facts straight." She gave me a little nod, so I went on. "I understand that you were unhappy with your wedding cake. Could you tell me why?"

J. J. barged in before she had a chance to answer. "What? They didn't tell you?"

"Edie told me that you were concerned about some differences between what you ordered and what we delivered."

He let out a harsh laugh. "*Some differences?* Are you freaking kidding me?"

I really didn't like this guy, but I couldn't

afford to make things worse between him and Zydeco, so I tried again to deal with his wife. "It would help if you could be specific about those differences. I may be able to explain why our cake artists had to change certain elements to maintain the integrity of the cake."

Charlotte looked as if she wanted to speak, but J. J. gave her a look that changed her mind. No question about who called the shots in this marriage. "We didn't get the cake we ordered," he snarled. "Is that specific enough? And I'm not paying you people another dime. You got it now? Or is that too complicated for you?"

There aren't many things that upset me faster than being treated like I'm stupid. I could feel my temper rising, but I managed to keep a grip on it. "I understand what you're saying, Mr. Hightower, but I'm confused. I've looked over the invoice and the photographs the staff took before delivery. There's no discrepancy that I can see." I held out a copy of each for them to look at. "You ordered a three-tier chocolate cake with white buttercream frosting and sunflowers —"

J. J. snatched the copies from my hand and studied them for all of about ten seconds. "What the hell is this?" he demanded, as he shoved them back at me. "Some kind of joke? Or are you people trying to scam us?"

"I can assure you —" I began.

"I don't want your assurances. I want restitution. You didn't give us what we ordered, and you ruined our wedding. And you have the nerve to ask me for money? I don't think so, sweetheart."

I clenched my teeth and tried to remain calm, at least on the outside. This kid needed a few lessons in manners. Or a punch in the face. Or both.

I took a steadying breath and reminded myself why I was here: to calm them down, find a resolution to the dispute, and salvage Zydeco's reputation.

"Those are copies of our records," I said when I trusted myself to speak again. "The original order you placed and photos of the cake just before delivery. As you can see, there are no differences."

J. J. gave the invoice another cursory glance. "Oh yeah. I can see that. But that's not what we ordered." He opened a file folder lying on the glass coffee table between us and thrust a computerized receipt at me. "It was supposed to be *five* tiers. White cake covered with white icing and then a bunch of orchids made out of . . . whatchama-callit . . . edible stuff."

Stunned speechless, I studied the receipt he'd given me. Sure enough, the invoice called for a five-tier white cake. White fondant. Lacy texture on one tier. Sugar beadwork on another. And gum-paste orchids — dozens of them. The kind Philippe had perfected while we were married. Most importantly, not a sunflower in sight.

Huge difference.

"A cascade of orchids," Charlotte said, pulling my attention away from the second invoice. "It was supposed to be light and elegant, and it was supposed to match my colors. Lavender and silver and white. Two of the tiers were supposed to match the beading and stitching on my dress. Instead, I got *that.*" Her lip quivered when she finished speaking, and tears brimmed in her eyes.

Now I wished she hadn't spoken. Those tears were far more convincing than her husband's anger. "How is this possible?" I said, more to myself than to them.

J. J. answered me anyway. "It's obvious what happened. Y'all messed up, big time, and now y'all are trying to cover your asses."

"That's not true," I assured him. "Nobody is trying to cover anything. I don't know how this happened, but I'll do my best to find out."

"Why bother?" J. J. tossed the receipt onto the coffee table and sat back. "It's not going to make one damn bit of difference. I'm not paying for your screwup."

"It's not just the cake, anyway," Charlotte said softly. "We might have been willing to work with you on that. It's what happened at the wedding that I can't forget."

I lowered the invoice to my lap and asked, "What happened at the wedding?"

"The fight," Charlotte said, watching my reaction as if that should be clue enough.

I felt a chill that had nothing to do with the air-conditioning vent overhead. "What fight?"

"Your boss," J. J. said. "The guy who died. He tried to deck me in the middle of the reception."

"Philippe?"

"I guess so. I told him that cake wasn't what we ordered, and he went off on me. Yelling. Threatening. The guy was a complete jerk."

I had some trouble taking that in. "At your wedding reception?" In front of potential customers? That was *so* not like Philippe.

"In front of three hundred and fifty guests."

My morning coffee churned in my stomach as I tried to make sense of what he was saying. "I'm sure there was some reasonable explanation for his behavior," I said, even though I wasn't sure at all.

"So now what?" J. J. asked with a smirk. "How are you going to make *that* go away?"

I tried not to let my panic show. "Let me figure out how the mistake was made on the cake," I suggested. "Then I'll try to find a resolution that will make us all happy."

"Good luck with that." J. J. got to his feet and stared down at me, clearly ready for me to leave. "We're through here," he said, grabbing his file folder and holding on as if it held the secrets of the universe. "Don't bother contacting me again. I came home from the honeymoon ready to file charges against your boss for assault. Can't do that now, but you'll be hearing from my attorney." He surged out of the room still clutching that file folder and leaving his wife to make sure I didn't pocket the family silver on my way out.

I held my head high, trying not to look beaten as I followed Charlotte to the front door. I stopped on the threshold and tried once more to get through to her. "Your husband is clearly upset, but there's no reason to make this worse. Give me a couple of days to figure out what happened at our end and come up with a resolution."

She shook her head and her lips narrowed so far they almost disappeared in her face. "It's not up to me."

"But you can talk to him. You can convince him to give me a chance to fix this."

"Fix it?" She opened the front door to shoo me outside. "I don't know how you can do that unless you can turn back the clock. But it's not up to me."

My spirits sank to a new low, but I couldn't give up yet. "This is a difficult time for everyone at Zydeco, and it may take me a little while to get to the bottom of this. Please. Can you talk to your husband and ask him to be patient for just another day or two?"

She shot a glance over one bony shoulder and dragged it back to me reluctantly. "I don't think it would do any good. J. J. is used to getting what he wants."

Including a bride with no backbone, I guess. She shuffled me out the door and shut it behind me, and I started toward the elevator weighed down by regret. I had no doubt that the saboteur had struck again, but that wasn't what worried me most. I'd blown it. Instead of coming away with a resolution, I'd just made the situation worse. Maybe Ox was right about me. Maybe putting me in charge of Zydeco —

even for a few days — was the wrong decision to make.

TWENTY-THREE

"It's just so hard to imagine anyone here making a mistake of this magnitude," I said to Edie, as she dumped a stack of papers on the desk in front of me and collapsed into an empty chair.

"It's even harder to imagine when you look at who took the order." Edie pointed to a small box on the form bearing the initials WO. Wyndham Oxford. I hadn't even realized the entry in that box was someone's initials.

I cut a glance at her. "Ox did the consultation? I thought this was Philippe's client."

Edie shrugged. "Philippe did the original legwork to bring the Hightowers in, and he delivered the cake to their wedding, but Ox was the one who took the order. He would also be the one who put it into the computer. There's no way he'd make a mistake like this. Either J. J. Hightower's lying, or the saboteur struck again. I've gone back to the beginning, and everything we have shows that they ordered a four-tier chocolate cake with sunflowers."

"You're absolutely certain? No question at all?" I desperately wanted her to be right, but I couldn't ignore the fact that Ox had been considering Dmitri's offer. Was he the saboteur? Had he been trying to drive Philippe out of business before jumping ship?

Edie leaned forward and pointed to the invoice I'd taken from the Hightowers. "Faking one of our invoices wouldn't be that difficult. Anyone with a little computer know-how could pull this off."

"Maybe," I said slowly. "But then why did Philippe lose control at the wedding reception? Did he realize that it was sabotage when he delivered the cake and they freaked out over the order?"

"That's my guess," Edie said. "But then he went off on the client? In front of all those guests?"

"I agree that it seems odd, but there are extenuating circumstances we have to consider. This particular client is not a nice guy. If Philippe got there with the cake and J. J. started complaining about the mix-up, it might have pushed Philippe over the edge."

Edie tucked a lock of her silky brown hair behind one ear. "So you think J. J. is telling the truth?"

"I don't want to think that," I said, placing both invoices side by side and hoping I'd find something I'd missed before. "I wouldn't put anything past him. But you didn't see the look on Charlotte Hightower's face this morning. I might believe that J. J. is trying to pull a fast one on us, but she doesn't seem the type."

"Besides, they were in Aruba," Edie reminded me. "I doubt they'd leave their honeymoon to come back and extract revenge over a wedding cake."

Except for the details of the order, the invoices looked identical. Surely there would be *something* different about them if one was a fake. Scowling in concentration, I tapped the Zydeco logo, the accordion-playing alligator cartoon, on the Hightower's invoice with one finger. "Let's say they did create a fake invoice. How would they get the logo?"

Edie shrugged and pulled a half-empty bag of M&M's from her pocket. "It's on the website. Supposed to be protected somehow, but that doesn't necessarily mean anything." She shook a few candies into her hand. "Or maybe they scanned the original invoice we gave them and turned it into a JPEG file. Who knows? People can do all sorts of things with computers."

I held the invoice up to the light. Nothing. "It seems like a lot of effort on their part, doesn't it? The amount they owe us is probably pocket change for them."

Edie lined up the candies in her palm by color and ate the brown ones first. "So? Some wealthy people are tighter with their money than folks without. That's how they get rich in the first place."

"Maybe you're right," I said, but I wasn't convinced. Still . . .

While Edie crunched on the orange candies, I studied both invoices for what must have been the hundredth time. Mistake or scam? Neither answer seemed to fit. The only possibility that made any sense was sabotage. If Philippe suspected Ox of purposely ruining the Hightower order and embarrassing him in front of hundreds of people, it helped explain why their relationship had grown so strained at the end. Believing he'd been betrayed by his closest friend might also explain why he lost control.

"We need to talk to Ox," I said. "Do you think he'd agree to meet with me here?"

Edie shook her head. "I don't know. He was pretty upset. Besides, what good would that do? If he did sabotage the order, he'll only deny it."

"Maybe. But what if he didn't do it? What if he's telling the truth? I think he deserves a chance to defend himself, don't you?" And I wanted to look him in the eye when I asked about the job offer from Dmitri.

Edie lined up the yellow M&M's, and lifted one shoulder. "I suppose."

"Would you call and ask him to dig up his original notes for this order? Right now, it's our word against theirs. Our invoice against theirs. If theirs is a fake, we can use Ox's notes to prove it. If the order was changed after Ox put it into the computer system, his notes will help prove that."

Edie picked up a red M&M's candy, but stopped short of putting it into her mouth. "And if it was changed in the computer?"

"Then we try to figure out who did it. Does everyone on staff have access to the computer?"

She nodded. "We've been trying to move into the computer age for a while now. Philippe wasn't all that excited about it, but the rest of us thought it was great."

"Is there any way to track changes made on the computer?"

"Probably. Everybody has a unique log-in, so somebody who knows what he or she is doing should be able to figure out who did what, and when."

That was the first good news I'd had in days. "Maybe this will give us a lead on the saboteur."

"I hope so," Edie said, pushing one last red M&M's candy around on her palm with a fingertip. "It's been awful around here — even before Philippe's death — ever since all this weird stuff started happening."

"And you have no idea who's responsible?"

"None. Somebody who has access to the equipment, that's all I know. But that means everybody on staff is on the list."

I chewed my thumbnail and debated the wisdom of asking her about the leak. But I had to trust *somebody,* and for all her quirks, I never really suspected Edie. "I ran into Dmitri Wolff at lunch yesterday. He knows about our missing design."

"He knows? How?"

"That's what I want to know. Have you told anyone but the staff about it?"

Edie rolled that poor piece of candy between her fingers until the shell cracked. "I haven't said a word, but it's pretty obvious someone here must've. Whoever it is should be fired. Immediately."

I agreed with her. But figuring out who to fire was the tough part. "I think we can agree that the saboteur and the leak must be the same person, and if that's true, he or she must be working with Dmitri to destroy the bakery." I had a pretty short list of possible traitors: Quinn and Ox. But I also wanted to allow for the remote possibility that it was someone else.

Edie leaned over to throw away the crushed candy. "Do you think that the saboteur is also the person who killed Philippe?"

"Maybe." But I couldn't imagine either of my sabotage suspects plunging a knife into Philippe's chest. "The question is, who would want to sabotage the business? What would they gain from doing it?"

"It doesn't surprise me that Dmitri's involved," Edie said, without hesitation. "He used to be the hottest thing in town until Philippe came back to New Orleans. He's wanted us out of the way since day one. But I don't know how Dmitri could have messed with the sheeter or ruined that cake, either. And this? I guess he could have hacked into the system and changed the order . . ."

I nodded and turned the idea over in my mind one more time. The fondant rolling machine, commonly called a sheeter, sat in the middle of the design center workspace. Whoever messed with it must have had after-hours access to avoid being spotted. But putting the sheeter out of commission was more of a nuisance than a serious threat. The Hightower order, on the other hand, was serious. "Changing that order would be a good way to ruin Zydeco's reputation and drive Philippe out of business."

"Yeah, but Dmitri couldn't have gotten at our equipment or the computer network without somebody knowing. Unless he had an inside source."

"Is anyone on staff friendly with him?" I asked.

"Not that I know of. Besides, nobody saw him around here the day Philippe was killed."

"Would anyone on staff tell Quinn about the missing design?"

Edie's expression turned sour. "I sure hope not. Why? You think *she* told Dmitri?"

"Maybe. Or maybe Dmitri told her. She's been seen with him a few times, that's all I know."

"Cheating on Philippe?"

"Maybe."

Edie muttered something under her breath, but I could tell from the look on her face that she was holding something back. "What aren't you telling me?"

Edie's eyes snapped up to my face, and she looked like a kid who'd just been caught with her finger in the frosting bowl. "Nothing."

"You're not a very good liar, Edie. Spill it."

Scowling, she put the candy bag on her lap and ran her hands across her thighs. Sweaty palms. That meant she was nervous. "There's nothing to spill. I don't know anything."

"But you suspect something."

She stared at me without blinking.

"Come on," I urged again. "You don't want to leave this kind of mess for Miss Frankie to deal with. Tell me what you know."

"But that's just it. I don't *know* anything. Nobody does."

"But — ?"

She let out a heavy sigh and slumped down in the chair. "But Philippe thought he had it all figured out. I'm pretty sure he'd decided it was Ox."

That had to be the worst-kept secret around. "What do you think?"

"I don't believe it."

I wondered what she'd say if she knew that Ox was considering leaving Zydeco, but I bit my tongue. If Ox wasn't guilty, I wanted

326

Miss Frankie to bring him back to Zydeco. He couldn't take over for Philippe if he was tarred with the brush of suspicion. "Did you mention that to the police?"

Edie shrugged and looked down at the mangled candy wrapper. "No. But only because I know it doesn't have anything to do with the murder." She looked up at me again, her expression earnest. "If I thought there was any chance at all that Ox killed Philippe, I'd say something. Really I would."

"I still don't understand how things got this bad between Philippe and Ox. This wouldn't even have been a question when I knew them."

Edie nodded miserably. "Nobody else believed it. But Philippe —" She broke off with another deep sigh. "I don't know what happened. They used to be so close, but all of a sudden Philippe got this bug about Ox, and everything changed."

"And you don't know why?"

"I have no idea. Ox won't talk about it. By the day of the murder, Philippe wasn't even speaking to him except to accuse him of doing something wrong."

"Why do you think Ox stayed here under those circumstances? And if Philippe really believed that, why didn't he fire Ox and put an end to it?"

Edie shrugged again. "Who knows? I wouldn't have stayed, I'll tell you that much."

"I don't think I would have either," I admitted. But that only made the possibility that he'd stayed to destroy Zydeco seem more likely. "And if I was Philippe, I sure wouldn't have kept someone on my payroll who I thought was trying to destroy my business."

Why *had* Philippe kept Ox around? Had he really believed Ox was trying to undermine the business, or was something else going on? My stomach hurt a little, just thinking that my old friend might have been behind the recent trouble. That Philippe's change of heart had driven Ox to consider Dmitri's offer, even for a minute. "What about the rest of the staff? Do they believe Ox is the saboteur?"

Edie looked miserable. "Like I said, nobody wants to believe it. But it's starting to look bad, you know?"

Yeah. I did. I was also more confused than ever. What was going on around here? None of it made any sense to me. I stacked the invoices in the file folder and secured it in the locked drawer of Philippe's desk. I battled another wave of guilt over hiding what I knew from Edie, and those sharp brown eyes and the worried expression on her face made me wonder about something. "Is there any chance Philippe was sick before he died?"

Her eyes narrowed in confusion. "Sick like what? A cold? The flu?"

I shook my head. "Something more serious. Had he been to the doctor recently?"

"Not that I know of. Why? Have you heard something?"

"Nothing direct, but I keep hearing about things he did and said that just don't sound like him. Going off on a client, suspecting Ox of trying to destroy his business . . ."

"People change," Edie said, her voice surprisingly gentle. "You two were good together. But Quinn?" She shook her head and glanced over her shoulder at the door to the foyer. "She brought out the worst in him. Every relationship he had suffered, not just his friendship with Ox. Working here was fun at first, but that changed for me, too."

I thought about Miss Frankie's claim that Philippe had stopped confiding in her and realized sadly that she was probably telling the truth. I pocketed the key to the desk drawer and stood. "All the more reason not to make any snap judgments about what Ox was doing. I'll wait and hear what he has to say."

Edie pushed to her feet and tucked what was left of the ragged bag of M&M's in her pocket. I waited until I heard her fingers tapping on the computer's keyboard, and then I checked the time on my cell phone. I had just two hours until I needed to head back to Miss Frankie's, so I decided to spend some more time working on the new design for the bid. With the deadline in just a few days, I couldn't afford to waste time. Besides, working on that design kept me from dwelling on the prospect of going to Philippe's house with Miss Frankie. It was going to be tough enough for me. I just hoped that I could stay in control enough to help her get through it.

TWENTY-FOUR

That afternoon, Miss Frankie and I spent a couple of hours putting together an obituary she was willing to release to the public. Neither of us brought up last night's disagreement, and after the first few minutes, the awkwardness between us began to melt. Afterward, we ate a quick dinner in the kitchen and I caught her up on the day's events before I finally made myself suggest that we drive to Philippe's house together.

Now that we'd moved past last night's anger, I found myself grateful for her company as I drove through the gathering twilight. It would be nice to have someone there when I walked into the house and saw Philippe's stuff and the antiques we'd bought together.

Miss Frankie directed me from her old, affluent subdivision to an eclectic neighborhood filled with ethnic restaurants and boutiques. Philippe's house number was painted on an old brick building nestled between a Thai restaurant and a knitting shop, but I had to circle the block three times before I finally found a parking space.

This neighborhood looked like Philippe, I decided as I drove. He must have loved it here. At last, I found an empty space beneath a massive oak tree. Miss Frankie and I took our time getting out of the car and gathering our things before setting off down the sidewalk. With my heart in my throat, I walked with Miss Frankie to the place Philippe had apparently called home after he left the one we'd shared.

The evening air was so muggy it felt like warm, damp satin on my skin. I fingered the key in my pocket and argued with myself about climbing the front steps. Writing the obituary had drained my energy, and I wondered if I had enough oomph left to paw through the clothing and other possessions of a man who'd stopped loving me.

Wishing I had a couple of margaritas from the Dizzy Duke to wipe away my apprehensions, I stood beside Philippe's mother outside the front door and took a deep breath for courage before slipping the key into the lock. Over the sounds of traffic, I heard claws scrambling across hardwood floors and a series of high-pitched yips protesting our presence. I jerked backward and checked the house number again, unnecessary, really, because the key fit and Miss Frankie had brought me here. But hearing someone — some*thing* — moving around inside a house I'd assumed was empty made rational thought fly right out of my head.

The door flew open and I found myself face-to-face with Quinn and a hideously ugly dog the size of a large rat. Quinn wore a flowery sundress made from some gauzy material and a pair of beaded flip-flops on her slim, tanned feet. Her pale hair was wound in a lazy knot on the back of her head. All very genteel and southern and sleepily sexy, like something out of a movie.

Her dog had a wild tuft of hair on the top of its head, a serious underbite, and a garish rhinestone collar around its scrawny neck — at least I *think* they were rhinestones.

Both sets of eyes flashed at me, but then Quinn gasped and threw her arms around Miss Frankie's very stiff neck. "Miss Frankie? What are *you* doing here?"

The dog probably asked the same thing of me, but it came out sounding more like *"Grrrrr."* Tough sounding on the surface, but since he also lapped at me with his tongue the whole time he was growling, it took some of the heat out of the threat.

I ignored the dog and focused on the real bitch. I had a dozen questions to ask her, but not outside on the front porch, where she had me at a disadvantage. While Miss Frankie disentangled herself from Quinn's melodramatic hug, I asked the question uppermost in my mind. "Do you want to tell me how you got in, or should I just wait and let the police ask you that?"

Quinn's blue eyes grew round and her lips pursed, giving us her Anna Nicole look that had probably made Philippe stand at attention. "You'd do it, wouldn't you?" she whimpered. "You'd call the police on a grieving woman?"

"A grieving woman who's guilty of breaking and entering? You bet."

"I didn't break in," she said, with a sniff. "I have a key."

I made a mental note to change the locks and moved toward the door. This was *my* house, not hers. Philippe was *my* husband . . . you know . . . technically.

For the first time since I met her, Quinn showed a modicum of common sense, stepping aside to let us in. "I suppose you've come to stake your claim."

"Something like that." I brushed past her into the house, but I stopped just inside the door, lost in the clean, sparse lines of the glass and chrome that seemed to be everywhere. The interior was at such odds with the turn-of-the-century exterior and Philippe's usual tastes, I couldn't find my voice. *"Grrrrr."* Lick, lick, lick.

The encounter with Quinn had put some starch in Miss Frankie. She touched my arm gently. "Is something wrong?"

I moved so Quinn could shut the door behind us. "No. It's just not what I expected."

Both women followed my gaze. Miss Frankie seemed to be taking a mental inventory, while Quinn took in our surroundings as if she were seeing them for the first time, too. "It took me a while to get used to," she admitted. "I'm still not sure I actually like it, but Philippe loved it."

When *we* were together, Philippe had been all about his history. He'd spent weekends trolling antique stores and browsing online, filling our Chicago apartment with an incongruous mix of historic French and American pieces. I'd expected to find our furniture when I walked through the door, but nothing I could see looked familiar. I was having trouble picturing him in this sparsely decorated house.

When I realized that Quinn was watching

me, pride kicked in. I wasn't going to get all maudlin in front of her. Later, I told myself. There'd be plenty of time to figure out what I was feeling after she'd gone.

Miss Frankie wandered away, and I decided to let her have some privacy. Determined to stay cool, calm, and collected, I nodded toward a corridor that stretched from the front door to the back of the house. "The house is larger than it looks from the outside," I said to Quinn. "Do you know how many square feet it is?"

She gave me an odd look and shook her head. "I have no idea. It has three bedrooms: two on the second floor and the master suite on the third. It has three full bathrooms and a utility room behind the kitchen." She walked as she talked, falling into tour-guide mode and leading me first through the large living room and then into a kitchen that looked out over a small well-tended garden. Too soon, she climbed to the second floor.

At the top of the stairs, she put the rat-dog on the floor. It aimed one last lick-infused *"Grrrrr,"* in my direction and trotted off, probably in search of some hideously expensive piece of furniture to lift his leg on. He was Quinn's dog, after all. Not an ounce of class.

As we moved from room to room, I tried to keep my eye open for the missing cake design, but instead I kept noticing paintings and pieces of sculpture that were obviously expensive. I didn't spot any gaping holes in the decorating scheme or faded spots on the walls where pictures used to be, but how would I know if something was missing? I'd have to count on Miss Frankie to know that. Still, I realized, she was right. I should have come here right away instead of waiting.

After my initial shock faded, I began to see telltale signs of Philippe everywhere — the stack of books at his bedside, hunting magazines in the study, a shirt and tie tossed carelessly over the back of a chair in the bedroom. The realization that I'd have to sort through all of his possessions landed on me like a weight. My thin veneer of calm threatened to shatter, and even breathing became a chore.

All of which might explain why it took me so long to notice the other little things, like the earrings and necklace casually abandoned on the desk beside the computer, the exfoliating facial scrub in the master bath, the body spray in the guest bath next to a small bowl of cotton balls — not things I expected Philippe used.

My stomach gave a little bump as their

meaning hit me. "You and Philippe were living together?"

Quinn had been about to start down the staircase to the first floor, but she paused with one hand on the banister and lifted her chin as she turned back to face me. "Not officially. I still have an apartment on the other side of town."

Because Philippe hadn't been ready for the commitment, or because she and Dmitri needed a place to conduct their affair? "But you were here often."

"Very often." She stared me in the eye, defying me to make something of it.

I considered saying something snarky, but honestly, I didn't have the energy. "Good to know. Then maybe you can tell me if you've noticed a cake design lying around somewhere."

"I don't know anything about that missing design, and I don't know why you think it would be here."

So she did know about it. Big surprise. "I think it *might* be here because Philippe lived here. It's not at Zydeco, so I wondered if he left it here."

She shook her head hard enough to make the knot on the back of her head slip. "Philippe never brought work home."

"Really? He used to work at home all the

338

time, especially when he was working on the early stages of a design."

"Well, not anymore. But I'm sure you don't believe me, so why don't you look and see for yourself?"

"I'll do that. Later." Demon Dog reappeared and sniffed my shoes and ankles as I moved past Quinn and descended the stairs. I could see Miss Frankie in the kitchen, looking a little lost, and I decided it was time to send Quinn on her way. At the bottom of the stairs, I blocked her path and held out my hand. "I'm going to need your key back. I'm sure you understand."

Her eyes flashed, and she tried to shove past me. "I'll give it to you if and when a judge orders me to." I refused to move, which only made her madder. She tried again to get past me, but I refused to budge. "Get the hell out of my way."

"This is my house, Quinn, not yours. Hand over the key. If you actually win in court, I'll give it back."

She opened her mouth to refuse again, but Miss Frankie stepped into the hall and came to my defense. "Give her the key, Quinn. You and Philippe weren't married, thank the good Lord, and you were seeing someone else on the side. You have no right to be here. Either hand over the key or *I'll*

339

call the police."

Quinn's nostrils flared and her eyes snapped with fury, but her mouth puckered up like she'd just sucked on a lemon. "That's not true, Miss Frankie. I would never have cheated on Philippe! I loved him."

"You were seen with the other man more than once," I snarled.

She recoiled and made an awful noise that had me worried she might swallow her tongue. "That's a lie."

"Save it," Miss Frankie snapped. "Not only do I know about your affair, but I know who you were seeing. Bad enough that you'd cheat on Philippe, but with his biggest competitor? The man who wanted to put him out of business? Please. Leave now."

"You think I was sleeping with Dmitri?" Quinn's face registered both shock and outrage.

It almost looked genuine. "Like I said, you were seen with him more than once." I wiggled my fingers in a silent demand for her key. "Did he tell you about the missing design, or did you tell him?"

"I'm not even going to dignify that with an answer."

"You can tell me now or you can tell the police," I said. I was pretty sure which one she'd choose, and she didn't surprise me.

Her mouth trembled, but she gave a curt nod. "I have nothing to say to you. You want the key so bad, I'll give it to you. But you're going to have to let me get by. It's in my bag."

I moved aside, and the dog came barreling down the stairs, teeth flashing, his sights clearly set on my leg. I sidestepped his snarling little mouth. "If he bites me —"

"She." Quinn scooped up her little bundle of fur and cooed at her for a few minutes. "Her name is Snickerdoodle, and she was a gift. From Philippe."

"He bought *that?*" I asked. Philippe, who'd loved hunting dogs with massive heads and thick, waterproof fur, had shelled out money for . . . Snickerdoodle? Had I stepped into an alternate universe?

"Yes. Surprised?"

"As a matter of fact, I am."

Quinn tossed her head and sashayed into the kitchen. When she came back, she shoved a key into my hand. "I guess you didn't know him all that well, did you?"

I wasn't about to get into a pissing match over which of us had known him better, so I ignored the question. "You never did tell me what you're doing here."

Quinn nuzzled Snickerdoodle's head and

blinked a couple of times. As if on cue, tears filled her eyes. "I just needed to be around him. I feel close to him here. And besides, some of my things are still here."

"I noticed. Do you want to take them with you now?"

Her eyes flew open wide, and her mouth formed a little O of surprise. "Now?" She looked around as if the idea frightened her. Considering the expression on Miss Frankie's face, maybe it did. "No, I — I — Can I get them later? I don't think I can handle it today."

I wanted to say no, but I *had* scored a couple of small victories, and she looked so genuinely distraught I felt myself soften a little. But just a little. "That's fine," I said reluctantly. "You can take a day or two. Just give me a call when you're ready."

"Yeah. Okay." She scratched the dog's head absently as she looked around the first floor. "I guess you're planning to move in, then, right?"

Me? Live here? Under other circumstances, I might have jumped at the chance. The house was beautiful. But living here wasn't an option. I didn't belong in New Orleans. I had family and a life, such as it was, waiting for me in Albuquerque. "I don't have any plans to move in," I said.

"But I do need to get it ready to put on the market."

Quinn's watery eyes widened in horror, and Miss Frankie let out an audible sigh. "You're going to sell it?" Quinn asked.

"I'm going to have to," I said, but I was looking at Miss Frankie, trying to make her understand.

"It isn't enough for you that he's dead, is it?" Quinn demanded. "You want to wipe out his memory, too?"

The little bit of compassion I'd been feeling for her evaporated. "Do you have to be so melodramatic all the time? That's not what I want. Our marriage might not have lasted, but I still felt a lot of affection for him. I'm just being practical."

"Affection!" Quinn spat the word out and tightened her grip on the dog. "He was your husband! *And* he was the nicest, kindest man who ever walked the face of the earth. And you were . . . you were *fond* of him?"

"Leave it alone, Quinn," Miss Frankie said. "Rita has to do what she thinks is best."

Quinn dug a tissue from the bottom of her purse and mopped at her eyes with it. "I don't know how she can be so cold. It's like she doesn't have any feelings at all."

Oh, if only she knew. A dull ache formed behind my eyes, and exhaustion rolled over me again like a wave. "I don't have to explain myself to you," I said. "My relationship with Philippe is none of your concern."

"But you think you have the right to know everything about me?"

Her attitude was seriously starting to bother me. "Philippe and I were separated," I pointed out. "Our relationship was complicated. I don't know why my reaction to his death bothers you so much. If we'd been together, you wouldn't have been in the picture at all. But maybe that's the problem. Maybe you know that he wanted to work on our marriage. Maybe he told you all about it the night you had dinner with Miss Frankie. Or maybe he found out about you and Dmitri. Maybe that's why the two of you were acting so strangely."

"I wasn't sleeping with Dmitri," Quinn insisted, her face clouded with anger. "And Philippe *loved* me."

"I'm sure he did." I may not have sounded sincere when I said that. "But that still doesn't mean I have to explain myself to you. Now if you don't mind, I'd like you to leave."

"I'm not going anywhere," she said, bracing herself as if she expected me to pick her up and toss her out the door. "I belong here. You don't."

I'll admit the idea of removing her by force was tempting, but my muscles had joined my head in the ache-fest, so I pulled my cell phone from my pocket and flipped it open. "Fine. You can explain everything to the police when they get here."

She growled in frustration. Or maybe it was the dog. It didn't matter because she pivoted away and flounced toward the door. "You haven't heard the last of me," she shouted, and slammed the door behind her.

Twenty-Five

Miss Frankie and I stood there for a minute or two, reveling in the silence as Quinn's footsteps faded away. I don't know what she was feeling, but I was trying hard not to envy Philippe's good fortune as I took in the opulence of the house. After our split, he'd come back to New Orleans and built himself both a successful business and an incredible home of his own. I'd gone back to Albuquerque to my childhood bedroom and a less-than-satisfying job with my Uncle Nestor. But, I reminded myself, Philippe's good fortune hadn't served him so well. *I* was the one who was still alive. I really should keep that in mind.

I flipped the dead bolt on the door and kicked off my shoes. "I don't know about you," I said, "but I need a drink."

"At least one," Miss Frankie agreed, and led the way to the pantry, where we found an unopened Riesling in a small wine rack.

I dug around in the kitchen until I located a corkscrew. Miss Frankie poured two glasses and replaced the cork.

"Lord have mercy," she said, after she'd fortified herself with a healthy sip. "I don't know what Philippe was thinking when he got involved with that woman. Do you think she was telling the truth?"

I let out a bitter laugh. "About being faithful to Philippe? I doubt it. Bernice said she saw her with Dmitri more than once. Who do you believe?"

Miss Frankie carried her glass to the table and sat. She looked tired, and I got angry all over again with Quinn for putting her through another round of melodrama. "I believe Bernice, of course, but Quinn seemed awfully upset by the suggestion."

"Well, of course she would," I said, settling into a chair across from hers. "If she's still trying to lay claim to Philippe's estate, she doesn't want you to think she cheated on him."

Miss Frankie sent me a weary smile. "I suppose you're right, sugar. That must be it." She raked a hand through her hair and sighed so heavily I could almost feel her exhaustion. "I guess there's no talking you out of selling this place."

I shook my head, but it was with more

than a dash of regret that I did. "It's a beautiful house," I said, running a glance over the bookshelves and Philippe's collection of recipe books. "Have you thought about moving in here? It's smaller than your place. It might be easier to take care of."

Miss Frankie laughed without humor. "Oh, sugar, this is no neighborhood for an old lady. The noise and traffic would make me crazy in no time. No, I'll stay where I am." She leaned her head back and closed her eyes. "Why don't you look around a bit? I'll stay here and finish my wine."

I got up and, on impulse, brushed a kiss to her cool cheek. She touched my hand but didn't open her eyes, and I carried my own glass upstairs to the master bedroom. The stack of books waiting beside the bed for Philippe to read them made me ache inside. I abandoned my wineglass on the nightstand and carried the books down one flight of stairs to the spare bedroom he'd turned into a library.

I was pretty sure Philippe had a system for shelving the books, but I wasn't going to worry about that now. I just wanted to put the books back on the shelf so they'd stop waiting for him to come back and pick one of them up.

As I contemplated what it would take to

get the house ready to sell, the sheer magnitude of the work made me weak in the knees. Could I afford to pay someone to do it for me? Probably. But that seemed too cold and impersonal. Difficult as I knew it would be, I had to sort through Philippe's things myself.

Later.

Right now I wanted to find Philippe's suit and the shoes Miss Frankie had requested to bury him in. I'd just opened the closet when the deep *bong* of the doorbell echoed through the empty house. Startled, I slammed the door shut — right on my finger.

Swearing under my breath, I stalked toward the stairs. It had been what? Five minutes? Ten? What did that woman want now? Finger throbbing, I padded on bare feet down the stairs, yelling to Miss Frankie that I'd deal with it, and thought again about Quinn's over-the-top theatrics. Just how far would she have gone to protect her relationship with Philippe? What if he had told her that he planned to get back together with me? Could she have killed him?

Of course she could. Everyone was capable of murder if they were provoked enough. And what if she had killed Philippe? Was she angry enough to come after me next? Had confronting her about the affair with Dmitri pushed her over the edge?

I paused with my good hand on the door-knob, suddenly afraid to answer the bell. My imagination was flying all over the place at the thought of Quinn as a killer. Maybe Quinn left when she did to establish an alibi before coming back to take us out. She'd put up little more than a token protest over returning the key, so maybe she'd just pretended to be angry about leaving to make us let down our guard. Maybe she'd stashed the dog so its excited yips wouldn't alert neighbors to the fact that Quinn was committing her second (and third?) murders in less than a week. My heart pounded in my chest and my breath grew ragged as I raced through my options. Run? Scream? Fight? Assume the fetal position and pray?

The bell pealed again, and my heart jumped right back into my throat. I stifled a scream and told myself not to make a sound. Quinn might *think* we were still inside, but she couldn't know for sure. If I remained absolutely silent . . .

"Rita? I know you're in there. I can hear you. Open the door."

A little common sense managed to work its way beneath my terror, and I realized that, unless she'd had a sex-change operation in the last ten minutes, it couldn't be Quinn on the front porch.

Inching onto my toes, I peeked through the security peephole at Detective Liam Sullivan's face. Somewhere deep inside, I wondered what he was doing here, but at that moment, I didn't really care. I'd never been so glad to see anyone in my life.

I flipped the dead bolt and wrenched open the door. "Liam? How did you know I was here?"

"I didn't until I spotted Quinn leaving. Only one person I know could have put that look on her face."

I laughed and stepped aside to let him in. "Yeah. Well . . . What can I say?" I felt giddy with relief. "Miss Frankie and I were just having a glass of wine. I'd offer you one, but you're probably on duty, right?"

He cut a glance at me, no doubt trying to decide whether I was about to hurl on his shoes. After all, the last time he saw me, I'd hardly been at my best. "Right," he said. "On duty."

"Coffee then? I'm pretty sure I can throw that together. I don't know about anything else."

"Coffee would be great. Thanks." He followed me into the kitchen, where Miss Frankie had roused herself and now watched him with curiosity.

"Good evening, Detective. What brings you here? I hope you're here to tell me you've caught my son's killer."

"I'm afraid not," he admitted with obvious regret.

I found several packages of gourmet coffee in the pantry. Choosing the Belgian Lace, I poured coffee into the filter and filled the coffeemaker with cold, filtered water. While the coffee brewed and filled the kitchen with its smooth chocolate aroma, I checked the freshness date on the carton of cream in the fridge and poured some into the silver creamer I found in the cupboard. Someone had given us the set for our wedding, and Philippe had taken it in the split.

"You have no leads?" Miss Frankie asked. "No suspects?"

Sullivan shook his head. "Nothing new, I'm afraid. I wish I could tell you otherwise."

"What *are* you doing to find my son's killer?" Miss Frankie demanded.

"We're doing everything we can, ma'am. Please believe that."

I filled the matching silver bowl with sugar and rounded up a couple of mugs and spoons, then dug into the pantry to see what I could find to serve with the coffee. I found homemade shortbread cookies in the cookie jar and nibbled one to make sure they weren't stale. The rich, buttery flavor and satisfying crunch assured me they weren't, but I ate a second cookie, just to be certain, before arranging the rest on a plate. I filled three mugs, and carried the whole thing to the table on a tray, all the while waiting for Sullivan to explain what he was doing there.

Once we were all seated at the table, Sullivan grabbed a mug and sipped. Apparently, he took his coffee black. I scooped sugar into mine and laced it with cream. Miss Frankie did the same.

The coffee was perfect, its flavor bold but smooth and satisfying. "So what's up?" I asked, when the curiosity finally got the best of me. "Or do you expect us to believe you just happened to be hanging around outside when Quinn left?"

He chuckled and helped himself to a cookie. "I don't expect you to believe anything. I was watching the place."

"Why?"

"Why not?" He finished one cookie and took another. "It's a thing of mine, I guess. Instead of banging my head against the wall when I run into a dead end, I hang out in places where the victim used to go. Sometimes I see something. Sometimes I hear something. Sometimes it's a waste of effort."

"And this time?" Miss Frankie asked.

He shrugged. "It's still too early to tell, I'm afraid." He turned his attention to me. "So what happened between you and Quinn? What did you do to piss her off?"

I answered with a casual shrug of my own. "I made her give me back her key. She didn't like that. In spite of the fact that she's been seeing someone on the side."

Sullivan looked up with a scowl. "And you know that how?"

"My neighbor told us," Miss Frankie answered before I could. "She saw them together more than once."

I explained our conversation, then told him about my run-in with Dmitri Wolff at lunch and Quinn's reaction when I asked her about the affair. "She denied it, of course, but I don't believe her. She already knew about the cake design that's missing, and the only way she could know about that is from Dmitri."

"Maybe she has friends at Zydeco," Sullivan suggested. "She would have been around there a lot when Philippe was alive."

"No." I purposely ignored the niggling doubts he'd raised. "No! Everyone I've talked to at Zydeco has issue with her."

"What issues?"

"No one likes her." I sounded childish, and I hated that. "They all think she was after Philippe's money." But even as I said it, I wondered if I was being entirely honest. Had I really talked to everyone? I couldn't remember. And those I had talked to had been split on the question of a possible affair.

"Quinn isn't Philippe's usual type," Miss Frankie said as she put her cup on the table. "But I don't know what to think about the affair. My neighbor did see her with the other man, but Quinn seemed quite genuine when she denied being involved with him."

"Oh please," I said, with a bitter laugh. "I don't think she knows the meaning of the word *genuine*."

Sullivan actually smiled, but not in a good way. "That's not jealousy talking, is it?"

The coffee grew bitter in my mouth. "No. Absolutely not. It's just hard to imagine the two of them together. But I've been told that the trouble between Philippe and Ox started when Quinn came into Philippe's life. Those two were as close as brothers. Closer, really. But she made Philippe suspect Ox of trying to destroy the business. I don't know how, and nobody else seems to either. Or maybe they just don't trust me enough to say."

"Trust isn't automatic," Sullivan said, going after his third cookie. "You have to earn it, and that's not always easy. Just don't give them any reason not to trust you, and it will come." He leaned back in his chair and linked his hands together over a remarkably taut stomach. "My turn to ask: What are you doing here?"

"We came to pick up Philippe's burial clothes."

"Besides, this is Rita's house now," Miss Frankie reminded him. "I thought she should see it before she makes any decisions about what to do with it."

Sullivan nodded as if our answers satisfied him. "Nice digs."

"My family has money, Detective."

"So I've heard. I'm told you're loaded." It was a crass way of putting it, but I caught him watching Miss Frankie's expression for a reaction.

"I suppose you could say that," she said.

He turned his attention to me again. "And now so are you."

"I don't care about the money," I said, with a frown. "I learned very early in our marriage that money really can't buy happiness."

"No, but it can make misery a lot more

356

comfortable." He grinned to show me he was making a joke.

I tossed him a thin smile to show that I got it. "So what do you think about Dmitri Wolff as a suspect? Do you think he killed Philippe so he could get Zydeco?"

"We've considered him," Sullivan admitted, "but he has an alibi for the day of the murder."

My heart dropped as my perfectly good theory crumbled like stale bread. "A good one? Airtight?"

"Airtight. He was delivering a cake in the Quarter at the time of the murder. Nearly two hundred people can vouch for him."

"But — Then —" Then the killer was probably someone from Zydeco. Someone Philippe had considered a friend. I didn't like that at all.

"If someone killed Philippe to get his or her hands on the bakery, it's possible that the two of you are in danger, too."

Everything inside me turned to ice. "You really think someone might hurt Miss Frankie?"

"It's possible. And since you're next in line —" He broke off and let me fill in the blanks for myself.

"But I'm not next in line," I protested.

He looked from me to Miss Frankie. "Do

you want to tell her, or should I?"

Miss Frankie's shoulders stiffened. "I told you that in confidence, Detective. I'd prefer not to discuss this with Rita until later."

The exchange between them made my fingers tingle. "Discuss what with me? What are you two talking about?"

Sullivan gave Miss Frankie another look, and she let out an exasperated sigh. "All right. Fine. I've made a few changes to my will since Philippe died, sugar. That's all."

"What kinds of changes?"

"Nothing big," Sullivan said. "Just that everything goes to you if she dies."

I jerked to my feet and stared down at both of them. "But that's ridiculous!"

"I don't happen to agree with you," Miss Frankie said. "You're the logical person to take over at Zydeco if something happens to me. And at my age —"

"You're not old," I snapped. "And how could you do something like this without discussing it with me?"

"If I'd discussed it with you, you'd have said no."

As if that made her actions acceptable. I could only stare at the two of them while my overloaded brain tried to process what he'd said. Oh, sure, I'd entertained a few errant thoughts about Quinn coming after me, but I hadn't *really* believed she would. But now . . . Well, now the possibility was a lot more real. "You think somebody might try to . . . to hurt the two of us?"

"It's possible." Sullivan stood to face me. "Look, I don't have any proof, and I don't want to alarm you. I'm running on gut instinct here."

"I feel so much better knowing that."

"Maybe I shouldn't have said anything."

"Ya think?"

"It's just that I believe forewarned is forearmed. I don't want you taking any unnecessary chances. Don't go to the shop alone. Don't stay after hours."

The acidic smell of the coffee made my throat tighten, and the butter in the cookies seemed to grow stale in my stomach. "I can't just hole up and hide," I told him. "I have to get Zydeco back on track. We have a bid coming up for a project that could really put us on the map, especially if I can find Philippe's design. We have two weddings this week and cakes due for an anniversary party and a grand opening. Curling up in a ball isn't an option."

"If the person we're after is someone at Zydeco —"

"Figure out who it is," I interrupted. "Lock him — or her — up and let the rest of us get back to normal."

"I'm working on it. Believe me."

A heavy silence fell between us and we stood there, ignoring the coffee and the cookies for a while. "What about Quinn?" I asked eventually. "Does she have an alibi?"

"No, but that's not unusual. She doesn't have a motive either. Philippe was her meal ticket."

My knees were a little wobbly, so I sat again and he followed suit. "Yeah, but what if he decided not to continue paying her way? Miss Frankie had dinner with them the night before the murder. She says they were both behaving strangely. Tell him, Miss Frankie." When she didn't speak, I filled in what I knew. "She told me she's convinced Philippe broke it off with Quinn after they left her."

"Because of you?"

I shook my head. "Philippe didn't even know I was coming to town."

"But he left a message the next morning saying he wanted to get back together with you? He must have known you were here by the time they had dinner."

The cookies rolled over in my stomach again. "It's possible, I guess. But he didn't say he wanted to get back together exactly. He said he'd made a mistake, and he wanted to talk."

"So he might have been talking about something else?"

I nodded slowly, uncomfortable with the thought that Philippe had broken up with Quinn because of me. "I guess he might have, but I don't know what else it could have been. Unless he wanted to talk to me about Quinn. Because, let's face it, she was a mistake. I just don't see him wanting to share that with me."

Sullivan had leaned forward as I spoke, his arms resting on his thighs, his gaze locked on the floor. But now he lifted his gaze to mine, and I could see that something was troubling him.

He didn't say anything, so I prodded him. "What?"

"There's nothing else you can think of that he might have wanted to discuss with you?"

"Nothing! We'd been separated for so long I wasn't involved in his life."

Sullivan's expression clouded. He shifted position on the chair but didn't say a word.

"What?"

"It's just that the idea of him wanting to get back together with you doesn't fit into the picture I'm getting."

"What do you mean?"

Sullivan reached for yet another cookie, and I made a decision. I was convinced that Quinn had murdered Philippe, but I had no way to prove it. Without proof, nobody would ever believe me. So one way or another, I needed to find evidence against Quinn. Just enough to convince Detective Sullivan.

I just hoped that I'd live to regret it.

TWENTY-SIX

Detective Sullivan walked Miss Frankie and me to the car after I locked up Philippe's house. I kept one eye on my rearview mirror as I drove home, half expecting to find Quinn following me. We scurried inside when we got back to Miss Frankie's, and for the second night in a row, Miss Frankie went to bed the minute we stepped into the house.

When I came downstairs the next morning, I found coffee, bagels, cream cheese, fresh melon, pineapple, and grapes along with a note explaining that she'd gone to breakfast with Bernice. I hated thinking of her running around town, ignoring the potential danger, but she didn't carry a cell phone and I had no idea where to start looking for her.

Promising myself that I'd touch base with her later, I drove to work and tried to immerse myself in the exacting job of creating have a few secrets in her closet was enough to make Philippe go nuts. But I made it worse. I wanted to make sure he knew what he was getting into, so I did a little digging. I didn't uncover anything at first, but then I got lucky, if you can call it that. Found out some pretty unsavory stuff. Turns out Quinn worked as a call girl for a few years and she was pretty desperate to keep Philippe from finding out. LeBeau wanted money for the information, but I gave it to Philippe for free. Turns out, he didn't care what she'd done; he just wanted to take *me* apart."

I took in what Ox was saying slowly, in tiny pieces, word by word, until I could process the whole thing. LeBeau was right. Quinn *wasn't* what she seemed at all. "Philippe loved her," I said after a few minutes. "I mean really. He actually loved her."

Ox nodded slowly, watching me the whole time for my reaction. "He did."

"More than he ever loved me."

"It was different," my friend said. "Not more, not less, just different."

I managed a weak smile, grateful for the kindness of his lie. "Okay." I took a couple of deep breaths and finished absorbing that idea. Giving myself a mental shake, I lifted my chin and plowed on. "Okay. Then why did Philippe call me the morning he died? Why did he ask me to meet with him? Why did he say that he'd made a terrible mistake?"

Ox actually looked sheepish. "He wanted to bring you in as a partner in the bakery."

The can of Coke slipped from my fingers. I caught it before it hit the floor, but a few drops spilled onto the carpet. With a cry of alarm, I got down on the floor. "Do you have a paper towel or a rag? I'm sure I can get it out —" Tears streamed down my face, and a strange mixture of anger and pain twisted through me. I looked around frantically for a piece of scrap cloth or a tissue.

Ox leaned forward and grabbed my wrist. "It's okay, Rita. I'll get it."

I jerked away and scrambled to my feet. "It's not okay. Just tell me where to find a towel."

Ox lumbered out of his easy chair and grabbed my shoulders gently. "Rita —"

Before I knew what was happening, I hit him. Hard. My fist landed on his chest with a thump that actually hurt my hand a little. But not enough. I hit him again. And again. And again.

I don't know how long he stood there and let me whale on him, but finally my anger, frustration, and hurt began to wind down,

I drove to the Dizzy Duke with the windows down, enjoying the breeze coming in off Lake Pontchartrain and the rare low humidity. I hadn't been back to the Duke since the night of Philippe's memorial. Maybe I shouldn't go back tonight, but with Ox off my short list, Dmitri cleared by an ironclad alibi, and Quinn off the hook, the only person left I could imagine who might have wanted to hurt Philippe was Guy LeBeau — the alligator wrestler.

Guy, who believed that Philippe had gotten what he deserved. Guy, who'd opened the Pandora's box of Quinn's past in the first place.

Sure, I was curious about his possible role in Philippe's death, but I wasn't stupid. I wasn't going to put myself in danger. I just wanted all the pieces in one place before I took my suspicions to Detective Sullivan. After my brief conversation with Old Dog

Leg outside the Dizzy Duke on the night of Philippe's memorial, I'd had every intention of following through with the musician's suggestion that I talk with Rikki, the harried cocktail waitress who supposedly knew about everything at the Duke. Since then, too many other things had claimed my attention. I'd all but forgotten about watching Guy LeBeau hit her up for money. Now I wondered if the rose-scented waitress held the keys to the puzzle after all.

My visit with Ox had left me exhausted, both physically and emotionally. I didn't want to think about the murder. Didn't want to think about Philippe's relationship with Quinn. I cast about for Gabriel, the cute bartender, but he was deep in conversation with a customer at the far end of the bar, so I placed my order with a young man whose dreadlocks fell below his shoulders. He gave the polished wood a swipe with a towel, and smiled. "You won't be sorry. We make the best margaritas in town."

"Potent, too," I said. "Go easy on the tequila tonight okay?"

He grinned. "You've been here before, then?"

"Yeah, but tonight I want to walk out of here on my own steam." He slid a bowl of roasted peanuts onto the bar in front of me, and the aroma reminded me that I hadn't eaten since breakfast. I pulled the bowl closer and helped myself to a few handfuls. Crunchy. Salty. And so peanutty I almost swooned. Until I caught Gabriel watching me from the other end of the bar, which convinced me to hold it together. I was not going to embarrass myself in front of him again.

My bartender returned with my drink and eyed the half-empty bowl in front of me. "Do you want me to start a tab for you?"

The offer surprised me. "You'd do that?"

"Why not? Gabriel says you're from the cake shop. We run tabs for y'all all the time."

After the day I'd had, the offer was tempting — which is why I turned him down. "Maybe next time. Before you go, can you tell me if Rikki's working tonight?"

"Rikki? Sure. She'll be here around eight."

I checked my watch. Not quite seven. It wasn't a long wait, but considering how tired I was, it felt like forever. "Do you have any jambalaya today? I'm starving."

"Sure. Full bowl or half?"

"Full, please."

He nodded. "Cornbread?"

"Perfect." Shifting on my stool so I could watch the door, I wolfed down a couple more handfuls of peanuts. A few customers were scattered around the Duke, but the atmosphere was much more laid-back than it had been the other night. Laughter and muted conversations rose up from the tables, and soft jazz floated out of the jukebox. Philippe would have loved the memorial party, but tonight's mood suited me better.

After a few minutes, I noticed people moving around near the bandstand. Two men and a woman fiddled with amplifiers and microphones, setting up equipment before their first set of the night. After a few minutes, I realized Old Dog Leg was sitting in the corner near the stage, so I picked up my drink and carried it toward him.

Maybe he'd cough up a few more answers and save me the wait.

He held a long-neck beer bottle in his hand and as I approached, a broad smile creased his face. "There you are, Rita. I wondered if we gone meet again."

"You can tell who I am?"

"It's not that hard." He patted the seat beside him. "Sit. Relax. Take a load off and make an ol' man happy."

I sat, turning my chair slightly so I could keep one eye on the door.

He tilted his head to one side and pursed his mouth. "You waitin' for somebody?"

"The cocktail waitress you mentioned the other day. Rikki. But how can you tell that?"

"Ain' no thing, my dear. Ain' no t'ing." He took a long pull on his beer and let out a satisfied sigh. "Something's on your mind tonight. Wanna tell me what it is?"

I shook my head in amazement. "As a matter of fact, something *is* on my mind. The other night you told me to talk to Rikki about Philippe. Why?"

"I tol' you dat. She knows 'bout everything goes on around here. What she tell you?"

"I haven't talked to her yet."

"No?" The smile on his face faded. "You goin' to though, right?"

"I'm hoping to talk with her tonight. Was she a girlfriend of Philippe's? Is that why I'm supposed to talk to her?"

"It bother you if she was?"

After what I'd learned earlier? I shook my head, then caught myself and answered aloud. "No, I don't think so."

"Dat's good. Jealousy is a bad t'ing, y' hear? Nothin' good comes of it. Ever."

"I'll keep that in mind." I sipped my drink, still determined to be a one-margarita kind of gal.

Old Dog Leg wrapped both hands around his bottle and regarded me with his sightless old eyes. Before he could say anything else, Rikki came in through the front door. The bartender motioned her over, spoke a few words, and pointed at me.

She stowed her bag behind the bar and crossed the room toward our table. Wariness clouded her eyes, but she brushed a kiss on Dog Leg's cheek and sat across from me. "Brandon said you wanted to talk to me?"

"That's right. Can I buy you a drink first?"

She shook her head and folded her arms defensively. "Just make it quick. I have to work, and I can't afford to miss out on any tips."

Right. "I'm Rita Lucero," I began.

"Philippe's wife," Dog Leg interrupted.

"Philippe's *ex*," I corrected. "At least, I would have been. Soon."

Old Dog Leg unfolded his white cane and stood. "On that note, I'm gone give you ladies some alone time. But you be careful, hear? Don't go diggin' places dat should be left alone."

We both watched him tap his way toward the stage; then Rikki tucked a lock of hair behind one ear and gave me a once-over. "I'm sorry about what happened. Philippe was a good guy. A really good guy."

"Yeah," I said on a sigh. "He was."

"You're the one who dumped the drink

on me, right?"

My cheeks burned. "Yeah. Sorry. My foot caught on the stool."

"I'll send you my dry-cleaning bill." She darted a glance over her shoulder. "Is that it? You want to apologize for making such a fuss?"

"I fell," I clarified. "Philippe's girlfriend made the fuss."

"Quinn made the fuss. You fell on your face. I'm not sure I see a big difference."

"Maybe there isn't one," I said, then took a breath and tried a new tack. "You were a friend of Philippe's?"

Rikki darted another look over her shoulder, then gave a reluctant nod. "You could say that."

"Were you more than friends?"

She let out a sharp laugh. "No, and I don't need you saying shit like that around here. My old man wouldn't like it. Philippe did me a favor once, that's all."

"Is that why Guy hated him?"

She seemed surprised that I knew her boyfriend's name, but she nodded. "That's right."

"What was the favor?"

"None of your business."

"Listen, my ex was brutally murdered, and your boyfriend seems happy about it. I think

382

that makes it my business."

Rikki's irritation turned to nervousness in a heartbeat. "He's not happy," she snapped. "Okay, so he didn't like Philippe. That doesn't mean that he wanted him dead."

"Are you sure about that?"

"Of course I'm sure." Rikki sat, checked behind her once more, and leaned in close. "Guy can be a jerk, okay? I'll admit it. And sometimes, when he has too much to drink, he loses control of his temper. But he doesn't mean anything by it."

I blinked. "He hits you?"

"A little. Sometimes. It's nothing major, okay? And he's always real sorry afterward."

My stomach rolled over. Twice. "I'll bet he is. What does this have to do with Philippe?"

Rikki sighed and plowed her fingers into her hair. "He walked in on us during an argument. He got in the middle of it. Guy was pissed about it, but that's all. He was mad. End of story. He likes shooting his mouth off, but he's harmless."

"Except for the part where he smacks you around. And the part where he tried to blackmail Philippe over Quinn's past."

Rikki's eyes flashed on me, and her expression grew grim. "That was nothing, okay? I told you he can be a jerk. He's always looking for a way to make a quick buck. He doesn't mean anything by it."

I stared at her in disbelief, wondering how any woman could let herself be so blinded by a man. "He threatened to expose a potentially harmful secret in exchange for money. How is that okay?"

Rikki's eyes grew cold. "She was lying to Philippe. Pretending to be something she wasn't. Philippe deserved to know."

"Maybe," I said, "but it was her story to tell, not your boyfriend's. And not in exchange for money. How did Guy take it when he found out Philippe didn't care?"

She shrugged. "He'd already lost interest in trying to get money from Philippe. Said he had a better deal worked out."

That sent a chill through me. "What kind of deal?"

"How should I know? Guy's always got something in the works. Maybe he found someone else who thought the information was valuable."

"Who?"

Rikki lifted her shoulder again. "Ask Guy if you want to know."

"I'm asking you."

She glanced around the room, her movements furtive. When she spoke again, her voice was hushed. "Look, I didn't want any

384

trouble for Philippe. I told Guy to just let it go, but he was still pretty pissed about Philippe getting in his face. He set up a meeting with some other cake dude. Fox or something like that."

My breath caught. "Dmitri Wolff?"

She nodded slowly. "Yeah, that's it."

"Guy sold the information about Quinn's past to Dmitri Wolff?"

"I don't know. He went to talk to him, that's all I know." Rikki stood abruptly. "I'm sorry Philippe is dead," she said. "He didn't deserve what he got. But it has nothing to do with me."

She walked away, and the story she'd told me echoed in my head. Was that why Quinn met with Dmitri secretly? Was he blackmailing her? I could believe it of him, but if Ox was right, she had no money to pay him off with. I suppose that meant she was telling the truth about not having an affair with Dmitri. But I wasn't ready to let her off the hook completely. She must have given Dmitri *something,* and I was almost certain that I knew what it was. Quinn must have stolen the design we'd been looking for, and maybe she'd been behind the sabotage, as well.

Something else bothered me about the conversation I'd just had with Rikki but my cell phone rang before I could decide what it was.

"Oh, sugar, I'm so glad you picked up," Miss Frankie said when I answered. "I just realized that we left in such a hurry, we forgot Philippe's things at the house yesterday. Can you swing by and pick them up on your way back here?"

Everything else moved onto the back burner at the mention of Philippe's funeral. I took a deep breath and tried not to sound distracted when I answered her. "Of course, Miss Frankie. Remind me what you need?"

The bartender delivered my jambalaya and cornbread as I jotted down the list, and after I disconnected, I dug into the meal with gusto. Huge chunks of chicken and sweet andouille mingled with shrimp, vegetables, and long-grain rice in a surprisingly well-made Creole version of the dish. The blend of garlic and cayenne pepper gave it a slow burn that crept across my tongue and made the roof of my mouth tingle. The amazing thing about a dish like jambalaya is that the combination of ingredients makes every bite taste just a little different from the one before. Paired with the slightly sweet cornbread — crusty on the outside, perfectly cooked on the inside — it was a meal to remember.

Half an hour later, I slid behind the wheel of Philippe's — *my* — Mercedes, and turned the wheel toward *my* house. I still felt a little bruised inside after my conversation with Ox and numb from my conversation with Rikki. Maybe a few minutes alone in the house would help me come to terms with the truth about my failed marriage and Philippe's relationship with Quinn. If I could wrap my mind around both those things, maybe I could finally decide what to do about my future.

TWENTY-EIGHT

I called Detective Sullivan from my cell phone as I drove. I wanted to tell him what I knew about Ox, about Quinn, and about Guy LeBeau. He didn't answer, so I left a message telling him I had some information for him and asking him to call me when he had a chance. I wasn't sure that I had all the pieces in the right places, but I was pretty sure that Guy LeBeau's attempt to extort money from Philippe was important, and so was the fact that Dmitri Wolff had been involved.

I found a parking spot in front of a closed pet store and walked back along the sidewalk, thinking about Miss Frankie's offer of a partnership and the life waiting for me back in Albuquerque. I wondered what it would be like to live here, and for the first time, I gave it some serious thought. I could do it if I wanted to. The only things standing between me and my dream were a sense of duty and fear of the unknown.

A stiff wind tossed the branches of trees overhead and sent leaves and bits of twigs and dirt skittering across the sidewalk in front of me. The scents of Thai food and pizza mingled on the breeze, and I could hear the muted sounds of accordion, guitar, bass, and drums from somewhere nearby, underscoring the laughter of a young couple as they passed me.

I let myself into the house and locked the door behind me. Leaving my bag and keys on a table in the entryway, I moved slowly from room to room, mentally rearranging furniture and deciding on the pieces I'd want to keep and those I'd want to get rid of. I'd change a lot, I decided. You know . . . if I decided to take the plunge.

After a while I moved to the second floor, where the glass of wine I'd left on the desk still waited for me. There was something oddly comforting in that. I'd never lived alone before. My whole life, there'd always been someone around to pick up what I put down. I liked knowing that here, in this house, what I put down stayed where I'd left it.

I carried the glass into the bathroom, dumped the wine, and rinsed the glass. After spreading a hand towel on the counter, I left the glass to dry and turned to leave. I ran my hand along the empty counter . . . and then froze.

Except for my glass and my towel, the counter was empty. But it hadn't been empty the last time I was here. There'd been something here. Body spray or exfoliating cream. I couldn't remember which. I only knew that it wasn't here now. Which meant that Quinn had come back. Without telling me.

My breath caught in my throat, but I told myself not to panic. Maybe I'd remembered wrong. Maybe she'd grabbed whatever it was without me noticing.

I hurried into the study and checked for the earrings and the necklace I'd noticed earlier. Gone. Upstairs to the master bath. Clean as a whistle. Anger boiled up inside me as I thought about her sneaking back into the house to get her things. Hadn't I told her to call me when she wanted to come back?

Contemplating filing a complaint with the police, I went back to the second floor. This time, I glanced into the library as I passed it. The books that had been shelved so carefully last time I was here were now scattered across the floor in careless heaps. I froze with one hand on the door and stared at the mess in disbelief. Quinn really was nuts. Why trash the library to get back at me? Or was she looking for something she'd hidden here? Like, say, the missing design?

A floorboard above my head creaked, and my heart stopped beating for a moment. Oh. My. God. She was still here.

I couldn't move. Couldn't breathe. Couldn't hear anything over the frantic beating of my heart. Quinn was here. Waiting for me. Had she killed Philippe after all?

The floor creaked again, and everything that had been frozen thawed. I looked around for a weapon. Something I could use to defend myself. I'd found a letter opener in the study, but that wouldn't be effective unless I let her get close to me, and I didn't intend to do that. Books? A paperweight? I spotted a sculpture on one of the bookshelves and lunged for it as the creaking overhead turned into measured footsteps.

Clutching the sculpture, I looked around for a place to hide. I could crawl under the desk in the study, but if she found me there I'd have no way to escape. Ditto for the closet. My only hope was to get downstairs before she came after me.

I turned toward the stairs, but movement from the corner of my eye stopped me cold.

391

I saw a figure standing on the third-floor landing.

But it wasn't Quinn.

It was Burt McGuire. And instead of flashing his dimpled and flirtatious grin, he was holding a gun and looking at me through eyes so flat and filled with hatred, I heard myself gasp.

"What are you doing here?" he demanded.

I tried to swallow, but my throat was too tight and dry. "I own the place," I croaked. I didn't want to antagonize him, but neither did I want him to realize how terrified I was. "How did you get in?"

A brittle smile curved his lips. "Does it really matter?"

Probably not. "What are you doing here?"

"What do you think? Looking for that stupid design."

It took me a few seconds to process that. His words had a hard time making it through the panic shrieking through my head. "You're here for the design?"

"Sure. Why not? It's going to make me a pretty penny if I can just deliver. What in the hell have you done with it?"

Burt. With a gun. Aimed at me. I'd been so wrong. I somehow managed to shake my head slowly. "I haven't seen it. It's not here."

"Sure it is. Where else would that dimwit

stash it?"

I stole a glance over my shoulder at the books on the floor. "You think Quinn took the design and hid it here?"

"I know that's what she did. She had one job to do. *One!* And she couldn't even manage that."

"Quinn was helping you sabotage Zydeco?"

Burt laughed. "Using her wasn't my idea, although I will say that she did have her uses. She managed to deflect Philippe's suspicions pretty well."

The fog in my head began to clear a bit. "You're working for Dmitri?"

"I like to think of myself as an independent contractor. Now stop yapping and tell me where the design is."

He looked so angry I almost wished I could tell him. "I have no idea," I said. "I haven't seen it."

He studied me for what felt like forever, then nodded. "Fine. Then shut up and come up the stairs. Slowly."

I briefly considered my chances of making a dash down the stairs instead, but I'd never be able to outrun a bullet.

"Now!" he roared.

With his voice still echoing through the house, I clutched the sculpture tightly and did as I was told.

"What's that in your hand?" he demanded, then without waiting for an answer, "Drop it. Right there."

I released my grip and the statue hit the floor by my foot. Time seemed to slow, and my legs wobbled as I climbed the stairs. The pounding of my heart made it hard to breathe. I might as well have been climbing Mount Everest. "You killed Philippe."

Burt recoiled slightly, but not enough to give me an advantage. "I didn't mean to. I didn't *want* to."

"But you did."

"Shut up. You have no idea what happened that day. You have no right to judge me."

I moved slowly, sizing up the situation and trying to figure out a way to overpower him once I got to the top of the stairs. Nothing brilliant came to mind, but I knew I had to keep him talking. "You're right. I have no idea what happened. Why don't you tell me?"

Burt tightened his grip on the pistol, using both hands to hold it steady. The flirtatious smile that was his trademark flashed across his face, and the dimples sliced into his cheeks for an instant. "Seems to me, you should be more concerned with what's going to happen tonight."

"Okay. Tell me about that."

He used the pistol to gesture toward a door at the end of the hall. "Open it."

I walked past him, watching for a chance to throw him off balance. But he was ready for me, his eyes narrowed, his stance solid. He was bigger than me and in better shape. I wouldn't stand a chance unless I could catch him off guard.

Praying that he wouldn't shoot me in the back, I opened the door and found another set of stairs, this one apparently leading to the roof.

He nudged me in the back. "Up."

"What's up there?"

"You'll see. Now go."

My legs were aching, and fear filled my throat, but I didn't want to make him angry. I couldn't afford for him to lose control yet. At the top of the stairs, he directed me to open another door, and I stepped out onto a rooftop patio that would have taken my breath away if I'd seen it under other circumstances. Large planters holding various trees and flowering bushes had been positioned along a wrought-iron railing around the rim of the patio. Stone chairs circled a round table in the center, and twinkling white lights gave the terrace a fairy-tale look.

"Nice, isn't it?"

I glanced over my shoulder at the crazy man behind me. "Seriously? We're going to talk about the garden?"

"Why not? It's going to be the last thing you ever see."

My throat tightened, and fear made me numb. "Why are you doing this?"

His lips curled into a bitter smile. "Because you won't leave well enough alone. What happened with Philippe was an accident. I only wanted to get his attention. But you . . ." He jerked his arms upward until I found myself staring down the barrel of his gun. I had no idea what caliber it was, and I didn't care. From my perspective, it looked like a cannon. "You just kept digging."

A strange calm settled over me. "So you're going to kill me."

"Nope. You're going to kill yourself. Throw yourself off the roof in despair. So sad."

"Nobody will believe it," I warned him. "They'll know something is wrong with that story, and they'll figure it out eventually."

"I wouldn't count on that," he said with a mock frown. "Everybody knows how upset you've been since Philippe died."

"But why does Dmitri want Zydeco out

of the way so badly? Why would he pay you to sabotage Zydeco?"

"There's big money on the line. People will do strange things for fame and fortune. What can I say about Dmitri? He's a twisted guy."

Unlike the loony tune standing in front of me? "But why? What did Philippe ever do to you?"

"It's what he didn't do, sweetheart. He didn't recognize what he had. He didn't understand the contribution I could have made to Zydeco. He passed me over time and time again because he was too stupid to see the value of what I had to offer."

"So you betrayed him because you wanted a promotion?"

He smiled again — a feral smile that chilled me from the inside out. "It's all about looking out for number one in this world. If you don't take care of yourself, who will?" His smile faded slowly. "Too bad you won't get a chance to figure that out for yourself."

The gun wavered in front of my face, and my life flashed in front of my eyes, only it wasn't the life I'd had. It was the life I wasn't going to get. Ever. Unless I did something to stop this crazy person from killing me.

"What happened that day?" I kept my voice low and soothing, hoping that giving him the chance to talk would calm him down again. "You said you didn't mean to kill him, so what happened?"

He motioned for me to move toward the railing. "It was the fight. That stupid, stupid fight. He wasn't supposed to come into the rose garden. He wasn't supposed to find me."

My mind worked like sludge, but slowly the pieces began to fall into place. "After you destroyed the cake."

"It was going to be the last thing. It was going to be over," Burt said with a shrug. "Ox was ruined. Philippe was so head over heels in love with that bimbo, he wasn't paying attention to anything. I could have had it all."

"Until he found you in the rose garden and realized that it was you who'd been sabotaging Zydeco and framing Ox."

He wagged the gun toward the railing again, and the coldness in his eyes crept onto his face. "Move. By the railing."

"I'm not going to jump," I told him, "and if you shoot me, you'll be caught. There are too many people on the street for you to get away."

"Of course you're going to jump. Like I

398

said, everyone knows how upset you are over Philippe's murder. Poor thing. I guess you just couldn't take it anymore."

His finger tightened on the trigger, and I knew it was now or never. Bending to get below the barrel of the gun, I rammed him with every bit of strength I could muster, using my shoulder to deflect his aim.

He staggered under the force of my weight but didn't lose his footing. "Bitch!" he shouted, and tried to get a bead on me again.

I had about half a second before I'd lose whatever chance I might have. I had landed on my knees, so I aimed for his legs next, throwing my weight into the move and praying this time I could make him lose his balance.

My shoulder hit the front of his knees, and I heard him grunt loudly, which gave me some hope. An instant later, I felt him falling toward me. I rolled out from beneath him and tried to find his hands and the gun in the dim light. It seemed to take forever to spot his hands and get my own around his wrist. I couldn't hope to overpower him for long, but I planted myself on his stomach and held on, using all my force to slam his gun hand against the closest planter.

Burt roared in pain, and the death grip he

had on the gun loosened slightly. Was it enough? It had to be.

Blood pounded in my ears, and my breath came in painful gasps as I fought to maintain my slim advantage. He bucked beneath me, twisting and turning as he tried to throw me.

He was too strong. Too crazy. Too determined. I couldn't do this alone, I realized. I needed help.

Hoping someone would be able to hear me on the street, I shouted at the top of my lungs. "Help! Call the police! On the roof!"

Burt growled in anger and bucked again, this time hard enough to roll out from beneath me. "You stupid, stupid bitch."

Too late, I scrambled to my feet and lunged for the gun he'd dropped. We reached it at the same time and fought bitterly for control. I yelled again, hoping someone would hear me. Praying someone would call the police before Burt could carry out his deranged plan to throw me off the roof.

He backhanded me across the face, and pain shot through my cheek and jaw. My eyesight blurred, and I staggered backward, tasting blood and trying to regain my focus. Before I could catch my breath, he slugged me in the stomach with his fist, and the air exploded from my lungs. I fell backward, gasping for air and still trying to make my eyes work.

"Get up."

I could see the barrel of the gun again, just inches from my face. This was it, wasn't it? The end of everything. I'd never know love again. I'd never have a family. Never own my own business or work at the thing I loved most. It was all going to end right here, at the hands of a deranged killer.

I moaned and rolled onto my side, hoping that he'd believe I was too worn out to fight any longer.

"Get. Up."

I moaned again, sucked air into my aching lungs, and took my last shot at staying alive. With one mighty heave, I threw myself at his legs and prayed that when he shot me, he'd miss my vital organs.

The gunshot exploded in the night, and I waited for the pain that never came. I heard a loud thump, the sound of hurried footsteps, and, finally, the touch of a hand on my arm. But I was too far gone to recognize it for what it was. I screamed and thrashed away, kicking as hard as I could to keep him from getting a good grip.

"Rita! It's all right! We've got him."

I scooted backward, too afraid to trust my

own ears. But very slowly, Detective Sullivan's face came into focus. A moment later, I realized that the huge black blur a few feet behind him was a couple of EMTs working on Burt, who lay bleeding on the cement floor of the deck.

Twenty-Nine

I held tightly to Miss Frankie's elbow as we walked across the lawn after the graveside service. Behind us, Dog Leg and a handful of friends played "Just a Closer Walk with Thee," and voices rose up from all around us as one friend after another took up the verse.

To anyone watching the two of us, it would look as if I wanted to make sure Miss Frankie didn't lose her balance on the uneven lawn. But I think we both knew it was more than that. The mausoleum was fine. Perfect, in fact. Philippe would be comfortable there. Nobody had to check it out to make sure.

"It was a beautiful service," she said as we stepped off the lawn and onto the pavement. "Don't you think it was?"

"It was lovely," I agreed. "Exactly right."

"I thought Ox's comments were especially nice. I'm glad he's agreed to come back to

Zydeco."

"So am I," I assured her. I loosened my grip slightly but didn't let go of her completely. Not that I didn't trust her, but . . . well, you know.

"I think his little vacation did him a world of good, don't you? It was good for him to get away from work for a few days."

Biting back a smile, I aimed the remote at the car. "Yes ma'am, I do. He looks well rested."

All around us, friends, relatives, and members of Zydeco's staff made their way toward their cars. Some offered last-minute condolences to Miss Frankie. Others seemed eager to return to the land of the living. I'd been overwhelmed by the turnout and by the warm reception I'd received from almost everyone there. Okay, so a few old friends and distant cousins had questioned Miss Frankie's decision to include me as part of the family, but nobody dared say so in front of her.

I watched Edie, Estelle, and Sparkle walking together toward the row of cars parked on the edge of the lawn, their heads down and shoulders slumped. A few feet ahead of them, Dwight scuffed toward his car, hands in his pockets, the picture of dejection. Ox, with one arm around Isabeau's shoulders, chatted with Abe near the mausoleum. It was nice to see that Ox and Isabeau had decided to go public, but they all looked as if the past few days had taken a toll.

A few feet farther on, I spotted Quinn standing quietly to one side of the road, her arms wrapped tightly around her middle. She'd returned the cake design and we'd managed to submit our bid on time. Now all we had to do was wait for the decision. I wasn't sure whether I wanted Zydeco to win the bid or not. All that publicity would be great for business and I'd love to see Philippe's last design honored in a big way, but I wasn't ready to have the business explode just yet. I could use a few months to settle in first.

Philippe's death had been hard on everyone at Zydeco. Finding out that Burt had been responsible for everything had been another blow. He'd been a friend, and it had shocked everyone to find out that he'd been working against them for months.

I caught a shadow from the corner of my eye and turned to find Detective Sullivan — Liam — coming toward us. "Good afternoon, Miss Frankie. Rita."

The rush of affection and gratitude I felt toward him was strong — he'd saved my life, after all, and I'd fallen a little bit in love with him as a result. "Good afternoon, Detective. Thank you so much for coming. That's above and beyond the call of duty, isn't it?"

He cut a glance at me and smiled. "The men and women of NOPD are here to serve the community."

"Well isn't that sweet of you?" Miss Frankie put a hand on his arm. "I'm glad you came. I wanted a chance to thank you in person for finding Philippe's killer and saving Rita."

"It was my pleasure, ma'am."

"Have you heard anything about Burt's condition?" I asked. "I tried calling the hospital, but they wouldn't tell me anything."

Sullivan's expression sobered. "He's fine. I didn't take a kill shot, and I didn't miss. He'll limp for a while, but he'll heal."

I'd be fine with that, I supposed. As long as he was doing his limping from behind bars. "Were you able to get a full confession?"

He nodded. "He didn't plan to kill Philippe. I know that doesn't help, Miss Frankie, but he only wanted to destroy the cake. One last attempt to discredit Ox and get rid of him. One last chance to ruin Zydeco's reputation and get rid of the competition for Dmitri Wolff. Philippe found Burt cleaning up in the rose garden, waiting for a chance to slip back into the bakery when nobody was watching."

"You're right," Miss Frankie said. "It doesn't help. He's crazier than a pet squirrel, and my boy is dead because that lunatic wanted more money." She fell silent for a moment, and neither of us broke the silence. After a minute, she forced a tiny smile. "You're coming to the Dizzy Duke aren't you, Detective?"

"I don't think so, ma'am. That's for friends and family."

She wagged a finger in his face. "Don't you even think about turning me down, young man. All of Philippe's friends will be there. Everyone from the bakery. Cousins nobody's ever heard of. You most certainly belong there, and I won't take no for an answer."

Sullivan laughed softly. "Then I'd be honored, ma'am, assuming my work schedule will allow it."

Her smile faded, and she took hold of my arm again. "I guess I can't ask for more than that, can I?"

He excused himself and left us alone. I watched him walk away before leading Miss Frankie toward the car. She and I still had a few things to sort out between us.

Miss Frankie's step slowed as she watched Ox and Isabeau leaving the cemetery. "I feel horrible for suspecting that boy. I should have known he wasn't behind all that mess." She cut one more glance at them over her shoulder and said, "They're sweet together, but it's not going to last."

"You don't think so?"

She shook her head. "She's too young for him. Mark my words. I give it three months, tops. But don't worry. I don't think their split will affect the business."

"I'm not worried."

With a sigh, she looked at me again and touched my cheek with her fingertips. "I'm so glad you decided to stay, sugar. I don't know what I'd do without you. We'll get the paperwork taken care of tomorrow."

"There's no rush," I assured her. I was still struggling to take in all the changes that had occurred in my life in the past week. "We can wait a few days."

"I've made an appointment with Thaddeus already. He's expecting us at ten."

I opened the door for her and helped her into her seat, but I paused with the door open and shot her a smile. "What are you trying to do, lock me into the partnership so I can't change my mind?"

She looked up at me with wide-eyed innocence. "Why, sugar, you know I'd never do a thing like that. I just want to make sure you're protected."

"Uh-huh."

"It's God's honest truth," she exclaimed. "You never know what's going to happen."

She had a point, I guess. I shut her door and walked toward the driver's side, then slid behind the wheel and started the car. I rolled down the windows to let the hot air spill out while we waited for the air conditioner to kick in. As we drove away from the cemetery, the sun burned down on us from a cloudless blue sky, and rays sparkled on the water of a nearby pond. I thought Philippe would approve of my decision to stay in New Orleans and run Zydeco, but I wondered if he'd approve of my decision to live in his house and watch over Miss Frankie.

We reached the exit and pulled into traffic. A breeze stirred in the trees overhead, bringing with it a welcome moment of relief from the heat. I wondered how long it would take me to adjust to the climate. How long it would take me to feel at home in Philippe's house and behind his desk — or if I ever would.

As we paused for a traffic light, a woman

stumbled out of a bar at the corner, and a few bars of Nat King Cole singing "Our Love Is Here to Stay" floated into the atmosphere behind her. Philippe and my song. Was it a sign? Or merely a coincidence? Miss Frankie turned her head and gave me a knowing look, leaving no doubt in my mind what she thought. And maybe she was right. I guess time would tell.

RECIPES

AUNT YOLANDA'S CHOCOLATE-BANANA COFFEE CAKE

1 1/2 cups semisweet chocolate chips
2/3 cup (packed) golden brown sugar
2/3 cup chopped walnuts (optional)
2 teaspoons ground cinnamon
1/2 cup butter, softened
3/4 cup granulated sugar
1 large egg
1 1/4 cups very ripe bananas, mashed
2 tablespoons sour cream (can substitute plain yogurt)
1 tablespoon milk
1 1/2 cups all-purpose flour
3/4 teaspoon baking soda
3/4 teaspoon baking powder
1/2 teaspoon salt

Heat oven to 350 F. (325 if using a glass pan). Grease an 8″ × 8″ × 2″ baking pan.

In a small bowl, combine chocolate chips,

brown sugar, walnuts (if desired), and cinnamon for the streusel topping. Set aside.

In a large bowl, beat butter, sugar, and egg with an electric mixer until fluffy. Add bananas, sour cream (or yogurt), and milk. Mix well. On low speed, beat in dry ingredients (flour, baking soda, baking powder, and salt) until just blended.

Spread a little more than half of the batter in the pan. Sprinkle with half of the streusel. Carefully spread the remaining batter over the streusel, and then top with the rest of the streusel. Bake until a toothpick inserted in the center of the cake comes out clean, about 40 to 50 minutes. Cool in pan on a wire rack. Serve warm or at room temperature.

This coffee cake tastes great the next day and freezes beautifully. Freeze it whole or cut it into pieces wrapped in plastic and placed in a zippered freezer bag.

ZYDECO BASIC WHITE CAKE
Yields one 10-inch cake (3 layers)

A classic cake, perfect for any occasion. The texture makes this cake a joy to work with, and it's amazingly versatile. Frost with buttercream or dust with powdered sugar for a great coffee cake. Split it into layers and add a fill-

ing, or serve it with berries and vanilla ice cream.

1 1/2 sticks butter (real butter is always best)
2 1/2 cups sugar
1 1/2 teaspoon salt
3 cups plus 2 tablespoons unbleached all-purpose flour
6 tablespoons cornstarch
1 1/2 teaspoons baking powder
3/4 teaspoon cream of tartar
1 1/4 cups milk
3/4 teaspoon vanilla extract (use real vanilla rather than vanilla flavoring if you have it!)
6–8 large egg whites (approximately 3/4 cup)

Preheat oven to 350° F. Prepare 2 10-inch round cake pans by spraying with nonstick cooking spray and lining each pan with waxed paper cut to fit.

Using an electric mixer, beat the butter and 2 cups of sugar at high speed until lighter in color and fluffy.

Sift the salt, flour, cornstarch, and baking powder together.

Mix the milk and vanilla together.

Add the dry ingredients and wet ingredients alternately to the batter, ending with

413

the dry ingredients.

In a separate bowl, beat the egg whites until foamy.

Add cream of tartar and beat until soft peaks form.

Slowly add the remaining 1/2 cup sugar to the egg whites, and beat until stiff peaks form.

Using a rubber spatula, gently fold a little of the egg whites into the batter, then the remaining whites, until just combined. Do not overmix the batter, or you'll lose all the air you worked so hard to incorporate, and the texture of the cake will change.

Pour 1/3 of the batter into one cake pan and the remaining 2/3 into the other two pans. Bake for 25–35 minutes. (Check after 25.) Cake is done when a tester inserted into the center of the cake comes out clean.

Cool the cakes in their pans for about 15 minutes, then turn out onto a wire rack to cool completely.

ZYDECO BUTTERCREAM ICING
Yields about 3 cups of icing

This recipe is perfect for spreading or decorating. Follow the directions to make it the consistency you need.

1/2 cup (1 stick) butter or margarine, softened (real butter is best if you have it)
1/2 cup solid vegetable shortening
1 teaspoon clear vanilla extract (use regular vanilla extract if that's all you have, but the clear variety won't change the color of your frosting)
4 cups sifted confectioner's sugar (approximately 1 pound)
2 tablespoons milk

For Medium Consistency

In a large bowl, cream together shortening and butter with an electric mixer. Add vanilla extract. Gradually add the sugar, one cup at a time, and beat well using medium speed. Scrape the sides of the bowl often to incorporate ingredients.

When the sugar has been mixed in, the icing will appear dry. Don't worry. This is normal. Add the milk, and beat at medium speed until light and fluffy.

Keep covered with a damp cloth until

ready to use. For best results, keep in the refrigerator when not in use. Refrigerated in an airtight container, the icing will last up to two weeks, but you'll need to rewhip before using.

For Thin Icing (Spreading Consistency)
Add 2 tablespoons light corn syrup, water, or milk.

For Stiff Icing
Omit the butter and substitute an additional 1/2 cup shortening. Add 1/2 teaspoon No-Color Butter Flavor.

MISS FRANKIE'S STRAWBERRY FREEZER JAM
Yields about 5 half-pint jars of jam

Once you've had this, you'll never want another strawberry jam. It's so easy to make, too! You'll need:

1 quart (4 cups) fresh strawberries, cut in half (Do not use frozen berries)
4 cups sugar
3/4 cup water
1 pkg (1 3/4 ounces) powdered fruit pectin

Using a potato masher or a food processor,

mash the strawberries until they're slightly chunky. Don't puree! You're looking for 2 cups of crushed strawberries.

Mix the strawberries and sugar together in a large bowl and let stand at room temperature for 10 minutes, stirring occasionally. Don't skimp on this process. The sugar needs the full 10 minutes to work on the berries.

Mix the water and the pectin together in a saucepan and heat to boiling, stirring occasionally. Once the mixture is boiling, let it continue to boil for 1 minute.

Pour the hot pectin mixture over the strawberries and stir constantly for 3 minutes.

Immediately spoon the mixture into prepared freezer containers (glass jars), leaving 1/2 inch headspace. Wipe the rims of the containers and seal. Let stand at room temperature for about 24 hours, or until set.

Store in the freezer for up to 6 months, or in the refrigerator for up to 3 weeks. Thaw frozen jam and stir before serving.

DIZZY DUKE JAMBALAYA
Yields 4 servings 1 1/2 cups each

Jambalaya is a versatile dish that can be made using many variations.

1 tablespoon olive oil
1 cup onion, diced
1 cup red bell pepper, diced
1 tablespoon minced garlic
6 ounces andouille, sliced into 1/4″ pieces
1 cup uncooked long-grain white rice
1 teaspoon paprika
1 teaspoon freshly ground black pepper
1 teaspoon dried oregano
1/2 teaspoon onion powder
1/2 teaspoon dried thyme
1/4 teaspoon garlic salt
1 bay leaf
2 cups chicken broth (can use fat-free and low-sodium varieties if desired)
3/4 cup water
1 tablespoon tomato paste
1/2 teaspoon hot pepper sauce
1 (14.5-ounce) can diced tomatoes, undrained (can use no-salt variety if desired)
1/2 pound peeled and deveined medium shrimp
2 tablespoons chopped fresh parsley

Heat the olive oil in a large Dutch oven ove medium-high heat. When hot, add onion, bell pepper, minced garlic, and sausage; sauté 5 minutes or until vegetables are tender.

Add rice and the next 7 ingredients (through bay leaf); cook approximately 2 minutes. Add broth, water, tomato paste, hot pepper sauce, and diced tomatoes; bring to a boil. Cover, reduce heat, and simmer 20 minutes. Make sure the rice isn't sticking to the bottom as it simmers, but don't over-stir during this stage. Too much stirring will change the texture of the rice. You can also omit the hot pepper sauce at this stage and allow diners to season to taste.

Add shrimp and cook 5 minutes. Let stand 5 minutes. Discard the bay leaf. Stir in the parsley and serve.

SOUTHERN STYLE CORNBREAD
Yields 4 to 6 servings

6 tablespoons unsalted butter, melted, plus a little more butter to prepare the baking dish
1 cup cornmeal
3/4 cup all-purpose flour
1 tablespoon sugar
1 1/2 teaspoons baking powder

/2 teaspoon baking soda
1/4 teaspoon salt
2 large eggs, lightly beaten
1 1/2 cups buttermilk

Preheat the oven to 425 degrees F. Lightly butter an 8-inch baking dish.

In a large bowl, mix together the cornmeal, flour, sugar, baking powder, baking soda, and salt.

In a separate bowl, mix together the eggs, buttermilk, and butter. Pour the buttermilk mixture into the cornmeal mixture and fold together until there are no dry spots (the batter will still be lumpy). Pour the batter into the prepared baking dish.

Bake until the top is golden brown and tester inserted into the middle of the corn bread comes out clean, about 20 to 25 minutes. Remove the cornbread from the oven and let it cool for 10 minutes before serving.

ABOUT THE AUTHOR

Jacklyn Brady is the pseudonym for a multipublished author in both mystery and romance.

The employees of Thorndike Press hope you have enjoyed this Large Print book. All our Thorndike, Wheeler, and Kennebec Large Print titles are designed for easy reading, and all our books are made to last. Other Thorndike Press Large Print books are available at your library, through selected bookstores, or directly from us.

For information about titles, please call:
  (800) 223-1244

or visit our Web site at:
  http://gale.cengage.com/thorndike

To share your comments, please write:
  Publisher
  Thorndike Press
  10 Water St., Suite 310
  Waterville, ME 04901